Jan Jongstra

THE RELUCTANT CRIMINAL

A Novel

Published by JanJongstraBooks

www.janjongstrabooks.com
jongstraj@gmail.com

ISBN: 978-1-7386706-0-4.

Fiction, Crime
2.Fiction, General

Typesetting services by Bookow.com
Cover design by ilanitshohat.com

Praise for *The Reluctant Criminal*

The Reluctant Criminal by Jan Jongstra sees the transformation of Frank from a mild-mannered man into a 'do whatever it takes' hero. *The Reluctant Criminal* pulled me right in and kept me reading. Frank is a likable guy who it was impossible not to root for and the bad guys were indeed evil. Jan Jongstra has created a credible crime novel with a strong plot offering murder, assassins, illegal schemes, and a hero. This book should be placed on your reading list if you are a fan of the crime genre with a strong affinity for integrity.

5 star rating — Readers' Favorite

Jongstra crafts an innovative crime novel while keeping the classic elements readers know and love intact. An absorbing and unique plot makes *The Reluctant Criminal* an enjoyable read.

BookLife Prize

Reading this exciting novel felt like a rickshaw ride through a busy street in Mumbai. I held on tight as the story took unexpected and dangerous twists and turns.

This new author has that unique talent and writing style that has him create for us a main character that is fascinating, broken, yet likeable.

I was quickly engaged in the story and as it evolved, I felt eager to stay on this ride until the end of the line. I was glad I did.

Harry Berholz

The Reluctant Criminal is a unique crime novel, beautifully written and featuring a protagonist who instantly grabs the attention of readers. The prose has the fluidity I enjoy in good writing, that music that sounds well to the ears. The author's economy of words had me thrilled as I went through the focused scenes, savoring the engaging dialogues, and getting immersed in Frank's occasional internal dialogues. The plot moves forward, propelled by the author's deft balancing of Frank's core values with external pressures. The characters are relatable and the conflict feels real. The conflict is well-imagined and brilliantly executed. Overall, this book has everything readers look for in a good novel — a genuinely flawed protagonist, a broken system exploited by criminals, and a finely drawn setting.

5 star rating The Book Commentary

Also by Jan Jongstra

How Benji Got His Name
A collection of children's stories for three-to-six-year-olds. November 2020

For my wife Jenny

ONE

A car idled on a dark stretch of road leading to the central train station of Antwerp, Belgium's largest seaport. The road was deserted. Inside the car were two burly men, one of whom was wearing black-rimmed glasses.

"I hate sitting around," he said.

His partner, Zachariah, known as Z to his criminal friends, said, "I know that. I remember Barcelona, where you got us into trouble with Mrs. Liu because you became so agitated that you attracted attention from passersby, and we had to cancel the job. So please—stop fiddling with your knife, and stop banging on the dashboard. Our target will be here soon. The train station closes in half an hour. She doesn't have much time left."

On cue, a young woman appeared, pulling a small pink suitcase. Her heels hit the sidewalk with a fast staccato. Z and the Man with the Black-Rimmed Glasses tensed up and focused on their victim. "That's her. Grab her before she runs."

The Man with the Black-Rimmed Glasses jumped out, grabbed the young woman, slapped his hand over her mouth, and moved her towards the car. He had trouble subduing his victim, who squirmed trying to get loose, and pummelled her attacker. She landed a few hits on his face, and the black-rimmed glasses fell onto the sidewalk. But she had no chance of getting away. Z handed his partner his glasses, and the Man with the Black-Rimmed Glasses took hold of the young woman's arms and pushed her into the back of the car. She noticed that a large plastic sheet covered the rear seats and she panicked.

"Why now?" she shouted. "I have left SunRise. I am going home. I did my job. Let me go. I have already forgotten . . ." She fell silent, out of breath, but after a few seconds, continued, begging, "Let me go, I will disappear and never mention the SunRise company again to anybody."

But Z and the Man with the Black-Rimmed Glasses ignored her pleas. Instead, Z said, "Too late. We have our instructions. You worked for SunRise, but you couldn't handle the responsibilities. We know you talked about your job with people you met in bars and restaurants and told them you worked for SunRise, which might be the reason the customs office shut us down. You mess with us; we mess with you."

Z looked at the Man with the Black-Rimmed Glasses and nodded. The men wrapped the lifeless body in the plastic sheet. The Man with the Black-Rimmed Glasses wiped his knife clean, and they drove away.

"Oh—did you take the suitcase?" Z asked.

"No, I forgot. We should go back."

"Let's not. Nobody can link the suitcase to us. There were no witnesses, so there won't be a problem. Instead, we'll get rid of the body and let Mrs. Liu know we finished the job. Then we can go for drinks. I can use a few strong ones."

The pink suitcase stood in the middle of the sidewalk, a witness to the heinous crime that had taken place. Several minutes after the men had driven away, a homeless man snatched up the suitcase and sold it to a used-clothing store for fifteen euros. It was a good day in his otherwise miserable life.

TWO

"FRANK, Mr. Young, and I, want you to come with us on a business trip to Shanghai next week. I'm sorry for the brief notice. We hope you can make it."

That announcement from his boss, Linda, threw Frank's quiet life into turmoil. His mouth opened and closed. Sounds, but no words came out. He stared at Linda, but he only saw her outline. *Travelling with Linda and with Mr. Young, the CEO?*

"You look surprised, Frank, but you shouldn't. We need more suppliers to satisfy our Canadian and European clients, so we've scheduled several meetings with Chinese wholesalers, and we want you to be there."

Frank, who was the data entry clerk at the Toronto YYZ Import/Export Company, could think of one simple question. "Why me?"

"You've been with us for a long time and you're familiar with the ins and outs of YYZ. Your experience convinced Mr. Young and I you can make valuable contributions to the discussions in Shanghai."

This made Frank even more confused. *For Pete's sake, I only enter data into the computer. What can I contribute to important business meetings?*

"Please tell us as soon as possible if you're coming." And with that, Linda left an unhinged Frank sitting behind his desk. Linda hadn't mixed him up with another employee, because for five years Frank had been the only office worker in the company. He did the data entry, and Linda and two warehouse workers did everything else. Mr. Young ran YYZ together with his wife, who had insisted Frank call her Linda. Her husband preferred to be addressed as Mr. Young, not by his first name, Leonard. Frank and the warehouse workers had little contact with Mr.

Young, who travelled often to visit potential and existing clients and was seldom in his office.

During the week between Linda's announcement and their departure to Shanghai, Frank kept busy with work. One day, he worked till well into the evening, something he had never done before, but this did nothing to keep him from thinking about why Linda and Mr. Young had asked him to come to China. Many times, he paced the hallway. Twice he made his way to Linda's office to talk with her, but the conversations did not diminish his anxiety.

"What do you and Mr. Young expect me to do in Shanghai?"

"Nothing difficult. Before we go, you'll transfer data we may need during the negotiations from your desktop computer to Mr. Young's laptop. You are coming with us in case Mr. Young needs help to pull up the right files. We want to make sure everything goes well, and he doesn't lose time in the meetings searching for specific transactions. Since you'll move the files, you should be able to find whatever he needs."

Frank fidgeted with his coffee cup. *I am* not *going; I can't do this. What if I must fuss with Mr. Young's computer while everyone is looking at me? I'll be too nervous and make mistakes.*

Frank returned to his office and put his head in his hands, trying to understand what had just happened. Shanghai, business meetings, helping Mr. Young in front of other business owners—it was too much. His life was one of quiet routines: wake up at seven, have breakfast, go to work, have dinner, watch TV, and go to bed at ten-thirty. He found comfort in doing the same work every day, five days a week, and he looked forward to his daily meetings with Linda, who checked his work. This gave him a sense of security and belonging. The invitation to come to Shanghai had shattered that. He visited Linda again.

"Do you need any specific data? I can work on the transfer now." Linda touched Frank's shoulder, who shivered as if the office were ice cold.

"Don't be so nervous. Tomorrow you'll transfer the data we have on the last six months of transactions with Chinese wholesalers to Mr.

Young's laptop, and I'll be there to help you find the proper files. So, please—relax."

Linda and Frank spent the next morning in Frank's office selecting data. When they finished, Linda said, "Why don't we have something to eat? Let's go to Mary's Diner." Frank didn't know what to say. He always brought lunch—two slices of toasted whole-grain bread with cheese and a yogurt drink. To have lunch with Linda broke his daily routine, and he took his time accepting the invitation.

After their meal, sipping their coffees, Linda asked, "Frank, we've worked together for five years now, yet I know little of your life outside the office. You're always on time in the morning, for example, at nine sharp. How do you manage? I struggle every day to be in the office on time. What's your secret?"

Frank thought this question was too personal. *Should I tell Linda the details of my morning routine?* Wake up at seven, go to the bathroom, shower, dress, eat breakfast, brush teeth, prepare lunch, and leave for work at eight-fifteen. *No way.* "I do the same things every weekday morning," he said. "I wake up at seven, and at eight-fifteen I leave the house to catch the subway."

"How do you feel about using the subway? I take my car because so many people use the subway during rush hour."

"You are right. Both in the morning and the evening. I hate that part of my life. I hate squeezing into a crowded train. But a few months after I started work at YYZ, I found a way I could avoid at least the misery of the evening rush hour. I stay in town to wait for the crowd to thin out. Often, I spend that time in a pub, the Silver Beaver, a few minutes' walk from the office. The food isn't special and I'm sure it's unhealthy, but together with a beer, it serves its purpose. Sometimes I splurge on a decent meal and a glass of wine in a nearby restaurant. Then I go home, and I can always find a place to sit in the subway."

"That's smart—a good way to avoid the crowd, and when you get home, no need to cook. What do you do for fun? It can't be *all* work. I know you take a few vacation days now and then. Do you travel?"

"I watch TV, and sometimes an old high school friend comes over to talk and we have a beer. I *want* to travel. Many years ago, my parents took me on a trip to the U.S. Southwest. Death Valley overwhelmed me. We travelled in April, and yellow, red, blue, and white desert flowers were blooming. Beautiful. I'd love to visit again. Before I saw Death Valley, I always thought of the desert as an expanse of dry sand and rocks, as you see in *Lawrence of Arabia*. The American Southwest is different, but you must go in March or April when the flowers bloom. We visited the Painted Desert too, and the many shades of red rock shimmering in the sun took my breath away. The next year, we went to New York City. I loved the city. Ever since those trips, going places has been on the top of my list of things to do, but my budget is small, so I don't travel often, and if I do, it's for a few days to a bed-and-breakfast up north, close to Toronto."

"Then you must look forward to your trip to Shanghai."

"Yes, I *am* excited, but the other day when I realized I may have to help Mr. Young retrieve data from his laptop in front of a room full of people, I had difficulty breathing."

"I'm sorry to hear that. But I told you, the chance that he'll call on you in the middle of a meeting is small. Enjoy the thought of going to China. There might be time for sightseeing."

Linda's words did not convince Frank, but her gentle voice and her smile caused him to volunteer more details of his personal life.

"I watch the local news," he said, "and on Tuesday evenings, I follow an interesting crime series. I keep up with sports, such as baseball and basketball."

"Don't you get bored? It doesn't sound exciting. Do you never go see a movie or visit a museum? Or attend a concert? There's so much to do in Toronto!"

"Exciting? No, my life isn't exciting, but I enjoy the routine, doing the same work every day. That's why I'm anxious about the trip to Shanghai."

THREE

THE flight to Shanghai seemed to go on forever. Frank occupied the middle seat of a row of three, in economy, with two large men on either side who kept up a conversation and intruded on his space. Whenever he objected, all he got was, "Sorry, bud—will try not to do it again." Of course, they did it again. Frank guessed being squeezed was the fate of every slim person on an airplane. He wondered how Mr. Young and Linda were enjoying their trip in first class, and he took a quick peek through the curtain that shielded first-class passengers from those in economy. Mr. Young was sipping wine and enjoying a sumptuous-looking meal, while Linda had stretched out her seat and appeared to be sleeping. *They deserve it. They carry the burden of the success of YYZ, and if they fail, I'm out of work.*

The next morning, Frank met Mr. Young and Linda in the hotel conference room and Mr. Young said to him, "I'm sure the long trip made you tired, and I realize you won't have much to do, but be alert. Don't embarrass me by making me wait for an answer when I ask you a question because you dozed off. The three of us must be on our best behaviour."

"Of course, sir. I'll be ready when you need me."

"What did you say? Talk louder."

"Sorry, sir. I said I will be there when you call for me."

Mr. Young busied himself with setting up his laptop, but from his frantic behaviour, Frank could see something was wrong. In the meantime, several Chinese businesspeople filed into the room. They shook Mr. Young's hand and bowed to Linda, who introduced Frank to them:

"My assistant." Frank concentrated on remembering the names of the people he had met and forgot about Mr. Young's struggle with his laptop.

"Frank," Mr. Young called out, and Frank's gaze snapped back to where it should be.

"Yes, sir. I'm here. Is something wrong?"

"Yes. The meeting starts soon, and my laptop doesn't want to start. I hope the trip didn't damage it."

"I'll try to make it work, sir. Did you charge your laptop last night?"

"No. I charged it before we left Toronto. That should have been enough."

"Is it possible you didn't switch it off by mistake and drained the battery? Do you have a charger with you?"

"Yes, but it's in my room, and we don't have time to go up there. Think of something else."

Frank spotted a Chinese gentleman sitting nearby using a similar computer. The large computer bag next to his chair looked promising.

"Do you have a . . . ?" Frank traced his hand from the gentleman's laptop to the bank of electric outlets on the table.

"Oh, a charger, one second." The man retrieved one from his bag. "Try this one. I think it will work."

Frank plugged Mr. Young's laptop in, waited a minute, and switched it on.

"Here you are, sir. Nothing serious. A small power problem."

Frank returned to his chair against the wall behind Mr. Young and Linda. *Wow*, he thought. *I helped Mr. Young and Linda out of a sticky situation. Who knows what else I can contribute? Let's hope whatever goes wrong next will be as easy to fix.*

No other problems needed solving in the next three days. Frank sat in his chair, drank coffee during the breaks, had lunch, and imagined leaving the meetings and doing a bit of sightseeing. Of course, he didn't, because his job was to help Mr. Young. In the evenings, he accompanied Mr. Young and Linda to dinner for more talks. These dinners were no fun because everybody ignored him, even more so than during the day when at least a few people had tried to converse with him in Mandarin, which he did not know how to speak. *Good for Linda and Mr. Young that they had followed courses in Mandarin. I could have done the same, but Linda didn't tell me I should.* Frank felt nobody tried to communicate with him in English, and twice, out of boredom, he spoke to the persons seated next to him. On the first day, he stated, "Toronto is a great city for doing business," and on the second day, "I would love to go on a tour of Shanghai." In both cases, he only received polite smiles. No one was interested in him, and looking at Mr. Young and Linda, Frank concluded they no longer needed him. This improved his mood, and by the third day, his nervousness had abated. Linda sat down next to him. "You look better. You're more relaxed than when we arrived. That's the right attitude."

On the last evening, he tried to find an excuse not to attend dinner, but Linda and Mr. Young insisted he came along. That evening was more interesting than the two previous ones because he met a woman Linda introduced as Mrs. Liu, the CEO of a Shanghai based wholesaler called SunRise Technologies. The company name sounded familiar to Frank. *I think YYZ has done business with them.* He and Mrs. Liu talked about life in Canada and how much he enjoyed living in Toronto. Frank inquired about Shanghai and what to see if he ever came back as a tourist.

"Sorry you did not have time to do a city tour," Mrs. Liu said. "Next time you are in Shanghai, contact me and I will organize a tour for you." Mrs. Liu continued, "Frank, what work do you do in Toronto? What do you know of YYZ's business?"

"I enter data into the office computer. I've never had much interest in YYZ's business or its clients and know little about how my bosses run the company."

"You are not loyal to your boss?"

"Of course, I am, but I have a lot of work to do, and digging into the company's business is not appropriate."

"What does 'appropriate' mean?"

"It means my job does not include the need to investigate what my bosses do."

Mrs. Liu smiled and nodded. "Good. Can you teach me some new English words? I can teach you a few Mandarin words." They spent most of the evening going over common words in both languages, and it was the most entertaining evening of the trip.

The next day, the three of them returned to Toronto. At the gate, waiting to board the plane, Frank asked Linda, "Were the meetings successful? I couldn't follow the discussions in Mandarin."

"The trip worked out well. Thank you for asking. The agreements we made with Mrs. Liu will be very profitable for YYZ."

She didn't elaborate. Frank suspected the agreements meant he would have to do more work and wanted to ask Linda about this, but there was a boarding call for first-class passengers. "We'll talk in Toronto," said Linda. "See you tomorrow in the office."

After the upheaval of the visit to Shanghai, Frank settled back into his usual life, except that he still struggled to figure out why Mr. Young and Linda had asked him to come with them. Other than starting up Mr. Young's laptop, he could not think of any meaningful contribution he had made to the business talks. Frank found no solace in his routine. The Silver Beaver looked dingy, and the smell of stale beer struck him hard. Dinner tasted worse than normal, and the number of beers he drank increased to two, then to three. He was not interested in his favourite baseball team's winning streak. Linda paid a lot of attention to him, visiting him two or three times a day in his office, smiling, and this added to his unease.

"Frank, do you want to come for lunch with me? Mr. Young is away on business, and I could do with some company."

"Eh . . . yes. Let's go to Mary's again."

During the meal, the conversation was smooth. Talking with Linda made Frank forget his anxiety.

"Remember the last time we ate here together?" he said. "I told you about my life, so now tell me something about yours. How did you get involved with YYZ?"

"Oh, simple. After I got my college degree in project management, I rotated through several jobs. One of these was at an auction house, where I met Mr. Young, who often came there to buy merchandise at a low price. I liked him, and after dating for six months, we got married. I started working with him on growing his business. We both worked hard, and after a few years, we did so well that we incorporated and called the business the YYZ Import/Export Company. Leonard—I mean, Mr. Young—owns two shares in the company, and I own one."

"Good for you. It's true you work hard. You're still in the office when I leave at five."

"Yes, I often stay in the office in the evening. But what else should I do? Mr. Young travels a lot, and I don't have many friends. Claudia is one, though. I've known her since elementary school, and you know her too. She told me you worked together at a summer job while you were both in college. She recommended you to me when I needed an extra hand for data entry. I still see her. We go for dinner every last Wednesday of the month."

"Yes. I remember Claudia. We had night jobs stocking shelves in a big grocery store and talked a lot about our plans after finishing college. 'I want to be a project manager,' she told me several times. I wanted to be an office manager. After we graduated, I ran into her once and she told me she'd found a job as an assistant project manager in a big international construction firm. My plan didn't work. I got my degree in office management, but I didn't interview well. I was nervous and mixed up my thoughts, so they must have thought I was incompetent. You hired me at YYZ a few years after graduation, the day after I turned twenty-five. A great birthday present. You must look forward to your get-togethers with Claudia. Having set events in your life is a good thing."

"Don't think of yourself as incompetent. You're good at what you do. And I understand you enjoy the routine of doing the same work five days a week, but I suggest you try to do more. Find another job with more responsibilities. If you do the same thing your whole working life, you'll stop living."

FOUR

A few weeks after their return from Shanghai, Linda came to see Frank. All smiles, she said, "Mr. Young wants to see you."

This was unsettling news; Frank had never been in Mr. Young's office, and his boss seldom spoke to him. Even in Shanghai, after Frank had solved his laptop problem, Mr. Young had not taken the time to thank him for his help.

"Let's not keep him waiting, There's good news for you."

Frank followed Linda. *What good news? An increase in salary?*

"Good of you to come, Frank. We're happy for you," Mr. Young said.

A few seconds passed before Frank could bring himself to ask, "What do you mean, sir?"

"Last night, we spoke on the phone with Mrs. Liu, and she told us she wants to offer you a job. You made a big impression on her. Not that I'm surprised, especially not if you talked import/export with her. You've learned so much about that in the five years you've worked at YYZ. Here's the good news—YYZ is going to help SunRise with their export business to Europe, through Amsterdam, and Mrs. Liu, Linda, and I agreed you should be our man on the ground in Europe." Mr. Young's announcement confused Frank. *Our man on the ground? That is straight out of a spy novel!*

"More good news," continued Mr. Young. "YYZ will promote you to the job of their agent in Amsterdam. We will give you a twenty-per cent raise, and because you'll handle only merchandise SunRise Technologies wants to import into Europe, they will also compensate you for your time. Guess what? This is great! You'll double your current salary. What do you think?"

Mr. Young's message stunned Frank. He wanted to point out he only did data entry, but his words came out garbled, and he gave up trying to explain he didn't feel qualified. A congratulatory tap on his shoulder from Linda brought him back to reality.

"What do I have to do in Amsterdam, sir?"

Linda answered Frank's question. "We'll go over that in more detail later, but for now, you should know that, as friends of SunRise, we want to help them make their export business easier. This means we'll buy merchandise from SunRise, import the goods into Canada, and then ship it in containers to Europe under the YYZ label, as we do when we supply our European clients with other Chinese goods, except then we use different suppliers, not SunRise. Our freight forwarder will handle the paperwork needed for importing the goods into Europe. SunRise will supply the certificates of origin, giving details of the Chinese manufacturers. The most important document is the commercial invoice, which describes the goods and lists the addresses of the buyers in various European countries. Your duties as the agent for YYZ are to make sure the shipments pass through customs in Amsterdam by presenting the forms, and to collect the invoices for customs and storage fees, which you'll send to me. Once the goods have cleared customs in Amsterdam, our transporter can distribute them throughout Europe and get the containers to SunRise's clients."

Mr. Young added, "The procedure sounds complicated, but it isn't. You'll learn in no time what forms you need to present to customs in Amsterdam, and once you know that, clearing the goods becomes routine. SunRise will give you an apartment in downtown Amsterdam with enough space so it can also serve as your office. There will be times when we will have few shipments, and during those times, we expect you to travel around Europe to meet SunRise clients and find new ones. SunRise will reimburse the costs of travel and accommodation. I think it's a great job."

At the mention of travel through Europe, Frank's heart skipped a beat, and he asked, "When do I start, sir?"

"As soon as possible. SunRise has a lot of goods in Shanghai ready for shipment to Europe. Mrs. Liu, Mrs. Young, and I hope you can start your new job next week."

"No problem. I have nothing special planned."

"I didn't think so," said Mr. Young. "Mrs. Young, on behalf of SunRise, will take care of your travel arrangements and teach you what you need to know about the paperwork, so stay in touch with her."

The meeting finished. Linda left, and Mr. Young started reading documents that were lying on his desk. Frank thanked Mr. Young for his promotion before returning to his office, where, for the rest of the day, he had trouble concentrating.

Later that day, Mr. Young met Linda in his office. Mr. Young took a sip from his coffee cup. "Frank's perfect for the job. I'm sure he's reliable. He's not ambitious or curious about what we're doing. And Mrs. Liu has taken a shine to him. Who knew Frank was such a charmer?"

"Yes, he's the perfect man to be our agent. He has the right looks and the proper manners, not like the Transport Coordinator in Amsterdam or the SunRise employees Mrs. Liu likes to hire. They come across as the rough, hardcore criminals they are. Frank will make a good impression on the customs officers, which will help him clear the containers. But I pity him. If the scheme falls apart, the Dutch police will arrest him, and Frank, and the two of us, will feel bad about that. Maybe we should have hired some hardcore criminal?"

"It was his choice," said Leonard. "It's a dream job. Those come at a price, and he should know that. And if he gets arrested, so what? The Transport Coordinator will contact you as soon as he thinks there is something wrong and we will shut down YYZ and be halfway the Caribbean by the time Frank figures things out. We don't owe him anything."

Leonard looked out the window. He turned to Linda and said, "Do you want to stay here for the rest of your life? Look at the weather, grey and wet. We're better off living on a Caribbean island. Forget about Frank."

He switched topics. "I went to see the people in the warehouse. They are important: they must pack the SunRise merchandise in boxes that are right for their destinations. They told me they promised you not to mention the SunRise connection to anyone, not even to their immediate families. Are you sure they'll do their job and be discreet?"

"They're reliable. Hand-picked by me. The SunRise merchandise is only a small fraction of the goods they handle, and they have no problem keeping their mouths shut. They see it for what it is, a side business."

"A side business for sure, but a profitable one."

* * *

Frank was ecstatic about the increase in salary and living in an old European city and travelling through Europe, but the promotion had been unexpected and disturbing. Various thoughts popped up in his mind. He knew that YYZ buying Chinese goods and then exporting them to Europe was nothing new. They did this often. YYZ had almost as many European as Canadian customers, and a professional broker cleared the goods through Amsterdam customs. *But what's so special about the SunRise goods that they'll pay me a salary and give me a free apartment to handle them? Why do they ship goods to Europe through Canada? What trouble is SunRise having exporting goods to Europe?* These were obvious questions, but he didn't know the answers and decided he shouldn't be busy with something that wasn't his business. Mr. Young and Linda were seasoned businesspeople. He was the data entry clerk, and he should trust that his bosses knew what they were doing.

Despite these questions and his mixed feelings, Frank got ready for his move. He wanted to change his old khaki pants and white shirt for something better suited to his new status. Encouraged by the impending increase in his salary, he dipped into his savings to buy a new business suit, two new white shirts, new shoes, and a suitcase to hold his clothing, toiletries, and a few knick-knacks. He emptied his apartment, giving away most of his few possessions to charity, cleaned out his fridge, and talked to the owner of his apartment about breaking his lease with only a week's notice.

On the day before he left for Amsterdam, Linda handed him the ticket.

"I'll miss you, Frank. It was great having you around the office."

"I'll miss you too."

"No, you won't. You're starting another life, and you're going to be busy with your work in Amsterdam and your travels through Europe. I'm happy for you. Send me an email now and then and tell me how much you enjoy your new job. I want to take you out for dinner tonight to celebrate, but I imagine you already have plans. Do you have to say goodbye to your friends?"

"Yes, I planned to, and I'll take a rain check for the dinner until I come back."

That evening, he visited the Silver Beaver and told the bartender that the next morning he was going to Amsterdam. "I got a promotion and will work for my company as an agent there."

"We hate to see you leave, but that's a significant promotion," said the bartender, who handed him a beer. "It's on the house. To celebrate your success."

Other men at the bar, regulars who knew Frank, congratulated him and called for a drink.

"You must love your promotion," the man next to him said. He was a regular, called Ethan, with whom Frank talked occasionally.

"It's great. I'm looking forward to living in Amsterdam, and I was told the job involved travelling through Europe, something I've wanted to do for a long time."

"You're lucky. I've never got a promotion. I've been working for the same company for twelve years now as a junior office manager, and I do my job well. When the office manager left, I expected my company to promote me, but no—a twenty-four-year-old with a B.A. who's worked there only three years got the job. To make things worse, my boss asked me to teach this guy the details of his new job." The bitterness in Ethan's voice did not escape Frank. "No one is interested in me," Ethan added.

"That's tough," said Frank with sympathy. "Hey, when I come back—and I can't tell you when that will be—I'll find you a better job at YYZ."

"Thanks, I'll wait for you. Let me buy you a beer."

Frank didn't want Ethan's negative mood to overshadow his feelings about going to Europe. He changed seats, and after a few more beers, headed home. The only thought he had was that the next day he would be on the plane to Amsterdam.

Well before it was time to go to the airport, Frank locked the door of his apartment, and arrived at the Departures Hall four hours early. He checked in and wandered around in his new suit and shoes until he had to board the plane. His new outfit, he noticed, made him feel important.

Frank arrived in Amsterdam early in the morning. Despite not having slept on the plane, he didn't feel tired. His excitement and a prominent sense of anticipation had increased his energy. After claiming his luggage, he scanned the Arrivals Hall and saw a man holding up a sign with his name written on it. Frank headed over, shook hands, and introduced himself.

"Welcome," said the man, who didn't bother to mention his name.

Frank didn't like him. The man had shaved his head, but a three-day stubble adorned his face. His shirt was an awful, fluorescent green with odd shapes and letters. Frank couldn't figure out whether there was any meaning to these decorations or if they were a sign of poor taste. He wore jeans held in place by a belt with a large, showy buckle, and his clothes smelled of cigarette smoke. The two of them walked to the taxi stand.

"How was the flight?" the man asked. "Did you get any sleep?"

"No, I didn't. I'm too excited to start the work here. Are you involved as well?"

"Fuck, yes. I coordinate the transport of the containers you clear through customs. I've been working for SunRise Technologies and YYZ in Europe for a long time and have lots of contacts in the trucking business, so we can move the merchandise out of the customs compound fast without having to pay storage fees."

The Transport Coordinator spoke with a distinctive accent that reminded Frank of a Dutch visitor to the YYZ office. His use of the F-word made him dislike the Transport Coordinator even more. His parents had taught him to use proper language, and on the rare occasions Frank used the F-word, he felt ashamed.

Frank enjoyed the ride through downtown Amsterdam. The contrast with Toronto couldn't have been bigger, and Frank realized how lucky he was to start his first trip to Europe in Amsterdam.

"It's a beautiful city—it looks special," he told the Transport Coordinator, who commented with a shrug.

"Look at these centuries-old houses and canals," Frank continued, "Imagine, people lived here three, four hundred years ago. I wonder what life was like then. What did they do? I can't wait to walk around town and enjoy the views. Travelling to Europe has been a long-time dream for me, and Amsterdam is an excellent place to start."

The Transport Coordinator looked at him. "I hope you know you are here for business. Not to stroll through the city and play tourist. In case travelling and tourism tempt you too much, know that we—SunRise and I—have a way to check up on you, so don't think you can do whatever you want. You fucking well better concentrate on your work and not make any mistakes."

A chill ran down Frank's spine. "Are you threatening me? I only arrived an hour ago! Don't worry, I'll do what is necessary to make my bosses at YYZ and SunRise happy."

"You better. The last agent, the one who worked with us in Antwerp, in Belgium, made mistakes and talked to people she met in bars and restaurants about SunRise and the merchandise in the containers she cleared. Shit, we couldn't tolerate that, so Mrs. Liu sent two enforcers to make her disappear."

"Why are you telling me that? What does that mean, 'to make her disappear?' Did you hurt her?"

The Transport Coordinator answered in a voice coloured with sarcasm. "I see you are a smart guy."

Frank's mood turned. *I hope they only scared her witless and didn't kill her.* But the Transport Coordinator's voice suggested otherwise. Doubts about whether he had made the right decision in accepting Mr. Young's offer crept up on Frank. *Should I have stayed home and stuck with my quiet life, or should I enjoy travelling and do what I agreed to as well as possible? I can still go back to Toronto and explain to Mr. Young I'm not fit for the job.*

Although the Transport Coordinator's words had put a serious dent in Frank's positive mood, one look out of the car window made him decide that accepting Mr. Young's proposal had been a good idea.

They got out of the taxi in front of a well-preserved old building on the Herengracht, one of the canals that form half-rings around downtown Amsterdam. The Transport Coordinator held out the keys. "Your apartment is on the third floor. You'll like it. Enjoy, but make sure not to mention your work to anybody. If somebody asks, say you are a freelance travel writer exploring the city."

"Why should I lie about my job? I'm an agent for YYZ, and that's a legit job. There's nothing to hide."

"It is better you don't mention YYZ, but if you do, be careful to whom you speak and what you say and never talk about SunRise. You don't want to suffer the same fate as your colleague in Antwerp."

Frank didn't hear that last remark. He had grabbed the keys and taken the stairs two steps at a time. A wave of happiness flushed over him when he entered his apartment, and a few small tears welled up in his eyes. The apartment was small, but SunRise had furnished it well with a small couch, a comfortable armchair, a dining table with two chairs, and a desk with a computer, a printer, and a fax machine. There was a well-equipped kitchen and a separate small bedroom. The view over the Herengracht was spectacular. *I love it here—so much better than anything else I've experienced in the last five years! I can live here for the rest of my life.*

After unpacking his belongings, Frank installed himself in the armchair and thought about the things he was going to do. Exploring the city was on the top of his list. Paris and the South of France, at the beach, were other destinations that popped up in his mind. But, after a while, his thoughts returned to what the Transport Coordinator had told him. That Mrs. Liu, with whom he had spent such a pleasant evening, had hired enforcers was disappointing. *Why does she have two thugs working for her? What's at stake here? It must be big and profitable to need enforcers to defend her interests. No doubt it involves the merchandise in the containers I'm to clear through customs. Should I try to find out more about the merchandise? Or should I quit now so nobody can implicate me in whatever is going on with these containers?* No, he decided, not yet. Mrs. Liu might use the enforcers to keep her competitors from muscling in on her business. He would learn about the merchandise from the paperwork Linda was going to fax him. No hurry to return to Toronto and his old data entry job.

Over the next few days, Frank didn't hear from Linda. This suited him, since it gave him time to explore the city. He visited the flower market and Rembrandt Square, where he made his way through a three-dimensional mock-up of Rembrandt's painting *The Night Watch*. He went to the Dam Square downtown, where he sat at the foot of the National War Memorial to take in the vibrant street life. But by far, his favourite activity was to walk along the canals, admiring the architecture of the seventeenth- and eighteenth-century houses lining these once important waterways. Merchants and other well-off citizens of Amsterdam had built these houses in an era when Amsterdam was a major trading centre. They sent ships to India and Southeast Asia, and the ships returned with spices, sugar cane, coffee, and many other types of merchandise. The centuries-old buildings inspired Frank, and he imagined himself as a spice trader selling his wares at auction. He would stand on a bridge looking out over a canal and draw a picture in his mind of people, including himself, dressed in seventeenth-century fashion, something he had seen in a brochure from the tourist information office. He saw himself walking along the canals.

"Hello, Frank," people said. "How is business?"

"Very well, thank you. I'm expecting a new shipment of spices to arrive soon."

"Good timing. Prices are on the rise. Can you please reserve a bag of nutmeg for me? I'm running low."

"Of course. I'll have someone bring it to your warehouse as soon as it arrives."

He repeated this once or twice a day, and the result of his imaginary meetings was that he felt more and more at home in this city that was so different from Toronto.

There were real meetings, too. The old barges tied up along the canals intrigued Frank. They were old merchandise transporters, long ago replaced by more efficient trucks and trains. He noticed people were living on these barges, and twice, while he was admiring a barge, the occupants invited him aboard and offered him coffee. He talked with them about his life in Toronto and his job as an agent for YYZ, but he never mentioned SunRise. Both times, his feeling that he was becoming part of the city grew. *I hope my job lasts a long time.*

Frank lunched on the many patios that had opened with the dry, sunny June weather, and he tried out several cafes to become familiar with Dutch beer. For his evening drinks, he settled on a cafe a short walk from his apartment. After a few visits, the regular patrons accepted him and reserved a place for him at the bar. Conversations were easy because most of the regulars and other people he met in Amsterdam spoke enough English to keep a conversation going. Frank fell in love with the city, which was a mix of the old and the modern. Amsterdam was inviting and stimulated his imagination, something Toronto had never done. *What a wonderful city! Amsterdam is my new home.*

FIVE

AFTER ten days, Frank received an email from Linda stating the first container was due to arrive soon and that in the meantime, he should meet SunRise Technologies' contacts in Brussels. "Not a business visit, more of a courtesy call." Instead of emailing or phoning, Linda preferred he go in person. She had written he was to catch an early morning Intercity train from Amsterdam Central Station, arriving in Brussels before noon. Someone was going to accompany him to the restaurant where the meeting was to take place.

Frank was excited. His first European trip! It was a sunny day, and his window seat gave him an unobstructed view of the Dutch landscape. For a while, he counted the cows grazing in the green fields, but after he had counted two hundred of them, he stopped. Frank looked at the fluffy white clouds and tried to recognize the shapes they formed: an elephant, a person, a ship . . . He had researched the tourist attractions in Brussels and was looking forward to visiting the Grand Place—the central square—of which he had seen stunning pictures on his phone. Frank wondered about the contacts. Who were they? And what was he going to tell them, other than a container was arriving in Amsterdam the next morning and they could expect it to arrive the next evening? Frank speculated on the contents of the container: handbags, clothing, jewellery, electronics, medicine? He didn't know, and he cared little. He met the Transport Coordinator in the railway station. Despite the threatening words at their first meeting, Frank greeted him without hostility. He asked the Transport Coordinator, "What do I call you?"

"You don't have to know my name. Many people who work with SunRise prefer to stay anonymous, but if you want to call me Ed, you can, as long as you realize that is not my real name."

"Okay, Ed, where are we meeting the SunRise customers? Is there time for a quick tour around downtown Brussels?"

"I don't fucking think so. You must take the three-p.m. train back, but you are lucky. We are going to meet the SunRise contacts in La Rose Blanche, on the Grand Place, so you will get an idea of what the square looks like even though you don't have the chance for a full city tour. Let's go. The restaurant is close, only a five-minute walk."

The beauty of the Grand Place overwhelmed Frank, and he slowed down to a crawl to look around the square. He forgot why he had come to Brussels. The Transport Coordinator waited, but after a few minutes said, "Hey, fucking time for our meeting."

They entered La Rose Blanche and made their way up to the second floor, where they met with two big, bulky men at a table in the back. Frank introduced himself as they shook hands. One of them wore black-rimmed glasses and grunted at Frank without giving his name. The other man was more friendly and told Frank to call him Z.

Frank enjoyed his food and the excellent wine that came with it. Halfway through the meal, he told Z that the next day, in the morning, a container would arrive in Amsterdam. He asked the Transport Coordinator if he had a solid estimate of the time of arrival. "Between six and seven tomorrow evening." Z liked that information and put up his glass to toast a continuing collaboration between YYZ and SunRise.

Encouraged by his role in this transaction—and by the three glasses of wine he had drunk—Frank said, looking at Z, "I haven't seen the paperwork yet. Tell me, what's in this container? Are they expensive items? Where are they going? How much profit is SunRise making on them? I'd like to know what goods I'm clearing through customs."

It was as if time around the table had stopped. Z's fork paused halfway between his plate and his mouth. The Transport Coordinator's wine glass touched his lips, but he didn't drink, and the napkin of the Man with the

Black-Rimmed Glasses hovered in midair. This lasted only half a second, and then the Man with the Black-Rimmed Glasses put his hand in the inner pocket of his jacket. Frank, to his horror, saw the handle of a knife. The Transport Coordinator mumbled several obscene sentences. Z's demeanour became hostile. He grabbed Frank's arm and said in a steely voice, "Come with me." Frank had no choice, and, unsteady on his feet, he walked with Z to the men's room. Z's hand lay heavy on Frank's shoulder. The Man with the Black-Rimmed Glasses was a few steps behind them. As soon as Frank and Z entered the men's room—the Man with the Black-Rimmed Glasses stayed outside—Z grabbed Frank by the lapels of his new suit and slammed him against the wall. Pain exploded in Frank's head.

"Why did you ask those questions? What's in the containers, where the goods are going, and how much money we make is not your business. You clear the containers and forget about them right away. Don't remember what's in the paperwork. Concentrate on your job. The agent in Antwerp had too much interest in the contents of the containers and talked about the goods with people she met in bars and restaurants. We couldn't allow her to do that. She might have caused our business a lot of trouble, and we took care of her. Remember, the moment you clear the container and the Transport Coordinator has it picked up, you will forget about it. Mrs. Liu told us you were reliable and not curious, but now I'm not sure we can work with you. Tell me, why are you interested in what's in the container? What do you have in mind? Stealing the container and selling the merchandise?"

Frank could not control his shaking. His head hurt, and he felt as if he had peed in his pants.

"I meant nothing, and I'm tired from the trip. I was just talking. I don't know what came over me. It was the wine," he blurted out as excuses for asking questions. He understood he had violated a code he had to follow.

"I did a stupid thing; it won't happen again," he added in a weak voice. Frank had difficulty speaking. He couldn't control the trembling of his lips.

Z looked at Frank with pity and disgust and slammed him once more against the wall, looked him over, and said, "We will let this go, but I assure you—the next time, we will eliminate you. My associate wanted to knife you right here, but he answers to me, so for now, you're safe. But I can't restrain him if you do something stupid again. We took care of the agent in Antwerp, and we can take care of you. Remember, you're only a small part of a large organization. We can replace you. For your own sake, no asking questions, no talking about your job. Clear the containers as they come and forget about them."

Frank's knees started wobbling. If Z hadn't held him by the lapels of his suit, he would have slid down the wall and ended up as a pile of fear on the floor. *These are Mrs. Liu's enforcers who killed the Antwerp agent.* Z's voice changed back to the friendly tone he had used over lunch. "Clean yourself up and join us for dessert."

It took a while before Frank could face himself in the mirror. He looked pale and his lips still trembled, but he felt good that at least he hadn't soiled himself. He arranged his suit jacket and left the washroom. The Man with the Black-Rimmed Glasses was standing next to the door. Frank did not dare to make eye contact and walked by him as fast as he could. After he joined the others, he ordered a coffee. While he waited, he stared at a table at the other end of the dining room. When he finished his coffee, the Transport Coordinator said, looking at Z, "I guess we're done with this meeting. The meal was excellent, thank you, and if we have nothing else to discuss, Frank and I will walk to the station and return to Amsterdam."

Z looked at Frank. "Thanks for coming. We got to know each other. We can work with you for now, but remember what I told you." Frank stood up, and without a word, he followed the Transport Coordinator. Once outside, Frank looked around, and it seemed to him the Grand Place had lost a lot of its lustre.

The train ride back was not as pleasant as the morning trip. Frank stared out the window but did not take in the landscape or the fluffy clouds he had enjoyed seeing in the morning. He still had a headache and wondered if he had a concussion. *I must see a doctor if it doesn't improve.* He thought of Mrs. Liu and how she had treated him so well in Shanghai and had offered to organize a city tour if he returned there. Mrs. Liu hiring goons such as Z and the Man with the Black-Rimmed Glasses disappointed Frank. *I must be careful not to make any more mistakes. Do my job and no more questions.*

The two men did not talk until halfway through the trip. The Transport Coordinator started, "Hey, perk up—nothing serious has happened. You broke the fucking rules, and Z took you to the washroom to remind you not to talk about your work. I can only guess what he did to you, but it can't have been too bad. You are still in one piece. By the way, a button is missing from your suit. Better get that fixed."

"These were the guys who killed the Antwerp agent, weren't they?"

"Yes, they were. You don't fucking well want them to visit you. When they finish with you, your mother might have trouble recognizing you. They checked you out today, and you gave them a reason to be concerned, but they gave you a second chance. Remember, if you stick to your work, they won't bother you."

Frank didn't react and continued staring out the window.

"We need to work out a protocol, for when our goods arrive in Amsterdam."

"We know what to do. I claim the container and do the paper work, and you organize the transport."

"Of course, I agree, and everything should go fine if we stick to a routine. I will inquire with customs about what time they will off-load the container and let you know. That is the time you get to the customs office, and you must fucking well call me within two hours to tell me you have no problems clearing the container."

Frank nodded and continued to stare out the window, but after a while asked, "Why two hours?"

"You must phone me as soon as you have signed the papers and the container has cleared customs. My experience tells me this takes one to two hours from the time you get to the customs office. If I haven't heard from you in those two hours, I assume something is wrong, and I must contact Mrs. Young in Toronto."

"Why Mrs. Young?"

"She has a lot of experience in clearing goods through customs. She may help with moving things forward."

"Oh, yes, I guess so."

The Transport Coordinator continued, "I am sure you have wondered whether you must do something else. Clearing one fucking container a week or every two weeks is an easy job."

"I thought of that. YYZ and SunRise pay me because they don't want to involve an official broker. I don't know the reason, but paying me might be cheaper for them than paying a broker? Not now, but it might if they come up with other jobs for me. Mr. Young told me that part of my job is to find new clients. When do I have to start with that?"

"Don't worry, Mrs. Liu will remind you. Almost everybody who works for SunRise—and that includes me and Z and the Man with the Black-Rimmed Glasses—must bring in new clients. But for now, clear the fucking containers."

"I will. Everybody has his job, don't worry."

After a night of fitful sleep, offset in the morning by two cups of strong coffee, Frank visited the customs office, which was a busy place. Many containers had to be cleared. Frank profited from the solid reputation YYZ enjoyed among the customs officers. On the rare occasions when officers had selected a YYZ container for inspection, they had found nothing wrong. Thus, when Frank introduced himself and showed a letter written by Linda on YYZ letterhead naming him as the YYZ agent, a customs officer named Tolman said, "Welcome to Amsterdam. If you sign these papers here, we will give you your container. Are there more coming?"

"Yes, there will be many more containers, and I will be around for a long time."

Frank signed the paperwork, and he was told the container should soon be ready. He phoned the Transport Coordinator to tell him that all was well.

After he saw the truck loaded with the YYZ container leave the customs compound, Frank walked back to his apartment. He emailed Linda, confirming the first container had cleared customs and was on its way to Brussels. Frank imagined how Linda hurried to Mr. Young's office to bring him the excellent news and tell him he, Frank, had done a good job.

SIX

FRANK cleared one container every two weeks. A few days before each container arrived in Amsterdam, Linda sent him an email telling him where to visit the SunRise contacts and the travel times. By now, he knew these visits were for the contacts, the men who ran the warehouses, to check him out, and so far, they had agreed to work with him. These emails were a mixed pleasure. The locations were places he could, not that long ago, have only dreamed of visiting—Paris, Barcelona, Berlin. But Frank looked forward to these meetings with trepidation because he didn't enjoy the people with whom he had lunch or dinner. They were variations on Z and the Man with the Black-Rimmed Glasses: rough and uneducated men who drank a lot and always ended up discussing women, saying they wouldn't mind having fun with the waitress or other women in the restaurant. Never a word on a subject other than money or sex, except for soccer, a sport that didn't interest Frank.

On a train trip to Berlin, he shared his compartment with a gentleman, well dressed in dark grey pants, a dark blue jacket, and a white shirt, open at the neck. His face was open and friendly, and he looked fit. Frank estimated he was in his mid-fifties.

"Are you Dutch?" he asked. "My name is Frank."

"Yes, I am Dutch. My name is Herman."

"I am Canadian, but I work in Amsterdam. As an agent for a Canadian import/export company." He remembered that the Transport Coordinator had told him not to talk about his work, but he had rejected that idea. He didn't have enough experience to pose as a travel writer. It would be awkward if people asked him questions about places to go or hotels to stay and he couldn't answer. Frank saw nothing wrong with mentioning his job as an agent. But he never mentioned he also worked for a Chinese company. *No need to complicate things.*

"What does an agent do?"

"My company exports goods to Europe, and I clear merchandise through customs. Since I'm new to this job, my bosses in Toronto insist I see their clients before the goods arrive. I guess these are 'get to know you' visits. That's why I'm going to Berlin today. I'll be back in Amsterdam tomorrow, and clear the merchandise destined for Berlin that will arrive in the Amsterdam container terminal in the morning."

"Sounds like you have a good job—not too stressful. What else do you do? Answer client complaints, organize returns, or promote your company?"

"For now, I only deal with the customs office. No stress, once you know what to do and how to behave." An image of Z and the Man with the Black-Rimmed Glasses flashed before Frank's eyes.

"What merchandise are you importing into Europe?"

"A variety of goods. The office manager in Toronto describes them in the paperwork she sends me, but I pay little attention to what she writes. The goods arrive in big containers that hold up to twenty-five thousand pounds of merchandise—impossible to remember all the individual items they contain."

"Imported from China, I guess. I don't know the situation in Canada, but in Europe, nobody, except for a few large plants, can manufacture anything anymore at a price competitive with what we pay for Chinese-made goods. It is a real shame we became so dependent on China."

"Yes, I agree, but most of the goods that come from China are of high quality. I know, because I worked in the Canadian office, and complaints from our Canadian clients about the quality of the Chinese merchandise were rare. Chinese manufacturing has caught up with what we make in Europe and North America, but at a much lower price."

"I suppose my idea that Chinese goods are of inferior quality was right some time ago. I am glad that is no longer the case. But I heard the counterfeit industry is big in China and Canada. Are you familiar with that?"

"No. This is the first time I've heard that. Are you sure?"

"I read it in the newspaper. There was an article that described a police raid on a shopping mall in a suburb north of Toronto. They found lots of counterfeit goods."

"But that doesn't mean a Canadian company manufactured them."

"No, of course not, and I am not suggesting you import fake merchandise."

For a while, both men were quiet. Herman was going to take a nap, and Frank felt like doing the same. He was always nervous on the day of travel, and despite the train leaving at eleven in the morning, he had woken up early, so a nap was a good idea before he arrived in Berlin and had to look sharp. As usual, Linda had arranged for the Transport Coordinator to meet him at the station. *We'll go for dinner*, Frank thought, and he slipped into a deep sleep.

Frank met the Transport Coordinator, and in the taxi to the restaurant where they were to meet their contacts, the Transport Coordinator told him, "This visit is important for you. The men you are going to see are picky about the people they work with. If you had pulled a stunt as you did in Brussels here in Berlin, it would have finished badly for you and me and your bosses in Toronto and Shanghai. So be alert, answer their questions, but don't mention what's in the fucking container that is coming."

"Easy. I don't know what's in the container because Mrs. Young hasn't faxed over the paperwork yet."

"Good. Remember what I told you when we first met? Mrs. Liu is a tough cookie and won't hesitate to punish you and replace you with someone she can trust."

Their contacts didn't bother to introduce themselves. Without trying to make conversation, Contact1 asked, "When does the container arrive?"

"It arrives in Amsterdam late tomorrow morning, so it might be here early in the morning the next day."

The Transport Coordinator nodded. "That's correct. I will phone you with a more precise time once I know."

"Are these the goods from China?" asked Contact1.

Contact2 added. "Are the gaming systems in the container?"

Frank hesitated for a fraction of a second. *These are test questions.* He answered, "I don't know. I haven't seen the paperwork yet. Besides, I'm not interested in the container's contents. My responsibility is to make sure the merchandise clears customs. It's a fine job, and I hope to do it for a long time."

The contacts nodded and Contact1 said, "Good. That is the way we work. If you stick to what you *have* to do, you will have a well-paid future with us."

Frank felt good that he had gotten the approval of the Berlin contacts. Pleading ignorance and a lack of interest in the contents of the containers had also worked in Paris and Barcelona.

The conversation continued, accompanied by a lot of beer. Frank wasn't keen on German beer. He found it too bitter. Remembering the consequences of his drinking in Brussels, he switched to mineral water. After a while, he left, leaving the contacts and the Transport Coordinator to their drinking, and spent the rest of the evening walking through Berlin's city centre, admiring the majestic architecture and visiting the Wall.

During the return trip, Frank had the compartment to himself most of the time. He arrived in Amsterdam at five p.m., walked to his apartment to pick up the paperwork Linda had faxed over, and went straight to the customs office to clear the container, which he did without difficulties. Frank then phoned the Transport Coordinator, who had taken an earlier train, to tell him everything was fine and sent off a similar message by email to Linda. He headed home, with a short stopover at his favourite cafe for a beer. He looked forward to at least a week of free time.

SEVEN

LINDA met with her best friend Claudia in a downtown restaurant. "Hey, Linda! Good to see you. I have something important to tell you," was the first thing Claudia said.

"What, another boyfriend?"

"No, not another boyfriend. I said 'something important.' Guess what —my company promoted me to project manager in our Paris office. They need someone to get three housing development projects back on track. One site is close, north of the city, and the others are further north, close to the Belgian border. I leave on Friday. The office manager of the Paris office will pick me up from the airport and bring me to a corporate apartment."

"Fantastic! And well deserved. You've worked so hard, and it paid off. Congratulations! You're leaving behind another heartbroken boyfriend. What's the name of the current one?"

"William, but I don't think he would have lasted long. The other night, he brought me to a pub called the Silver Beaver—what a dive—and guess what? I saw *Frank* there, but he didn't notice me. You remember him, don't you?"

"Of course—you put me in touch with him. He's been working for us for the last five years, and a month ago Leonard promoted him to be our agent in Amsterdam."

"Great! Frank was always talking about his wish to travel."

"Yes, but I'm uncomfortable because he doesn't know the true nature of his work. His job includes irregularities that could land him in trouble. I played a big role in Frank landing this job, but I'm having second thoughts."

"Tell me another time," said Claudia, who preferred to talk about how she was going to enjoy her stay in Paris over discussing Frank's possible problems, and soon the two women were engaged in talking about the main tourist attractions of Paris and what Claudia would do for her job. They finished their meal by sharing a big slice of cheesecake, split the bill as usual, and left.

"You must come and see me," said Claudia. "We can tour Paris and enjoy the food and wine."

"I will. I could do with a vacation."

Claudia's departure affected Linda more than she had expected. She realized how important the monthly dinners had been for her. The thought she had no other friends to go out with was devastating. Yes, she went out with Leonard, but those outings differed from her dinner dates with Claudia. Often, they ended up in a pub, the Silver Beaver, and most of the time they drank too much. Leonard always had a good time talking to his drinking buddies, but on those evenings, Linda felt abandoned. She would talk with the few women in the pub, but never enjoyed these outings much. She was tired of the Silver Beaver, and she didn't want to go out with Leonard anymore. He wasn't the right person. She wanted to go for dinner in a proper restaurant, go to the movies or the theatre or a concert or the ballet—events they could afford, but which didn't interest Leonard. She didn't want to go alone, and taking advantage of the many cultural events Toronto offered remained an unfulfilled wish.

Over time, Linda had become convinced Leonard was interested only in making money. He had told her his money-making ventures had started in high school, where he bought six-packs of Coke and sold them to his friends at a markup. Linda suspected that in the pub or in his sleep, he was designing profitable trading schemes. Linda also enjoyed making money. Despite knowing the criminal nature of the trading scheme, she had gone along with Leonard's latest plan of lending YYZ's excellent reputation to SunRise. The business was profitable. Each time Frank cleared the merchandise through customs in Amsterdam, a generous payment from Shanghai followed two or three days later. *Too bad—one day a customs officer will choose our container for inspection, and we'll have to leave YYZ behind and travel, in a hurry, to a Caribbean island.*

Now that the SunRise-YYZ collaboration was operational, it bothered Linda she had proposed Frank as the European agent. *I should warn him and tell him to get out while he still can. I should talk with Leonard about hiring a hardened criminal to do Frank's job.* The cost would be much higher than what they paid Frank, but they could afford the extra expense. The problem with this idea was that SunRise had to agree with it, and she wasn't sure how to approach Mrs. Liu. Regardless, she proposed to Leonard they replace Frank. This discussion took place in the Silver Beaver and was short.

"No," said Leonard. "Frank could have said no, but he didn't. He *wanted* to go to Europe with two salaries and a free apartment. We won't change that. He doesn't cost us anything extra, except the trivial amount we spend on the increase in his salary. SunRise pays the other expenses —rent and travel and whatnot. I am not going back to them asking for more money to hire another person. Oh, and something else. I spoke with Mrs. Liu this afternoon, and she wants us to ramp up the volume of goods we're shipping. This means we must hire two more people for the warehouse. This will be good for us and make Frank work harder."

"Are you sure you want to increase the volume of goods? We, and Frank, are taking most of the risk. We may have to give up on YYZ and move out of Toronto."

"That's why SunRise pays us as much as they do. Don't make problems. We have a unique opportunity to get rich. Then we can do without YYZ and Toronto and have a wonderful life. We'll buy whatever we want, and we'll be happy."

He's right, Linda thought. *Frank will have to take care of himself. He's well paid for the work he is doing.* But her feeling that their treatment of Frank was not fair remained. *Of course, I'll support our cooperation with SunRise. I won't make problems. We're a team; we're a couple.*

EIGHT

"HERMAN, how are you? I haven't seen you for a while, not since what happened in Antwerp."

The Transport Coordinator was meeting Herman in a small cafe off Dam Square.

"I'm well, thanks, except for this warm August weather. Yes, what happened in Antwerp was unfortunate. We had a good thing going, like we do now here in Amsterdam, but you can't control the customs officers. If someday they empty your container, all you can do is walk away."

Herman wiped his forehead.

"You're right, we ran," said the Transport Coordinator.

"No, not we. *You* ran. The police arrested *me*. Thanks to the lawyer hired by Mrs. Liu, I beat the charges."

The Transport Coordinator nodded. "I remember. That's why you are still here. We had a good run of importing through the port of Antwerp. How long were we busy there?"

"Almost eight months."

"Eight profitable months," said the Transport Coordinator.

"Let's hope our Amsterdam operation lasts at least as long," said Herman. "But now Toronto is an extra step in getting the goods into Europe, which increases the chance someone will make a mistake. But if everything goes well, the current operation should be at least as profitable as the one in Antwerp. I need the money because I want to retire. It's getting hard for me to do my job. The constant travel to check the various players is taking its toll. I don't enjoy going all over Europe to make sure nobody is skimming off the top. I like the accounting, but the travel gets too cumbersome."

Herman paused for a moment, thinking about his first travels years ago, and how he had enjoyed exploring new cities, beaches, and forests. *I'm getting older, so no surprise the constant travelling makes me tired.* He shrugged off these thoughts. *Getting old is natural and I can still enjoy my life.*

"Hey, nice to meet you," said Herman, "but why are we here? Any complaints or directives from Shanghai?"

"No. I have concerns about the fucking new agent. His name is Frank —but you must have heard that from Mrs. Liu."

The swearing of the Transport Coordinator made Herman wince. It was one of his complaints about the distributors he dealt with. *Why can't they speak as most people do? Why the rough language?*

"Okay," he said. "Tell me what disturbs you so much that we must meet. Mrs. Liu told me Frank was the ideal candidate, and she was, and as far as I am aware, still is, satisfied with him as the agent. For now, I have no reason to disagree. He looks solid. Mrs. Liu asked me to check him out, so I travelled with him on the train to Berlin, sharing a compartment. I asked him about his work, but he told me nothing that could compromise the operation. I asked if he was familiar with the sale of counterfeit merchandise, but he said he was not. When I pressed him further, he insisted the Chinese goods they imported were of excellent quality."

"Yes, he also talked well to our contacts in Berlin, so there should be no doubt the prick is suitable for the job. But there were a few slip-ups, and I'm worried."

"I want to hear them, but let me order two coffees first."

The men waited for the server to leave before continuing their discussion.

"You know what happened to the Antwerp agent," said Herman, "the Man with the Black-Rimmed Glasses used his knife. You may straighten Frank out by telling him that story."

"I told him, but he doesn't get the fucking message. From the start, the prick showed more interest in travelling and playing tourist than in taking care of business."

Herman shrugged. "As long as he does his job, that shouldn't be a problem. I must confess, I sometimes go to concerts or museums."

"Shit—you're kidding me. Good for you, but you going to artsy places and whatnot doesn't interfere with your work. In Frank's case, it could. We work on a tight two-hour schedule, and I'm afraid this could become a problem with Frank. Let me give you two examples. There was his behaviour in Brussels. The first thing he asked when I met him at the train station was if he had enough time for a city tour. No questions about the contacts he was to meet or what to tell them. Just 'Can I do a city tour?' It's a bad sign. You can see what a man's interests are from the fucking questions he asks."

Herman nodded and took a sip of his coffee.

"Later, during lunch," the Transport Coordinator continued, "after he'd drunk three glasses of wine, the prick asked Z what was in the container that was to arrive the next day. He asked—imagine—where the goods were going and how much profit we're making on them. Z took him to the washroom and slapped him around. But it worries me the prick asked questions like that. Z's treatment is no guarantee he won't do it again. What if it was the alcohol talking or he was in a talkative mood? Neither is good for us. We must find out whether he is a risk to the organization."

"Why do you call him a prick?"

"I call him a prick because he looks like one. All dressed up in a business suit and necktie. Shoes polished to a shine, but no fucking clue about his place in the SunRise network."

The Transport Coordinator paused for a minute, waiting for Herman to comment, but Herman stayed silent, and the Transport Coordinator continued. "Business is most successful when everybody gives it their full fucking attention. I can't put my finger on it, but I am convinced something is wrong with Frank. He doesn't commit to his work; this tourist stuff is distracting him. He may be Mrs. Liu's pet agent, but I'm not sure he's fit for the job. What do you think?"

"What you told me isn't too serious," Herman said, "but I agree. He shouldn't travel around Europe for fun. There's always the possibility he can't make it back in time. I often get stuck somewhere because the trains go on strike or poor weather grounds the planes. If anything like that happened, it could force you to call Mrs. Young and close down the entire operation. We can't take that risk."

"Thank you for agreeing with me. But what are we going to fucking well do?"

"Based on what you told me, we can't go to Mrs. Liu and ask her to find someone else. Frank worked for YYZ, and that made it easy for her to choose him as an agent. And knowing her, she must see something in him that makes him suitable for the job. She doesn't act on a whim."

"You're right. We need more fucking proof of the danger the prick poses before asking her to fire him."

"I propose we keep better track of him. I can take time off from checking up on the distributors and tail Frank for a while to investigate whether he's prone to making mistakes. Mrs. Liu won't mind me getting involved."

The Transport Coordinator agreed. "But since you already met Frank, tailing him might not work. What if he recognizes you?"

Herman nodded. "You're right. A better approach would be to contact him. I can, 'by chance,' run into him and set up a relationship with him. Who knows? We could become friends! That would make it easier for me to find out how much job-related information he'll share. Once I find out, I'll tell you, and then you can decide whether to continue to work with him."

"That's a good idea. Make friends with him and tell me if you see or hear anything serious enough to get rid of him. I don't want to do that too early, because I must admit, once he's in the customs office, he does well—never a problem. He told me he deals with a particular officer,

Tolman, and they seem to like each other. Besides, finding a replacement for Frank would be fucking difficult."

"Don't thank me. I have a big stake in the SunRise-YYZ collaboration too, and I could use a break from dealing with these distributors. Not the nicest people on earth. Making friends with Frank in Amsterdam will be much better. Who knows? I might take him to a concert. Loosen him up and find out if he still only talks about the high quality of Chinese products. He may know nothing about counterfeit goods, but by now he could suspect something. The subject is in the news a lot, and although Frank doesn't read Dutch newspapers, his drinking buddies might tell him. It will be important to see how much detail he wants to give me."

Herman stood up, ready to leave, but the Transport Coordinator stopped him and signalled he should sit down again.

"There's more," he said. "Something I can talk about only with someone I have worked with for a long fucking time. What? Eight, ten years? And there's never been a major problem between us."

Herman put down his coat and sat down again. "Tell me what you have in mind. I am curious."

"Are you aware that the amount of money involved in these counterfeit trading schemes is enormous? Someone told me that worldwide, it could be a few billion dollars every year, and the profits are fucking well immense. You know that. Many people are cashing in on the sale of fake brand-name goods. True, you and I receive a good share of the profits, but screw it—most of the profit ends up in Shanghai. I don't know how you're getting paid, and you don't have to tell me, but I get paid for every container for which I organize transport to warehouses in Europe. The problem is, Mrs. Liu pays me only a shitty thousand dollars per container, and I wonder if I can increase my income."

These words made Herman's skin crawl.

"I hope," he said, "that you don't suggest short-changing Mrs. Liu, because one of my jobs is to keep everyone involved in our scheme straight. And because you asked, I'm paid a fixed sum of money each month—a salary, if you will. Besides checking up on people, I also go around Europe and buy the products Mrs. Liu is planning to import. I take pictures of the packaging so the Chinese manufacturers can replicate it and make it look real. For shipments to France, for example, they must label the packaging in French, and it must carry the correct safety symbols. It's a lot of work."

"That's fucking interesting. I never thought about the labels. I'm sure that was your idea?"

"Yes. You can't put the entire operation in jeopardy because of the packaging. It would surprise you how often companies change the pictures and the labels, so when I'm in a store, I always check for changes."

"Listen," the Transport Coordinator said. "My proposal does not involve the freaking SunRise-YYZ collaboration."

"Then what are you talking about?" Herman was fidgeting with a napkin. He was sure the Transport Coordinator would propose a harebrained scheme to make money and ask him to take part.

"I want to start up our own fucking business. You and I, together with Mr. Young, can find another Chinese company to supply the merchandise. We can use the prick to clear it through fucking customs; he wouldn't know it's not coming from SunRise. There's enough demand for those goods in Europe for Mr. Young and us and Mrs. Liu to all make loads of money."

Herman remained silent for a few minutes, switching his empty coffee cup from one hand to the other. The Transport Coordinator stared at him as if he could force Herman into responding. After a while, Herman said, "I am going to pretend I didn't hear what you said. My loyalty is to Mrs. Liu, and starting up our own company would put us in direct competition with her. You might think the demand for counterfeit goods in Europe is high enough to satisfy both you and Mrs. Liu, but I'm sure she won't see it the same way. She'll see it as a betrayal, and I can imagine how she'll respond. Think of what happened to the Antwerp agent. And in that case, we weren't sure what she did wrong other than talking too much. I know for certain that if Mrs. Liu gets the idea you betrayed her,

Z and the Man with the Black-Rimmed Glasses will visit you to teach you a lesson. It will be painful, and you might count yourself lucky if they only torture you—cut you a bit, slice a few fingers off—but let you live. They are mean, corrupted men and enjoy inflicting pain on their victims. I can't tell you not to go ahead with your idea, but I don't want to be involved. I don't want to be worked over by two depraved thugs."

Herman's refusal to work with him disappointed the Transport Coordinator. He had worked out a profitable scheme, and loyalty had no place in it. Herman saw the disappointment on his face, but didn't change his mind.

"If you *are* keen to start up a new business," Herman added, "don't tell me about it, and don't use YYZ and SunRise resources. They pay Frank, so don't involve him, and don't sell stuff to Mrs. Liu's clients. That would only increase the chance of Mrs. Liu finding out. She probably follows what Frank is doing and might know how many containers are being cleared each week. If she finds out he clears more containers than what SunRise knows about, you will be in serious trouble. Take your time and think hard before you start something."

Herman was ready to leave and said, "I'll keep an eye on Frank and tell you what I find out, and because we've gone through so much together, I have already forgotten what you said about striking out on your own. You should forget it too. It's too dangerous."

Herman left the cafe, disturbed by what the Transport Coordinator had told him, and he shivered despite the August heat. He had worked with the Transport Coordinator long enough that he knew the man was going ahead with his plan. *He's putting me in a difficult position. I must report him to Mrs. Liu, but I don't want to, because that will be his death sentence. But what if Mrs. Liu finds out about the new project and blames me for not telling her? Why these complications? Why are people not satisfied with what they have? It's not possible to change the SunRise network and trying to do so is dangerous. How do I get out of this jam?*

NINE

THE number of containers arriving in Amsterdam had increased in the last few weeks, which meant Frank only made trips within the Netherlands. He planned to travel the country and visit The Hague, which was the seat of the government and Parliament. For now, he walked around Amsterdam and, on a whim, visited the Rijksmuseum, where he tried to see *The Night Watch*, the famous painting by Rembrandt. It took ten minutes before he could get a good look at it because of the busloads of tourists trying to do the same. The wait paid off, and when Frank faced the portrait of the seventeenth-century militia company, he was breathless. The details with which Rembrandt had painted the different persons and reflected the light were exquisite, and a specialty of Rembrandt. Frank understood from reading a booklet that the way the characters were positioned on the screen was unconventional at the time of painting. To add the little girl had been a stroke of genius, he thought. It brightened up the entire centre-left of the picture.

He must had stood in front of the painting for at least ten minutes when someone tapped him on his shoulder.

"I see you are interested in old Dutch art."

Frank turned his head and recognized Herman.

"Yes," Frank said. "I'm surprised, though. In Toronto, I was never interested in paintings. When I was much younger, my parents brought me to New York and took me to the Metropolitan Museum. It was interesting, but it didn't grab me. But this painting is exceptional. I could stand here all day."

"You changed. You are older, and you appreciate the extraordinary effort Rembrandt put into this work. It is funny that now we consider it such a magnificent piece of art. In 1642, it was a commission, and because Rembrandt did not depict the militia in the usual fashion, the painting was controversial. The original was larger than what you see here. When the militia company moved to another place after a few years, the picture didn't fit, and they cut strips off the four sides. Imagine that! You take a knife to the painting now; you'll end up in prison."

"I'm surprised at myself," said Frank. "This painting is something special, and I can't take my eyes off it. It's surprising I'm even in this museum. But what are *you* doing here? When we met on the train to Berlin, you were going to see friends."

"You must have forgotten I told you I am Dutch; I live in Utrecht, and sometimes I come to Amsterdam to visit a museum or go to a concert or walk around town."

"Great! Does that mean you're retired?"

"Yes, and I am enjoying every moment of my retirement."

Frank and Herman kept discussing *The Night Watch*, pointing out details of the ornate uniforms and the weapons the militia used, but after a while, a group of tourists pushed them aside. The two men walked to the cafeteria to have coffee and lunch.

"I love the coffee in the Netherlands," said Frank.

"Yes, Dutch coffee is excellent, although I rarely notice it anymore. I drink too much of it."

"That's how it goes, I guess," said Frank. "After a while, you don't recognize what you have. Things become routine."

"Like your job?"

Frank was ready to answer, but then paused and wondered if that was true. Had his job become routine? Did he no longer appreciate what he had here in Amsterdam?

"No," he said, "my work isn't routine. Every day, I realize how lucky I am to have gotten this position. Life for me is so much more attractive than in Toronto. The strange thing is, I was content with my life in

Toronto. I guess I didn't know any better. Here, I am interested in museums, I go to the movies—when they're in English—and I'm planning to go to a concert at the Concertgebouw. Living here has changed me."

"It will be a shock then for you when you have to return to Toronto."

Again, Frank paused before answering. He knew, of course, his job was not permanent, but he seldom thought about the day an email from Linda would arrive saying no more shipments were coming.

"I am not going back," he said with a conviction in his voice that surprised Herman. "If my current job finishes, I'll find another one right here."

"Good for you. Listen, you mentioned going to a concert. This is a good time. September means the classical music concert season has started. We can go together next week. It is an all-Mozart program. I will buy the tickets, and we can have dinner before the concert."

Frank's heart skipped a beat. A concert! Mozart! *This is an occasion to get acquainted with classical music. And with a companion, so I don't have to face my first concert by myself.*

"Great," he said. "Let's do it."

"Excellent. I will organize the whole thing and let you know. Give me your email, so I can write you when and where to meet."

Frank wrote his address and handed it to Herman, who noticed Frank's hands were shaking.

"I'm looking forward to this," Frank said. "My first classical concert!"

"I hope you enjoy it. For me, classical music is an escape from the actual world. When things don't go as well as I want, to listen to classical music helps me to relax. It might do the same for you."

"I don't need to go to a concert. My life is perfect right now."

"Glad to hear that. It must be your job—or did you meet the love of your life?"

Frank smiled. "I have the perfect job. Well paid and a lot of free time."

"That's great. I'm glad to meet someone who likes his life. These days, too many people are complaining about how bad things are."

Herman waved his hands as if that would keep the complainers at bay, and he changed the subject. "Do you remember our conversation about counterfeit goods on the train to Berlin? I asked whether the Chinese goods you import could be counterfeit. After that, I became curious about how big the trade in counterfeit goods is. So, guess what—I learned that every year, worldwide, half a trillion U.S. dollars in counterfeit goods change hands, which makes up three to five per cent of total global trade. It's a big business, and profitable too."

Frank didn't know how to respond. The enormity of the trade in counterfeit goods fascinated him, but he couldn't connect this with his work. After the incident in Brussels, he had thought little about the goods SunRise imported into Europe with the help of YYZ—*his* help—and although Herman had mentioned in the train to Berlin that the trade in fake goods was large, Frank didn't think the SunRise merchandise could be counterfeit. *Mr. Young and Linda won't make me do illegal things.*

"Those numbers are interesting," he said, "but our goods are genuine."

"Of course, I wasn't suggesting you were importing counterfeit goods, but given the money involved, one can see how people might try to get a slice of the profits."

The whole week after meeting Herman, Frank had trouble concentrating on his work. He was so excited about going to the concert that he couldn't resist asking the Transport Coordinator whether he was interested in attending too. The Transport Coordinator gave him a disapproving look and said in a loud voice,

"Hell, no. I have work to do."

Frank nodded. "I don't know why I thought you might enjoy it, but don't get upset with me for asking."

"Do you like classical music?"

"I don't know yet, but no harm in finding out. A few days ago, I met someone who told me classical music helps him relax when things aren't going well. We're going together."

"I don't need music to relax. A stiff drink or two will do the trick. It's amazing you have time to go to concerts—your company doesn't work you hard enough. To claim two fucking shipments a week is only four or five hours of work. Nice job."

"Everybody has his job to do, and if that's what my company wants me to do, then that's what I do." Raising his voice a bit, he continued, "Why does this concern you?" *Why is the Transport Coordinator busy with my job? Let him worry about his own.*

"I got a message from Mrs. Liu for you," the Transport Coordinator said. "SunRise can ship more goods than they do now, but they need more fucking customers here in Europe, and they want you to do your part to find them. Start trying to figure out how you will get SunRise new clients. If you can't do it or won't do it, I can see they will hire someone else to do your job. Shit, I might volunteer, so I am sure someone does the job right."

The first real threat to my stay in Amsterdam.

"Any suggestions?" Frank asked. "What goods am I supposed to sell?"

"Anything. SunRise has a supplier for any fucking product for which you find a client. Start by identifying firms with specific needs. Construction companies need plumbing and electrical equipment and other supplies. Transport companies need tires, batteries, and engine parts. *You* fucking figure it out. Talk to them and find out what they need, what their biggest expense is, and tell them you can supply these parts at a twenty-five per cent discount compared with what they pay now. I bet you get orders soon."

"Twenty-five per cent off the current price? Without knowing how much they pay? Does SunRise make any profit on sales like that?"

"They may or may not—I don't fucking know. But twenty-five per cent off is a teaser rate. If your new clients become regulars, SunRise will increase the price."

"Ah, a door crasher. Good strategy. How about the shipments and payments?"

"Don't worry. That is not part of your job. In the time between clearing merchandise, you contact potential clients, take orders, and send them to Mr. Young. He organizes with SunRise and arranges the shipment and payment. If you get questions you can't answer, refer them to Mr. Young."

A sales job seemed odd to Frank. He had never done something like that, but he realized he couldn't refuse. He put on a confident face and said, "No problem. I have never done a sales job, but you can count on me. I'll do my best."

"I hope so. I can work with you, and I don't want you to leave. You never know what person will replace you." The Transport Coordinator emphasized the word *replace*.

On his way home, Frank thought about what had happened to him over the last few months. He felt he had changed. In Toronto, he never went to museums, let alone classical concerts. He also would never be as assertive as he was now, but then, his life in Toronto had been a routine of work, visits to the pub, and many hours of TV watching. It had satisfied him then, but he didn't want to return to it; he had tasted a more exciting life. *Let's keep it this way for as long as possible.* He would find new customers. He had no choice.

The day of the concert, Frank was so excited that he arrived at the customs office with a few minutes to spare. The Transport Coordinator was ready to contact Linda, but Frank phoned him in time to tell that all was well and the container could be picked up.

"What the fuck happened?" asked the Transport Coordinator. "I was thinking of flushing the entire operation down the drain. Why were you so late?"

Frank realized he had made a mistake, but he couldn't tell the Transport Coordinator he had come in late and the container had been standing around for a while when he arrived at the customs office because his thoughts were with the concert, not with his work.

Frank forced himself to speak in a calm voice. "Sorry, there were problems with the paperwork, but nothing important. A form was missing. It turned out it had fallen on the floor, so it took longer than normal."

"Remember our freaking timeline. If you have a problem, you *must* contact me. If I don't hear from you within two hours after customs have offloaded the container from the ship, I assume something is wrong and I will phone Mrs. Young."

"Yes, you don't have to remind me. I'm sorry—I should have phoned you earlier. But all is well. You can pick up the container. Don't worry; it won't happen again. I'll see you in a few days. I'm sure another shipment is coming."

With these words, he left the Transport Coordinator stewing and made his way to a restaurant near the concert hall. When he entered, Herman had already found a table. Frank took the chair opposite him and they exchanged greetings.

"Excited?" asked Herman. "It is a wonderful program. Symphonies number forty and forty-one are among my favourite music."

"I wouldn't know, but I *am* eager to listen."

During the meal, they made small talk about the weather, which was turning colder, the traffic, which was increasing in the city, and the food, which was tasty but not outstanding. Herman changed subjects and told Frank he had seen another story in a national newspaper describing the large number of counterfeit products that were for sale in Europe. The article stated that many of these counterfeit goods were of inferior quality and did not conform to European standards.

"I guess you didn't read the article," he added. "You don't read Dutch, I assume, but the problem is real. I am happy you import only genuine products."

"You're right, I didn't see the article, but two of my drinking buddies in the cafe near my apartment told me about the big trade in counterfeit goods. They also told me most of these goods come from China."

Herman looked at Frank. *He won't talk, or he doesn't know. But let's ask him again after the concert when his mind is still busy with the music.* "Have you seen the concert hall on one of your many walks around town?"

"No, I haven't, but someone told me I should attend a concert."

They made the five-minute walk to the concert hall. Herman explained, "The Dutch call it the Concertgebouw, which means concert building. It is on the south side of a large, almost triangular plaza called

Museum Square. The famous Rijksmuseum, where we met earlier in front of *The Night Watch*, is on the north side. You might not have noticed the plaza we're looking at now, because you most likely used the front entrance. What you see now is the rear of the museum. This is an area of museums," Herman continued. "Besides the Rijksmuseum on the north side, the famous Van Gogh Museum and the City Museum are on the west side. There is also a small museum called Moco that exhibits modern works from Banksy, the Iranian brothers Icy and Sot, and Andy Warhol. You should go visit. And of course, you can't miss the Van Gogh Museum. Many of his famous paintings are there."

"Amazing," said Frank. "It'll take time to see all this."

"I am glad you are interested in going. Art is an essential part of my life. It lifts my spirits."

"I'll try to find the time, but I've got more work to do. And let's first see whether I enjoy classical music."

The concert hall overwhelmed Frank the moment he entered. The elegant decor, the quiet buzz of the audience that waited for the concert to start, and his anticipation made him feel sophisticated and insecure at the same time—sophisticated for being part of a cultural event in such a dignified setting, and insecure because this was the first time, he had been in a concert hall. He looked in awe at the musicians who walked on stage and tuned their instruments, and he applauded when the conductor took to the stage. Throughout the music, he sat motionless in his chair, mesmerized and enveloped by magical sounds. During the intermission, Herman bought two glasses of white wine, but Frank didn't stop talking about how beautiful the music was and how much he liked the violin section. How he didn't understand the conductor's movements. He wondered how anyone could write music for so many instruments and make it sound coordinated. When the bell rang, calling the audience back into the hall for the second part of the concert, Frank's glass was almost untouched. After the concert, Frank applauded until the last musician had left the stage. In his entire life, he had heard nothing so beautiful. The sounds of the instruments were still playing through his head. Herman had to coax him back to reality.

"No need to ask whether you liked the concert. I can see it written on your face. I'm sure, if I had a way of looking inside your head, I would see and hear the orchestra playing the music. I am happy you liked the concert that much. Shall we have a drink in the cafe across the street?"

Sipping their beers, Frank said, "Herman, I am happy I met you on the train to Berlin. Without you, I would never have ventured out to a classical music concert. I was thinking about attending one, but you made it happen. Thank you very much. I hope we can do this again soon."

"I'm also happy we met. It is better to go to concerts with other people who like the music, than to go alone. This was a novel experience for me too."

Frank ordered two more beers. The men remained silent for a while, then Herman said, "The concert was the perfect end of the day. What are you going to do tomorrow? Clear more containers?"

"Yes, and I must find new clients. I'll be busy. I hope I can put the music out of my head."

Recognizing an opportunity to catch Frank off guard, Herman dropped a question on him. "You know, ever since you told me the goods you clear are genuine, I have been thinking about how you know that. How can you be so sure the merchandise in the containers you clear is not counterfeit? Do you ever see those goods? Do you know the retail prices? Don't you have any doubts?"

Frank, still listening to the music in his head, answered, "Yes, I do have doubts. We *could* import Chinese counterfeit goods. That could be the reason SunRise sends the merchandise to Canada, so the goods enter Europe as YYZ merchandise. I noticed on the paperwork that the supplier is not SunRise, but other Chinese companies. Yet my bosses in Toronto told me we're helping SunRise import goods into Europe, and for that, SunRise pays me a salary. It looks like YYZ and SunRise work together to export SunRise merchandise to Europe. Whether they are counterfeit . . . ?" He stopped talking, realizing he already had said too much.

"I understand," Herman said. "Listen, don't worry—your secrets are safe with me. I consider you my friend, and friends protect friends. I won't talk to anyone about what you just told me."

"Thank you, Herman. It's great to have a friend who knows so much about music. The concert was fantastic. I'm looking forward to the next concert. Email me anytime."

"We will repeat this, but now I must catch a train home."

After a firm handshake, the two men parted ways.

Frank crossed the road to look at the big museums. He walked around the City Museum and then circled the Van Gogh Museum and decided he had to visit both.

When Frank got home, reality struck. How was he going to find more clients for SunRise? Frank thought about the Transport Coordinator's suggestions and decided he would make a few cold calls. He looked up transport and construction companies online, then narrowed the results to those that were in or near Amsterdam and used their websites to decide which ones were big enough to make interesting targets. *Tomorrow morning, I will phone them*, he decided. That night, he went to sleep with the theme of Mozart's *Symphony No. forty-one* playing through his head. He had seldom felt this good about himself.

* * *

Over the next few days, Frank was busy trying to find potential new clients. He had identified suitable construction and trucking companies and was ready to phone them. But something stopped him, something he had not experienced yet during his stay in Amsterdam. *Why follow the Transport Coordinator's suggestions? I can come up with my own ideas.* Frank phoned the head of purchasing of a company called Golden Pastures that operated retirement homes and long-term care facilities throughout the Netherlands. He was proud of this find, and he hoped to convince them he could supply adult briefs and other incontinence-related products at a significant discount compared to what they paid now. That, he was sure, would enhance his status with Linda and with SunRise. *Linda and Mrs. Liu might phone me and tell me what a good job I'm doing.*

"Hi, my name is Frank Cordelero, and I work for a company that specializes in supplies for the elderly. The company is Canadian and wants to discuss with you the cost of adult briefs and other products you need for your residents with incontinence problems. We offer you these items at a much lower price than what you pay now."

"That sounds interesting, but how can you make such an offer without knowing what we pay our current supplier? We already get a significant volume discount."

"I am sure you do, but my company wants to branch out into the Netherlands and other European countries, and we selected Golden Pastures as our first potential client. Because of that, we can offer you a twenty-five per cent discount on what you are being charged with now. How does that sound?"

"Interesting. That is a large saving, but how good are your products?"

"No problem with quality—we sell only brand-name products. We deal with companies in China that manufacture goods to the precise agreed to specifications, like the products you use now. The reason we can give you a large discount is that the volume discount your local distributor gives you is only a fraction of what he gets from the manufacturer. We will give you a much larger slice of the manufacturer's volume discount."

"Well, that seems worth discussing. Can we meet?"

"Any time that is convenient for you," answered Frank. "But I am tasked only with making the first contacts. The head office in Toronto negotiates the size of the orders, the delivery schedules, and the prices. I will give you their email address so you can contact them whenever you want, or I can ask them to contact you. As you prefer."

"I will speak with them as soon as possible. There are questions I must ask before considering doing business with your company."

"Of course. Direct your questions to the Toronto office, and I am sure the answers will satisfy you. I will send you their email address. Thank you for taking my call. I hope our discussion is the start of a great and profitable relationship."

Frank was proud of his approach, and he liked the fact he could deflect the questions to Mr. Young, so that if Golden Pastures did not want to do business with YYZ, Linda and Mrs. Liu could not blame him. *I must protect my job.*

It was time to go to the customs office to clear a container of merchandise destined for Berlin. He would mention his phone call with Golden Pastures to the Transport Coordinator to show he was busy finding new clients. *If I do well, there will be no more talk of me being replaced.*

After he finished the formalities at the customs office, Frank phoned four more companies. He couldn't convince them all that it was worthwhile to pursue his offer. One purchasing manager told him he had no confidence in the quality of cheap Chinese goods. "We are a high-end company; I cannot take any risks with the products we use." But two construction companies and a big trucking company promised to contact the YYZ office in Toronto. This made Frank feel sophisticated and successful. *I'm contributing to the SunRise-YYZ business and reducing the chance Mrs. Liu will end my job.*

He took advantage of a free afternoon and spent over two hours in the Van Gogh Museum. The paintings overwhelmed him, and he enjoyed seeing the details so much that the security guards reminded him not to lean in too close. He couldn't help himself. The paintings spoke to him, and he became part of the scenes. He wandered through the orchard with blossoming apricot trees and joined a family of farmers in their meagre dinner of potatoes. He spent a long time in front of the sunflower painting and imagined how a vase of sunflowers would brighten up his apartment. *Why did I never visit any of the many art exhibitions in Toronto.* This thought, however, was short lived. *Why bother with the past. The present is a lot more interesting.*

TEN

THE Transport Coordinator met Mr. Young in the same cafe where he had talked with Herman and asked him to watch Frank, and where Herman had told him not to set up a trading scheme involving Mr. Young. During a follow-up meeting, Herman had assured the Transport Coordinator he had tried his best to get Frank to admit YYZ filled the containers with Chinese counterfeit goods, but Frank had no doubts the goods were genuine. "He's solid. No reason to worry about him." Once the Transport Coordinator heard that, he forged ahead with his new money-making plan that involved Frank.

The Transport Coordinator agreed with Herman that using YYZ or SunRise assets in his new import business, such as having Frank clear the merchandise or selling to SunRise's clients, would be dangerous. But there was no choice; he didn't have any contacts in China. To source products in China, he needed Mr. Young's help, and he needed Frank to clear the goods through customs. To minimize the risk of Mrs. Liu finding out, his new scheme should be time-limited and should concentrate on Eastern Europe and the Balkans, where Mrs. Liu had few customers. If they could import twenty or thirty containers, he would accumulate enough money to help him retire to a place where Mrs. Liu couldn't get to him. He could still do a few minor jobs, but no more Mrs. Liu breathing down his neck.

"Mr. Young," he said. "Nice to see you. How are you? You must travel a lot, so thank you for making time for me. I have something special to discuss with you."

The Transport Coordinator knew how to get Mr. Young's attention. Mr. Young had agreed to meet after the Transport Coordinator had emailed him that there was a way to increase their payouts.

"Tell me," Mr. Young said. "Why did you want to see me?"

"To discuss growing the business of importing Chinese counterfeit goods into Europe."

"You want to work with *me* on that? Why?"

"You have the sources in China and can clear them through customs, while I have access to transportation and new customers all over Europe. We would make a great team."

Mr. Young was silent. What he heard was a duplicate of the SunRise scheme. *Why risk my business with SunRise?*

The Transport Coordinator waited for Mr. Young's response but got none.

"I know this sounds familiar," he said, "but think of this idea as a variation of the ongoing SunRise-YYZ scheme, except the source is different and the clients are different." He paused for a few seconds for dramatic effect and added, "And the fucking profits are bigger."

This piqued Mr. Young's interest. "How so? After the goods arrive in Toronto, the shipping and distribution expenses are the same as in the current scheme. How do you generate increased profits?"

The Transport Coordinator had expected this question and had prepared an answer he was certain would make Mr. Young agree to work with him.

"Right now, you are acting as a service company representing the interests of SunRise. You are helping them to export their goods to Europe. I am not sure how much SunRise pays you out of the money they receive from their clients, but I doubt you control that. This means you are an employee of SunRise. They are in charge and pay you whatever they see fit. Like a salary. They do the same to me. One thousand dollars per container, a fucking pittance."

Mr. Young wanted to say something. The Transport Coordinator's words had struck a chord. He did not appreciate being described as a service provider and an employee without control of his earnings. That was the dependent person he disliked. Like his warehouse workers. "But I . . ."

"My scheme will be much more profitable," the Transport Coordinator continued, ignoring Mr. Young trying to say something. "You buy the goods from a Chinese source and sell them at a price *you* control. All the fucking profits go to you, and the only person you must share the money with is me. You will be in command."

Mr. Young paid close attention. He was warming up to the idea of buying goods cheap and selling them at a healthy profit. *I will be my own man.* He resented Mrs. Liu and her constant demands on him. Being his own man was attractive, and who knows—if this new business went well, he could get rid of Mrs. Liu and SunRise Technologies.

"What about Frank?" he asked. "Will he suspect anything?"

"Not if Mrs. Young adds the extra containers in her messages to him. That way he can't distinguish between containers that contain goods from SunRise and those from your new supplier. Frank won't give it any thought. He is solid, doing an outstanding job."

"What about your clients? How many do you have lined up already? Are you sure they don't overlap with Mrs. Liu's?"

"Don't worry. Give me two weeks, and I'll show you a list of clients and their needs. I have plenty of contacts with a lot of demands."

"Great. Once you give me the list of what your clients want to buy, I'll contact my sources in China. It shouldn't be difficult to find one that manufactures what we need. By mid-October, we can ship the first container."

After negotiating the schedules and payments for the Transport Coordinator—five thousand dollars per container—the men agreed to start with one container a week to test out the market and the profits. They shook hands and the Transport Coordinator left, claiming he had to take care of a container that had arrived. Mr. Young stayed for another coffee. *This is great.* He missed being in control of YYZ.

Close to two months after this meeting, the first container filled with counterfeit electronics arrived in Amsterdam. It had been easy for Mr. Young to find a supplier. The only hiccup he had encountered had come from Linda, who resisted the idea of a parallel trading scheme.

"You're going too far," she said. "This won't finish well. Your greed is getting out of control. If Mrs. Liu finds out, she'll think you're moving in on her territory. Who knows what she'll do to you? And to me and Frank. One thing is certain—you'll lose your business."

"She won't find out. We'll keep separate files on the two streams of goods, and if I satisfy her demands, there shouldn't be any problems. There will be no reason for her to question what we're doing."

"You can't be sure. You can't control everything. Mrs. Liu has an extensive network of distributors and clients in Europe, and how do we know your parallel network doesn't have one or more people in common with hers? I won't take that risk. I want nothing to do with this. If you want separate records, you can teach the data entry clerk what to do."

Of course, Leonard had ignored Linda's objections. He was right. Linda's sense of loyalty to him and YYZ—and the additional money—got the upper hand and she, despite knowing she was putting herself in unnecessary danger, included the containers that were part of the new trading scheme in her messages to Frank.

ELEVEN

A few small tears trickled down Linda's cheeks. "I want to leave Leonard," she blurted out. Linda had come to Paris to talk to Claudia. She was the only person Linda trusted, the only one with whom she could discuss her problem with Leonard. The two women were having lunch in a quiet restaurant when Linda gave Claudia the unexpected news.

"Why? You two have been together for a long time. Why separate now?"

"It's difficult to explain, but either Leonard or I have changed over the years. I don't have the same feelings for him as when we were just married. In the beginning, I didn't mind the most important thing for Leonard was making money, 'like my father,' or that we never went out to any place other than the Silver Beaver, never to a show or to the movies. We never took a holiday and only travelled for work, never for pleasure, and we were always discussing new projects and trying to find new clients, and that was okay. Our business provided us a comfortable living, better than I had as a young girl."

She stopped talking and wiped away the tears.

"I should have listened to my mother. When Leonard and I announced we were getting married, she told me not to. She said, 'The man has no soul. All he wants to do is make money. Yes, he will love you and treat you well in the beginning, but over time, that will change. His soul will fill up with money, which will push out whatever love it has now.'"

Claudia had never heard Linda complain about her husband, and Linda's story made her uncomfortable.

"Of course," Linda said to Claudia, "I didn't listen. I was in love with a handsome man who promised to make us rich. To make money was good, but with time, I realized it wasn't the only important thing in life. We live in Toronto. You can go out every night to the movies, or a concert, a play, the ballet . . . but we got no further than the Silver Beaver. And after a few years, Leonard changed. He often left the pub drunk. He always insisted on having sex after we came home, but it differed from when we married. Quick and rough and sometimes violent. I dreaded going to the pub for what would happen after."

Linda paused for a few seconds and then explained the SunRise-YYZ trading scheme to Claudia. "We can supply anything at a large discount. In the beginning, I was excited to be part of an extensive network of manufacturers, wholesalers, shipping agents, buyers, and distributors, but lately, my involvement in this agreement with SunRise has disturbed me. I didn't marry Leonard to become a criminal, and I argued with him often to stop the trading schemes, but I had no choice but to go along with the project. Leonard always does what he wants—if it involves making money."

"Wow, what a story," said Claudia. "I didn't know your life was so animated. I thought you had a steady but somewhat boring job."

"I wish it had been boring! What you call 'animated' is illegal and dangerous. Mrs. Liu will resort to extreme violence to defend her interests. Our transporter told me she had her agent in Antwerp killed."

Claudia didn't know how to react to the mention of violence and said nothing. Linda continued. "There's more. A few weeks ago, Leonard started up a *second* money-making scheme. It's like the one involving SunRise. Same idea, but different suppliers and different clients, and still involving Frank and the usual transporter. I'm scared. It will end in violence once Mrs. Liu finds out, and I'm sure she will. This second scheme convinced me Leonard had pushed his greed too far, and that's when I thought about leaving him."

"Will you divorce him?"

"I prefer to settle this between us. Involving lawyers and judges will lead to a lot of scrutiny of the business practices of YYZ and where all the money came from, and that is not something I want. It will add to my problems."

The revelations that the illegal money-making schemes involved her best girlfriend and Frank shocked Claudia. They ate their dessert in silence and ordered coffee.

"I'm not surprised Frank got involved in this," Claudia said. "He was never that smart. When we worked together stocking grocery shelves, he worked hard, but when the product displays changed, he needed time to figure out what to do."

"Frank trusts people," Linda said. "He trusts *me* not to get him into trouble, which makes the situation we're in now even more unpalatable. Leonard and I are living in different worlds. Leonard took me to his world, and now I've realized that isn't where I want to be. He'll make money no matter what—legal, illegal. I want to be in a world where money is important not for money's sake, but for the comfort it gives you and the nice things it allows you to do. To explore interesting cities or to go on beach vacations. Money enables you to lead a comfortable life."

"You said Frank knows nothing about the illegal trading schemes. What's he going to do when he finds out? You think he'll quit?"

"I don't know how flexible his conscience is," said Linda. "I guess it depends to a large extent on what his alternatives are, but I'm sure his experiences in Amsterdam will make it difficult for him to go back to his quiet, routine life in Toronto. He's tasted the good life, and he won't be interested in returning to Toronto to be a data entry clerk."

"He may *have* to go back. It depends on the visa he has now."

"I know. Before he left for Amsterdam, we arranged all the paperwork. His work permit is occupation specific. He may have to apply again for another work permit if he finds a job that is classified differently from what he does now. I do not know how difficult that will be."

"He has to figure that out himself," Claudia said. "How about Leonard?"

"Leonard's greed is getting the better of him. No sane person would start a trading scheme competing with Mrs. Liu. Who is to say he won't transition to something more serious? Getting into money laundering, for instance. And I don't want to be part of dealings like that. I want out *now*, and the best thing to do is to work out a separation agreement with him."

"Does Mrs. Liu have to approve you leaving YYZ? She might not agree. She might be afraid you'll talk about the SunRise-YYZ collaboration."

"You're right. She won't like me leaving, but she can't stop me. I'll deal with her when the time comes."

Linda spoke in a confident voice, for Claudia's sake, but she wasn't sure her interaction with Mrs. Liu would be smooth, and right then she decided if she ever saw Z and the Man with the Black-Rimmed Glasses nearby, she would take refuge in a police station and confess her involvement in the YYZ counterfeit trading scheme.

TWELVE

THE day after Linda left Paris, Claudia remembered something that had caught her attention in the office, because it had led to a big discount on the price of the construction materials she needed. Three weeks before Linda arrived, two men had visited. The men were burly, and one wore large, black-rimmed glasses. They, her boss, and the office manager had holed up in the boss's office for the better part of the morning. After the visitors had left, the office manager had told her, "We have new suppliers who can sell us most of what we need at a great discount, twenty-five per cent less than what we pay now. They source our orders in China and will deliver the fire-retardant insulation panels you use a few weeks after receiving the order. From now on, I will do all the ordering. You tell me what you want, and I will take care of the rest."

"Why you? As the project manager, I'm responsible for the quality and the cost of the materials we use. I'll order the materials we need."

"Listen, the boss and I negotiated with the new suppliers. To keep in contact with them, I want to order the materials they can supply. Other materials you can order yourself. If you don't like this arrangement, talk to the boss. But you should know it was him who proposed this division of responsibilities, so good luck."

The big discount puzzled Claudia. *Who are these men who can sell materials at such low prices?* She felt faint for a moment. Something Linda had talked about came back to her in a flash. 'We can supply almost anything at a large discount,' she had said. Did that mean the office manager was doing business with YYZ? Involving Linda and Frank? How good were those cheap materials? Linda had admitted the merchandise they sent to Europe on behalf of SunRise was counterfeit. *Had anyone tested those fire-retardant panels?* She decided that because she didn't know the answers, she should let things be for now.

A few weeks later, the office manager was walking around the office with a big smile on his face. "The new supplier delivered our first order. We saved a lot of money this way, and everybody will profit from that. It increases the status of our office, and if this business repeats often enough, we might all get a raise."

The office manager's statement brought back the questions Claudia had after hearing of the new supplier, and now that materials were arriving, getting answers became more pressing. Claudia was most worried about the quality of the fire-retardant insulation panels she had ordered. She needed to be sure these cheap materials were up to European standards. That was *her* responsibility. She decided she should investigate them and planned a visit to the three building sites she supervised to ask the site managers for their opinion about the new materials. Because of her heavy workload, she didn't get away from the office until a few weeks later. In the meantime, their new supplier delivered another shipment of fire-retardant insulation panels and several shipments of electrical components, kitchen cabinets, and plumbing supplies to the three sites.

She first visited the two development projects near the Belgian border. The company was building modest townhouses and mid-rise apartment buildings. Her visits went well. The site managers thanked her for her support in getting materials delivered on time.

"You might have noticed we have a new supplier," she said. "Did you have any problems with the electrical and plumbing supplies you received? How about the fire-retardant insulation panels?"

Both site managers told her the new supplies were identical to the ones they had used earlier. Neither had realized the materials came from a different source.

"That's good to hear," Claudia said, "but if you have any doubts, please phone me."

Claudia's conversations with the site managers suggested the savings were real, and the materials were of good enough quality.

The project north of Paris was building the same mix of townhouses and mid-rise apartment buildings, and her visit was like the earlier two.

"Thank you for your support," the site manager said, "and for always being available to discuss my needs for materials and workers. Thanks to you, I expect the project will be finished on time. That will make us look good."

She was about to go back to her office when she spotted two stacks of insulation panels. She walked over and inspected them.

"Are you happy with these?" she asked.

"Yes, or to put it in a different way, I have no reason to be *un*happy with them. I assume they perform as well as those we used to install."

"Are you saying you have doubts, and you think they differ from the earlier panels?"

"Difficult to say, but the texture of these panels seems different. They are more brittle and more difficult to install. Whether that affects their capacity to insulate, I can't tell."

"How about their fire resistance?"

"We haven't tested that. We rely on the results of the French National Centre for Fire Safety. Their stamp of approval is on every panel. That is new," he said, looking at one. "The stamp used to be only on the packaging, never on the panels. But things change, and we have no reason to doubt the quality of these materials."

"Glad to hear," said Claudia. "The last thing we want is a problem with the materials we install."

Although the site manager's comments helped to put her mind to rest, when Claudia passed a big pile of leftover pieces of insulation panels, she picked up a piece and tried to fit it in her purse. But it was too big, and she asked the manager for a bag to carry the piece of the panel with her. "Just so I know what we're talking about."

"You are welcome to it. Do you want samples of the electrical and the plumbing supplies as well?"

"No thanks. I assume that the Chinese supplier had them manufactured to the right specifications, and we should have no doubts about using them."

Claudia caught a local train to Paris. She looked at the piece of panel. She turned it around in her hands and noticed the stamp of the French National Centre for Fire Safety. *Why am I doubting the quality of this material? Why did I take this sample?* It had been an impulsive action, and now she didn't know what to do. She tried to set aside her doubts. The three projects were progressing well, and the managers' praise made her feel good. It would enhance her status in the office and could lead to a raise.

It took Claudia over two months to have the piece of insulation tested. Between her return from the site visits and the time she sent the sample to the Fire Safety Centre, she was uncertain about testing the sample. *It isn't my problem. The office manager ordered these panels. Why should I be busy with this?* But this argument did not satisfy her. As the project manager, she had to check the quality of the materials used in the construction projects. The final decision about having the sample tested came when the office manager boasted to her about how profitable the business with the new supplier was.

"We are saving so much money that I am going to ask for a raise," he said. "And don't worry—I will include you. Do you know what is amazing? The new guys are efficient. It takes five to six weeks after we order the goods for them to arrive in Amsterdam, and then our suppliers deliver them to the construction sites within two days."

"That *is* quick," Claudia said. "Do you think someone had these fire-retardant panels tested?"

"I assume so. I never thought about that."

"Well, I did. We can use only materials that meet European standards. These panels being cheap doesn't mean they're inferior, but don't you think we should make sure?"

The office manager dismissed Claudia's suggestion with a shrug. "We rely on the French National Centre for Fire Safety. Every panel we install has its stamp of approval on it. That's good enough for me. The site managers have no complaints about the panels, and we are happy with the price. No need to dig into this testing business."

"You're right—no reason to question the Fire Safety Centre stamps."

But while Claudia talked to the office manager, she decided to have the sample analyzed. That afternoon, after phoning the Fire Safety Centre, she sent them the piece of fire-retardant insulation panel that had been in her office for over two months. There had been a slight difficulty in having the Fire Safety Centre accept the sample because they dealt only with samples from companies, not from private individuals. They needed a corporate account for billing. But Claudia convinced them she worked for a company, but sending the sample for testing was her initiative. After some back and forth, the Fire Safety Centre agreed and accepted her credit card as payment.

"Very irregular," said the man on the other side of the phone, "but we will make an exception. Expect the results in two weeks."

Ten days later, Claudia received an answer, and the results were devastating. The panels were inferior, well below standards. A report describing the test sample stated that in case a fire broke out in any of the homes in which Claudia's company had installed these panels, there would be minimal to no protection. The person who had performed the test objected to the stamp of the French National Centre for Fire Safety on the sample. "The Centre would never approve panels of such inferior quality. These panels are fake, cheap imitations, counterfeit." Although she had expected a bad outcome, the negative results shocked Claudia. *How could the office manager and the boss agree to use this material before making sure the quality is up to accepted standards? Money must be the reason. They must take the savings for themselves.*

Claudia hated the position the report put her in. She wanted to do her job and enjoy her life in Paris, not be busy with inadequate fire-retardant insulation panels.

For a while, she had told herself that she could ignore the results. *She* hadn't ordered the panels and thus, she argued, was not responsible for their use. The blame lay on the shoulders of her boss and the office manager. *They* had made a deal with the new supplier that was too good to be true, and *they* should have made sure the panels performed well.

It isn't my job to make trouble and question the quality of the cheap supplies. But that had been before she received the results. Now that she knew the dangers of using these panels, she should do something. Doing nothing would turn her into a criminal.

Claudia had several options with whom to discuss the test results. She could talk to the office manager or her boss or to the head office in Toronto. But what might the consequences be for her? The head office might blame this disaster on *her*. They would think that making sure the company completed the projects on time and complied with European standards was her responsibility. For anyone not familiar with the Paris office's purchasing policy, it would be easy to blame the project manager for using low-quality materials. Any investigation would find her guilty of using them. It would be her word against those of the boss and the office manager. And what would happen with the faulty panels if she told the company? The company would have to replace the panels that they had already installed at a large cost. That was going to mean a significant delay in finishing the projects. Missing the deadline would harm her excellent reputation and could lead to her losing her job. Claudia didn't know what to do. And what if YYZ had supplied these panels? The fact their supplier imported them through Amsterdam and sold them at a price that was so much lower than the panels they had used till then suggested to Claudia that YYZ could be part of the supply chain. *If so, are Linda and Frank aware of the inferior quality of these panels? Will they get in trouble if I talk to the head office?* These questions were begging for answers. She needed more time; she would gain nothing by making a rash decision.

THIRTEEN

Frank realized his stay in Amsterdam had changed him. He now did important work. Important for YYZ, Linda, and SunRise. Much more important than his job as a data entry clerk in Toronto and much more interesting. He was meeting and talking with different people, like Herman, Mr. Tolman, his colleagues at the customs office, and the people he met on his train travels through Europe. In the YYZ office, often days had passed with no conversation between him and Linda or Mr. Young, the only other people in the office. Now that he had a new life in Amsterdam, he wondered whether his routine life in Toronto had dulled his senses, whether he had mistaken fixed habits for contentment or even happiness.

Other thoughts popped up in his mind. Herman had told him how lucrative the trade in counterfeit goods was, and the thought that YYZ filled the containers with fake merchandise took hold. How else could he explain the low prices of, for instance, the brand-name labelled adult briefs he sold to Golden Pastures? But what to do with these suspicions? Quit? Leave Linda and Mr. Young scrambling for a replacement? And given how well he did his job, Mrs. Liu might not approve of him leaving. He thought about the fate of the SunRise agent in Antwerp. *I have no choice; I must play along if I don't want to disappear.* The thought of what Mrs. Liu had done to the Antwerp agent was always close to the surface.

These dark moments became more prominent and put a damper on Frank's happy feelings about his new life in Amsterdam. He felt lost. Nothing in his life had prepared him for the situation he was in. He needed help, or at least he needed to talk to someone.

"Herman, you remember that after our first concert I mentioned the goods I clear might be counterfeit?"

"Yes, I do, and as promised, I did not talk to anyone about that."

"Good. Ever since I told you that, I've been thinking about it. I suspect I *am* dealing with counterfeit goods. After SunRise told me to find them new clients and I found out their merchandise is cheap, I began to suspect I am clearing counterfeit goods. What else could explain the deep discounts I was told to offer new clients or the violent behaviour Mrs. Liu uses when somebody does the wrong thing? Mr. Young mentioned SunRise had problems importing goods into Europe, so we should help them. Those problems must have been serious. It couldn't be only a few defective products. If *that* was the case, SunRise should have been able to work something out with the Antwerp customs office. But customs banned SunRise from importing into Europe altogether, and that suggests a much more serious problem, like trading in counterfeit goods. So YYZ might be a conduit for counterfeit goods SunRise wants to export to Europe. And I'm part of that."

Herman looked at Frank. *Why has it taken him such a long time to figure out what is happening?* He smiled when he realized *his* questions about counterfeit goods had contributed to Frank getting the idea he was importing them.

"Who is this Mrs. Liu?" he asked. "Is she the principal person in this trading scheme?"

"Yes. She's the CEO of SunRise, a wholesale company in Shanghai. When I met her there, she was nice to me, but later I heard the SunRise agent in Antwerp disappeared when she made mistakes. Easy to guess what happened to her."

Herman winced at the mention of the Antwerp agent, but didn't respond.

"Herman, what should I do? If I'm right, I'm involved in something illegal, and if Amsterdam customs inspects a container and discovers the counterfeit goods, the consequences may be severe. The Dutch police will arrest me, and I will go to prison. Should I quit, go back to Toronto?"

"Well, if this Mrs. Liu is as violent as you say she is, then you can't just quit. She might not like losing you and would punish you for leaving. To quit and not suffer from violence by the SunRise enforcers, you must dismantle the entire organization and send Mrs. Liu to prison. And only if you can do it so she does not suspect *you* brought down the house. That won't be easy."

"What you're saying is I have no choice but to continue clearing the containers because dismantling the SunRise-YYZ scheme would be difficult and dangerous and needs a lot of planning?"

"You are right. It might be difficult, or it might be as simple as sending an anonymous note to the customs office telling them you think the YYZ containers are full of counterfeit goods. That's the simple part. The complicated part is preventing Mrs. Liu from suspecting *you* sent the note."

Frank remained silent for a while. Dismantle YYZ and SunRise? *That sounds like treachery. Mr. Young, Linda, and Mrs. Liu gave him an opportunity to change his life. I can't destroy their business. Sure, the goods I handle may be counterfeit, but I have no solid proof. I didn't see any of the merchandise, and I'm only speculating about why SunRise no longer imports goods into Europe.*

"I can't be sure," Frank said out loud, "because I have no proof. It might be too soon to try to end the SunRise-YYZ collaboration. The scheme works well for me. It lets me stay in Amsterdam, and my life here is much better than in Toronto. I don't want to go back and get a low-level, low-paying job again. Besides, Amsterdam has adopted me. I *can't* leave. This is my new hometown. I should wait before doing something as dramatic as sending a note until I find out more."

"That is a good idea. You should not give up this lucrative scheme on a whim. You only *suspect* the goods are counterfeit. What if they are not? Chinese-made goods that aren't counterfeit are a lot cheaper than those manufactured in Europe—that could explain the low price. Right now, many European companies, and I am sure many American and Canadian companies, get their products made in China."

"Thank you. I agree. Better to wait until I have definitive proof."

"You are right, and we can talk more later, but now we must hurry. Our concert starts soon."

But Frank couldn't concentrate on the music. *Am I making the right choice by waiting until I know more? Or should I be more proactive? What should I do?*

FOURTEEN

SEVEN months after Frank had cleared his first container through Amsterdam customs, his job came to a sudden end. Not because a customs officer inspected a container, not because Frank failed to show up at the customs office, and not because Claudia talked about the test results, but because Linda left Leonard and YYZ.

After her return from Paris, it took Linda a week to work up enough courage to confront Leonard. She met with him in his office, and with no introduction or small talk, told him, "Leonard, I want to separate." She was prepared to go over the arguments, the same ones she had given to Claudia, but she didn't get that chance because Leonard's answer was immediate.

"No way. YYZ *cannot* afford to lose you right now. Business with China is increasing, and I need you in the office."

"Leonard, I didn't come here to talk business. I came here to talk about our marriage, our relationship. I didn't say I was leaving YYZ, but that was your first thought. That tells me I'm right to want a separation. And you're correct: I *will* leave YYZ. Our marriage is no longer important to you. All I am for you is an office worker. But that's not good enough. That's not how we started. I don't know how we got to this point, but I want to be more than an office worker. When we got married, I imagined something else, something more romantic, a marriage built on love and respect. Being only an important office worker is not acceptable to me, so it's time for a separation. Not a divorce—not yet—but prepare for life without me. Get another office worker to replace me. Go by yourself to the Silver Beaver to get drunk and have sex with other women."

"What are you saying? Have you gone crazy? Have I not always taken care of you? You know how much money we make! Soon we'll be living a life of luxury you and I have never experienced. Imagine that and abandon your silly ideas."

"Leonard, money is not the only thing in life for me. Yes, we need it, and it allows us that life of luxury you mentioned. But I want to share it with someone who loves me and respects me, and you are no longer that person."

Leonard stormed out of his office. He was in no mood to agree to a separation.

Later in the day, Linda returned to Leonard's office to work out a settlement and found him pacing his office. "A few minutes ago, I got an email from Mrs. Liu saying if YYZ does not pick up the pace of finding new clients, SunRise will find other ways to import their goods into Europe and they might cease working with YYZ. I can't imagine that in a critical moment like this, you want to leave."

Linda read the email on the computer. "Leonard, she's bluffing. Who is she going to find to do the job we do for her? What company will sell its excellent reputation to accommodate SunRise? Don't worry too much about them walking away from our agreement. I remember YYZ agreed on a specific volume of merchandise, and we're already moving more."

Her reaction surprised Linda. She realized how difficult it would be to leave YYZ.

"Besides," she continued, "this email isn't all bad news. It could give you a way out of working with SunRise, without having to wait until you get caught and must abandon YYZ. All you need to do is to point out to SunRise you're holding up your end of the contract and you'll annul the agreement if SunRise doesn't back off. This is the best news you've received from SunRise for a while. You've made enough money from this scheme. Getting out now doesn't mean poverty for you."

Leonard was looking at his wife in disgust. "I don't want to get out. The profits of our collaboration with SunRise are unbelievable. A few more months of this, and you and I won't need YYZ anymore. If there are complications and the police are looking for us, you know we have a plan to leave at a moment's notice. Why abandon a profitable operation early? Is making money that repulsive to you?"

"I told you my reason for wanting to separate from you. But you haven't talked about that—you're more worried about me leaving YYZ. That means you didn't understand a thing I said. I *will* leave you and YYZ. Let's talk about *my* wishes and plans. After we separate, I'll need cash to give me a reasonable way of living. I must rent an apartment, and unless you sign one of our cars over to me, I need to buy or lease a car." Leonard started fidgeting in his chair, ready to interrupt, but Linda didn't let him.

"Since I own one of the three shares in the company, I want a third of the cash in the corporate bank account. That money comes from the legitimate transactions we've made over the years. I don't want any of the money we've gained from our business with SunRise or from the parallel scheme you started. If you agree, you'll never hear from me again. I promise I won't talk to anyone about the business between YYZ and SunRise or the parallel scheme. When these deals collapse—and they will—it won't be because of me."

"You want one-third of *my money?*" Leonard asked as if Linda had proposed to donate his kidneys, ignoring the fact Linda had made it clear she was only talking about the money in the corporate account. "What makes you think you deserve that much?"

"First, I gave almost eight years of my life to keep this company running without a formal salary. Second, where are you going to find a new office manager? You'll realize soon enough how much you'll have to pay that person to be discreet about your business. You will appreciate how valuable I am, was, for the company."

"This sounds like blackmail to me. I suppose if I don't give you the money, you're going to talk to the police?"

"No, I won't, but I might meet up with your current Canadian customers and drop a hint that YYZ engages in illegal trade with a Chinese wholesaler. I bet you won't hear from many of those customers again. Think of my ask as something you can appreciate: a straightforward business proposal. Pay a little money and continue doing big business or pay nothing and see your business collapse."

"A business deal? No way. This is straight blackmail, and I don't agree with it. You won't get a penny from me. If you leave YYZ, you better find a fantastic job or a rich boyfriend. Turn your idea around, stay and work for YYZ, and you'll earn a lot of money. Leave and get nothing. The only thing I agree with is if you no longer want to live with me, you're free to find another place."

Linda walked back to her office. How could she have imagined it was going to be easy? She should hire a lawyer and file for divorce, but, as she had explained to Claudia, that would cause too much scrutiny of her involvement in the YYZ business, legal and illegal. Things would be much easier if she was able to convince Leonard to agree to settle their differences between themselves. But Leonard was obsessed with money, and he wasn't willing to pay her only to see his office manager leave. She should have known. At least he agreed to a separation, which was something, but not enough. She felt depressed. How was she going to live? She would find another job, but that could take a while and, in the meantime, she would have to live with her parents. *But I have the right to a part of the corporate money. I've spent endless hours keeping the office running without a salary. I've supported the deal with SunRise and helped Leonard run the parallel scheme he started, despite my objections.* She convinced herself one-third of the balance in the corporate account was a reasonable ask, and since Leonard would not give it to her, she was going to take the money. That would be easy because she had signing authority on the corporate account and knew how much money there was—a little over five hundred thousand dollars. She stayed that night at her parents' house. She wasn't afraid of what Leonard was going to do after he learned of the cash withdrawal. He was knee-deep in two illegal trading schemes and would be reluctant to stir up any publicity about his office manager walking off with one hundred seventy thousand dollars.

She couldn't help pondering what would happen to YYZ. Without a competent office manager, the company would collapse. Linda felt a twinge of guilt, but decided not to think about this any longer. YYZ was no longer her business.

As soon as the bank opened the next morning, Linda asked to set up a personal bank account, something she hadn't had since college. *Why am I so nervous? I'm doing the right thing.* The clerk pointed out to her he could reactivate her old account, which was simpler than setting up a new one. Linda agreed. She liked the idea because she saw it as a measure of progress. In her college days, there had seldom been more than a few hundred dollars in the account.

"Please transfer one hundred seventy thousand dollars from our corporate account to mine," she told the clerk.

"Of course, right away." And with a few clicks on his keyboard, the clerk completed the transaction. Linda signed the transfer slip, and the clerk printed out a receipt that stated her new balance. She looked at it and smiled. Not bad, but then the money was a reward for years of hard work and dedication to the progress of YYZ. She withdrew ten thousand dollars and put it into her purse. After leaving the bank, she visited the travel agent she and Leonard used for their business travels and bought a ticket to Amsterdam.

"This is the second time I've sold a ticket to you alone," the travel agent said. "Is Mr. Young not coming with you? Is he all right?"

"Yes, he's fine, but sometimes I need to travel by myself. I have personal business in Amsterdam."

FIFTEEN

LEONARD was sitting behind his desk, trying to come to grips with Linda's departure. *Her defection*, he thought. The full reality of not having Linda running the office had not yet sunk in, and he was reading a contract he had to sign when two burly men entered his office, followed by the data entry clerk, who was wringing his hands and said in a small voice, "Sorry, Mr. Young, I tried to stop them. I asked them to wait, but they didn't. They looked in all the offices till they found yours and entered without asking."

"That's okay, thank you. Go back to work. I will speak with them."

Leonard looked at the two men. "What do you mean by barging into my office unannounced? What do you want?"

"Hello, Mr. Young. My name is Z, and this is my partner. We have a message for you from Mrs. Liu. She sent us here to remind you that you work for *her* and that she expects your full attention to your mutual business."

"Why send you? She could have phoned me if she has a complaint, but I'm sure she doesn't. We put in as much effort as we can."

Has Mrs. Liu discovered the parallel trading scheme? Leonard started shaking and his throat constricted.

"Hey, relax. Mrs. Liu has no complaints about you. If she did, we wouldn't be this friendly, and we wouldn't meet in your office. Too many witnesses. We would have to deal with your friendly clerk and the lady at the print shop downstairs who saw us go up the stairs. Think about that and relax. You're safe here. We are here because Mrs. Liu thinks it's a good idea to remind the people she works with what she expects from them."

Leonard's fear abated. *She doesn't know. This is her idea of a friendly visit.*

"I get the message," he said. "You can tell Mrs. Liu we are holding up our end of the agreement. No problem. Anything else?"

"We also need to speak to Mrs. Young. We understand the arrangement with Mrs. Liu includes her."

"Leave my wife out of this. She's not in the office today. I'll talk to her."

"We'll come back later. Or if you have coffee, we can wait here."

"She's travelling to meet clients."

"I was told that's *your* job," Z said.

"I do most of it, but Linda needed a break from the office."

"Too bad we can't talk to her. We'll have to leave a message."

"Write it down and I'll make sure she gets it."

Z nodded at the Man with the Black-Rimmed Glasses, who took out his knife and jammed it into the top of Leonard's desk.

Leonard froze. He tried to move away but couldn't. When he finally managed, he took a few steps towards the window and stared at the afternoon traffic. *What people have I gotten myself involved with? They're hardcore criminals, and they might kill me if I make a mistake.*

"Why don't you sit down," suggested Z. "It's easier to talk."

Two minutes went by before Leonard turned around and sat down again. "I'll talk to my wife," he stammered, "No need for violence."

"I told you to relax. This is not violence; this is a message for Mrs. Young. And for you."

Leonard was mesmerized by the sight of the knife standing straight up with its tip buried into the solid oak wood for almost half an inch. *This guy must be strong to drive the knife in that deep.* He wanted to protest, but had neither the courage nor the words to speak.

"Well, that's the end of our visit," announced Z. "Make sure you show Mrs. Young our message. We will hold *you* responsible for her actions. You are her boss."

The Man with the Black-Rimmed Glasses took back his knife and put it in his pocket, but not before pointing it at Leonard, who recoiled in fear. The men left the office. Leonard heard Z say goodbye to the data entry clerk, and a few seconds later, he heard the door of the office suite close. He stared at the knife mark on his desk for a long time. Leonard could think of only one thing. *I must stop the parallel trading scheme.* It also occurred to him he could no longer control Linda's actions, and he hoped she wouldn't do anything stupid.

Mr. Young sent the Transport Coordinator a rambling email saying they should stop their new trading scheme. This put the Transport Coordinator in a foul mood. The reason Mr. Young had gotten cold feet was, as far as he could tell, a visit from Mrs. Liu's enforcers. *That's the problem working with people who are new to the world of illegal money-making. They fall apart at the first sign of danger. No reason for Mr. Young to be so upset.*

The Transport Coordinator wrote back, trying to calm Mr. Young: "Don't worry. This was a routine visit. Mrs. Liu does this with all new people to make sure they behave well. You should realize she will never harm you. Her entire fucking operation depends on the resources you bring to the table."

The Transport Coordinator waited for the response to arrive. When after half an hour it hadn't yet, he thought, *Good, he's thinking what to do. Let's hope he comes to the right conclusion.*

Then Leonard wrote, "Okay. We can continue for now, but I will, at the slightest sign of trouble, quit this scheme and blame it on you." This irritated the Transport Coordinator. *We started this together, and now he's ready to blame the whole thing on me? Well, let him.* He knew Mrs. Liu would believe him if he told her he thought all the YYZ containers he picked up in Amsterdam carried SunRise goods. He would point to Mr. Young as the mastermind behind this scheme because Mr. Young shipped the merchandise and had the resources to send out a few extra containers. The Transport Coordinator emailed Mr. Young that message. He added, "Don't threaten me. I can talk with Mrs. Liu, and she will agree with me and identify you as the most important organizer of our collaboration. I know the situation is difficult, but *never* snitch on me, because you will be fucking sorry."

The answer surprised the Transport Coordinator: Mr. Young only asked whether Frank would also get a visit from Mrs. Liu's enforcers. He didn't comment on the Transport Coordinator's latest email, and the Transport Coordinator took it as a sign that Mr. Young had digested his message. *At least I can teach him how things work.* The Transport Coordinator wrote back, "No, of course not. Frank would fall apart if they threatened him with a knife. He would become unpredictable, and he might go to the police to ask for protection. Mrs. Liu would never take that chance. She only targets her senior workers. Please put this episode out of your mind—and make sure you ship the merchandise on time."

After this email exchange, Leonard turned his thoughts to what he needed to do to run YYZ. He realized he was in a critical situation. Linda's departure had immediate consequences for the smooth running of the office. Without her, the only person in the office was the data entry clerk, who was not interested in his work and made many mistakes in entering orders and payments. Ever since Frank had gone to Amsterdam, there had been a noticeable increase in phone calls from clients complaining about missing items or problems with billing. Frank's replacement couldn't run the office by himself. It had always been Linda who talked with dissatisfied customers and straightened everything out in a friendly way. Instead, Frank's replacement panicked and told them to stop bothering him. When they didn't, he used undiplomatic language, and the customers hung up on him after saying that they were going to speak with Mr. or Mrs. Young. This meant that Leonard, who didn't like to take part in the everyday running of the office, had to field many angry phone calls, and because of the time spent on the phone, he had missed important business meetings.

After two weeks, Leonard received an email from Mrs. Liu questioning why she had not received any reports of shipped merchandise. This, he realized, meant she had a way to follow the containers from the YYZ warehouse to the moment the freight forwarder loaded them on a container ship. *How does she do it? Does she pay the freight forwarder?*

The thought that Mrs. Liu was keeping a close watch on him was unsettling. The Transport Coordinator had convinced him not to quit the parallel scheme, but Mrs. Liu knew more about his business than he had thought. His instinct to stop his scheme with the Transport Coordinator might have been right. But after a while, he decided he couldn't forego the big profits associated with the parallel scheme. Besides, YYZ had bought a lot of merchandise from various Chinese sources based on what the Transport Coordinator said his clients wanted. Quitting now would leave him with two containers full of unsold goods. He had to ship these goods and the SunRise merchandise without delay. That was his priority. The Canadian clients would have to wait.

The next day, he drove to the YYZ warehouse and found the four employees who prepared the merchandise for shipping sitting around a small fold-out table drinking coffee. His reaction was immediate and harsh.

"What's going on here? Why aren't you working? Our clients are going to complain that we don't ship merchandise. Don't sit around here doing nothing."

"We *are* working," said the oldest of the four men, "but right now we're taking a fifteen-minute coffee break."

"A coffee break? Why? Do you think *I* take coffee breaks? No. Only thirty minutes for lunch, no more. No need for the four of you to stop working and drink coffee. Who told you about having breaks?"

"Mrs. Young told us to take fifteen minutes in the morning and fifteen minutes in the afternoon and thirty minutes for lunch. It's not possible to work eight to nine hours straight. We must make sure we put the right items in the right packaging. You would get a lot of complaints if clients received Nike sneakers in toaster boxes. And we need to match the language on the packaging and in the manuals with the destination. This takes time and a clear mind. How many complaints have you gotten about discrepancies between the goods and the packaging? I bet none, and that's because we're doing a good job. And to do that, we need regular breaks."

Leonard paced around the warehouse for a while, and when he had calmed down enough to speak, he said, "Look, I'm the boss here, so you four are going to do what I tell you to do and forget the fifteen-minute breaks. We need to increase our output, not decrease it by sitting around drinking coffee."

The four men looked at each other and one of them said, "Can we talk to Mrs. Young?"

"Mrs. Young is not in the office right now, so talk to me."

"Okay, you are the boss, but you depend on us, and we're not happy with the pace and volume of goods we must prepare for shipping. It's too much. For us to continue, we have a few demands. A ten per cent salary increase, time and a half for work done during the week after six p.m., and double pay for work done on the weekend. Not negotiable. If you don't agree, we will walk out of here right now. It's easy to find another job that pays the same wage you pay us. We can make more money flipping hamburgers." Leonard was beyond himself, and he yelled at the men. "You're useless! You can leave right now. I can find people who'll work for less."

The four men didn't respond.

"I need air," said Leonard. "I'll be back soon."

His mind was a mess. *This is the second time in two days people try to blackmail me. Why? I'm taking care of people, just not as much as they want. I'm not their babysitter. If they don't want to work for me, they can leave. Linda did.* Thoughts of firing the four men swirled through his mind, but he realized he didn't have the time to replace them. Firing them would lead to more delays in shipping the SunRise goods, something he couldn't afford. The men in the warehouse were an asset; they were doing their job. If he wanted to save his relationship with SunRise, he had to agree to their demands *and* hire another two men, which was going to cost money, but it would be only a small fraction of what he received from SunRise. *Let's call it an investment.* He calmed down and returned to the warehouse and told the men he agreed to their terms and would hire two more workers.

"I don't have time to search," he added, "so if you know people you trust, bring them to the warehouse and email me the details. They can start right away."

He didn't wait for the men's reactions and left without saying goodbye and drove straight home. In retrospect, he thought, he should have gone to the office to check up on the data entry clerk, but he felt drained by the experiences of the last two days. He needed to clear his mind to make the right decisions. Leonard felt good about the way he dealt with the warehouse workers, and once at home, he took a short nap and then headed for the pub.

The next morning, at breakfast, Leonard felt pressed. Yes, he had dealt with the crisis in the warehouse, but the big problem that Linda's departure posed was far more difficult to solve. *And I'm not free to do what I want. I have obligations to Mrs. Liu. I must find a replacement for Linda if I want to stay out of trouble with Mrs. Liu.* With this feeling of urgency, he entered the YYZ office suite convinced he had one or two days to set things right. But his mood became worse when he heard the telephone in Linda's office ringing and nobody picking up. *Where's the data entry clerk? Why isn't he answering the phone? Why do I pay such useless people? Does the entry clerk think I'll answer the phone early in the morning? Time to talk to him and let him know he must be at work before the calls come in.*

Leonard didn't get the opportunity to talk with the data entry clerk. In his office, he found a note from the data entry clerk taped on his computer screen and it read:

Dear Mr. Young,

Because Linda is no longer working here, the office is like hell. I get no work done because the phone is ringing all the time, and when I pick up, the people on the other side are complaining about faulty billing, missing items, and late delivery of orders. I don't know what to do. One caller spoke Chinese, which I don't understand. The office needs Linda back. She was the one who took care of these phone calls, and in her absence, I quit. Without notice.

Leonard's head spun. How could he run the office and take care of his business relationships and find new customers by himself? Who was the Chinese caller? He was in full crisis mode. He could deal with the five containers on their way to Amsterdam, four of them filled with goods from SunRise. Talking to the freight forwarder and getting hold of the arrival times of these containers would allow him to transfer this information to Frank and the Transport Coordinator. This would give him breathing room in his dealings with SunRise, but he needed to ship at least two containers of SunRise goods within a week to prevent a large period of inactivity. *Why has Linda left? Am I that bad of a husband?* He didn't think so. He didn't understand. Leonard sat down behind his desk and prioritized what he needed to do.

The first thing was to find another office manager, a competent person who could take care of the smooth running of the office and who could ship the merchandise. That person also had to contact the freight forwarder to learn when containers were to arrive in Amsterdam. But finding a new office manager would be difficult. Leonard did not know how to do that. He phoned his business friends, but they weren't able to help. They only promised to ask their contacts.

The second thing to do was to find a new data entry clerk. He phoned a temporary work agency and was told, "No problem. We will send you a candidate this afternoon for an interview, but no, right now we have no candidates for the office manager position." *An interview. What am I going to ask this person?* Linda had found and interviewed Frank and his replacement. How much salary should he offer? Perhaps he could look at the financial statements. In Linda's office, he ignored the ringing of the telephone, looked over the latest financial statement, and found what he wanted. Linda had entered the payments to the four warehouse workers, Frank, and Frank's replacement. After leaving Linda's office, he saw that mail had arrived through the slot in the front door of the office suite. One envelope was from the bank. Others were from clients and might contain buy orders or cheques. He opened the envelope from the bank and read a statement of withdrawal of one hundred seventy thousand dollars. Leonard knew what that meant. Linda had wanted money, and when he'd refused to give it to her, she had taken it. *I should never have given her signing authority on the corporate account.*

Leonard's reaction was not what one would expect. No thoughts of revenge, no cursing, no yelling or shouting. He became calm, sat down in his office, and analyzed the situation. All the things that had happened in the last two days—Linda leaving, the visit of Mrs. Liu's enforcers, the data entry clerk quitting, losing a large sum of money—were direct challenges to the way he had organized his life, and there was only one way to respond to it: overcome the current difficulties, work twice as hard, and earn more money than he ever had. Linda might have given up on YYZ, but he hadn't. He was going to grow YYZ and make it thrive.

The rest of the day was hectic. Leonard fielded many phone calls and had to interview the potential data entry clerk. The interview went well, and within twenty minutes, Leonard had hired the candidate, with recording the buy and sell transactions and keeping track of payments as his major duties. After agreeing with the salary Leonard offered him, the new data entry clerk said, "I'll start tomorrow." *Good. One thing done. The next thing is to find a competent office manager who can take care of all the other things necessary to run the office.* It occurred to him Linda had done an excellent job, but he suppressed that thought because Linda taking out money that, in his mind, did not belong to her disgusted him.

In the evening, he visited his favourite pub to eat something and have a few beers. He settled at the bar and chatted with the usual customers about the weather and the local sports teams. The bartender asked how business was, which made Leonard wonder whether word of Linda's leaving had already spread to the Silver Beaver. He didn't think so, and answered, too loud and too determined, "YYZ is doing well. No problems we can't handle."

"I'm glad to hear. We don't want to lose you as a customer."

Leonard's brash proclamation attracted the attention of a man who sat two stools further down the bar. The man turned to Leonard and said, "Hi. I'm Ethan. I heard you talking about YYZ and how well you're doing. Are you the owner?"

Leonard looked at the man and recognized him as an occasional customer of the Silver Beaver.

"Yes, I am," he said. "What's your interest in my company?" *He might be a new client.*

"Oh, I talked with Frank a short time before he moved to Amsterdam. A great opportunity for him. His promotion thrilled everybody here."

"Frank is doing a good job for us."

"We talked about how lucky he was to get this promotion and how the company I work for has never promoted me but promoted a much younger person. And we talked about Frank trying to find me a job at YYZ after his return to Toronto. I know Frank isn't back yet, but now that I've run into *you*, I might as well ask if you have any jobs open for a person like me who knows a lot about managing an office. In the company I work now, I get no credit. I'm looking for a new job."

Leonard couldn't believe his luck. If this man had the experience he claimed, he was an excellent candidate to replace Linda.

"This isn't a good place to talk," Leonard said, "but I need someone to run the office, do the payroll and the month-end financial statements, take care of the paperwork needed to ship goods, manage my other employees, and keep my customers happy so they don't phone me all day. If you're qualified for a job like that, we can talk in my office tomorrow morning at nine."

"Thank you for the opportunity," Ethan said. "I *can* do the job; it's much like the work I do now, except I have no experience in shipping goods. But I'm a quick learner. I'll see you tomorrow at nine—and thank you again."

"No thanks needed. Be in my office on time."

The men shook hands. Leonard paid his bill and left. He felt good. *If this works out, we can clear the backlog in the warehouse in a week or two. That will satisfy Mrs. Liu, and the new clients the Transport Coordinator has identified.*

The next morning, at nine sharp, Ethan entered Leonard's office. He was eager to speak about the job opportunity.

"Sit down," Leonard said. "Call me Mr. Young. There's not much time. I have seven employees, and they need supervision. That would be part of your job description. One works here in the office and enters the relevant data about our business transactions in the computer; the other six work in our warehouse preparing goods for shipment to clients in Canada and Europe. These people slack off, so you need to make frequent visits to the warehouse to set them straight. You can do this job if you have the experience you say you have, and I will gamble on that."

"I won't disappoint you," said Ethan. "Show me the details of importing and exporting goods. I'm sure that is not too difficult."

"It's not. But tell me a few things about your current job. What problems have you dealt with in the last two months?"

"Well, it has been hectic selling and servicing heating furnaces and with the temperatures dropping, there's a lot of demand. Our technicians have been busy, and I found out a few were cutting corners. I had to deal with a lot of complaints from our clients. One technician was selling new furnaces at a marked-up price and pocketing the difference—but that didn't bother me much. After I spoke with him, he promised not to do it again. A few irregularities are normal when work gets hectic. I couldn't fire him because it would leave the company shorthanded."

"So, you have a flexible attitude? Business first—is that it?"

"Yes, you could put it that way. Business first, and if we need to bend the rules a bit, so be it."

"Good," said Leonard. "I like your approach. Our business is simple. We hire a freight forwarding company to pick up merchandise that needs to be moved, and they put it in a container and ship it to Europe or elsewhere in Canada. I'll show you what forms to fill in for each shipment. You can start tomorrow. How about it?"

"I'd love to, but I must give my present employer two weeks notice."

"I need you tomorrow, not in two weeks. Tell your current boss you quit today." *Like* my *employees do.* "Before you say yes," Leonard continued, "One more thing. I need someone who is *discreet* about YYZ's business. There are things we do that could attract the scrutiny of the customs office, and we don't want that aggravation. But it's a good job for someone with the right attitude, which you appear to have."

He wondered if he had said too much to this man he had met only the previous day. But then, he liked Ethan's "business first and bend the rules if necessary" point of view.

Ethan thought about what Mr. Young had told him. Was this job landing him in trouble? It could. Mr. Young couldn't have been clearer about that. But there may be a bit of excitement associated with the job, which would be a welcome change from his current one.

"No problem," he said. "I won't tell anyone outside the company what happens in YYZ. But I understand there might be risks involved, and for that reason, I am asking for a salary twice that of your earlier office manager."

Leonard smiled for the first time in a long time. "Good—you agreed to a zero salary. My previous office manager was my wife, and she never had an official salary. So, two times zero is fine with me."

Ethan looked at the floor. He should have made inquiries, he realized, before discussing salaries.

"Don't worry," said Leonard. "Of course, YYZ will pay you."

He made Ethan a proposal. After negotiating for a while, the men agreed on a salary and shook hands.

"Great," said Leonard. "Welcome to YYZ. Be here tomorrow morning at nine and I'll show you the place."

"Thanks, Mr. Young. Looking forward to it. I'll go tell my boss this is the last day. If he wants to know why, I will explain to him promoting a young guy to a job I was more qualified for was a mistake. You never know—he might learn something about managing people."

Ethan left Leonard in as good a spirit as was possible under the circumstances. *If this guy works out, he's the perfect revenge for Linda having abandoned* YYZ. The rest of the morning, Leonard spent teaching the new data entry clerk what to do. He told him about keeping a separate file on transactions involving SunRise Technologies—the volume of goods received and exported, and the associated payments. His first impression was that the new clerk was going to work out well. He seemed intelligent and hardworking. This instilled in Leonard an optimism that he was able to grow YYZ without the help of Linda. Before long, he could leave this whole terrible episode behind and go back to taking care of his customers and looking for new ones.

Leonard drove to the warehouse to see what goods were ready to ship. When he arrived, the six workers were having their lunch break. In an unusual display of good management, he told them that *after* they finished, he wanted to see what goods were ready to ship out by tomorrow. In the meantime, he made the rounds of the warehouse. He had brought an inventory list put together by the previous data entry clerk and noticed quite a few discrepancies. Goods marked as shipped were still there, and goods listed on the inventory list were missing. *It's a good thing Frank's replacement quit.* He would ask the new data entry clerk to go to the warehouse, and find out why the inventory list didn't match the goods in the warehouse. This could be the reason for the many phone calls. He felt energized and eager to correct these mistakes. *It's one more thing to get YYZ back on track. If Linda thinks that her leaving will make the company collapse, she is wrong.*

SIXTEEN

LINDA met Frank in the lobby of her Amsterdam hotel.

"Nice to see you," Frank said, "but why are you here? I'm surprised you have time to travel besides taking care of the shipments and everything else you do. How long are you planning to stay?"

"Only a few days. I came here to tell you I'm no longer working for YYZ."

This announcement stunned Frank. He tried to imagine the office without Linda, but images of her making phone calls, organizing the constant shipments, checking the accuracy of his data entry, making coffee, and doing myriad other things were too prominent. He could think of Linda only as the office manager, and he was sure the YYZ office would not run well without her.

"Why did you leave?" he asked. "Please tell me. The office might stop working if you aren't there."

"Let's go to the dining room. I need a decent lunch after the flight from Toronto."

During lunch, Linda said, "The simple answer is, the relationship between Mr. Young and me has changed to where I no longer want to share my life with him. We're separating. For now, let's leave it at that."

"Is someone else in the office going to organize the shipments?"

"I'm not sure; I didn't leave on good terms with Mr. Young. Short term, don't worry. We shipped five containers in he two or three weeks before I left, and they should arrive soon. What happens after that, I can't tell. That depends on whether Mr. Young can find someone to replace me or whether he'll take care of the shipments himself. It's unlikely he'll do that. He never had much interest in the paperwork."

Frank panicked. He looked out the window, and in the soggy December weather, he saw a flock of black crows looking at him. *Is this the end of my job? Do I have to go back to my routine life in Toronto?*

"This is unexpected," he said. "I always saw your marriage with Mr. Young as solid."

Linda did not elaborate, other than saying her marriage was no more like what it was when they had just married. "I ended it. No point pretending everything's fine."

"That makes sense, but I can't imagine you as anything other than the YYZ office manager. You were so busy; you almost ran the entire office by yourself. My contributions were modest."

"Don't underestimate what you did and still are doing for YYZ. Correct records of business transactions and maintaining an up-to-date inventory are crucial. I realized how important these records were when it turned out your replacement made many mistakes, leading to a lot of complaints from our customers."

Linda's remarks flattered Frank and lifted his spirits, but only for a short time. Throughout the rest of the meal, he felt as if he had to go to his apartment and pack his suitcase.

"Who will tell the Transport Coordinator the arrival times of the containers? He always got this information from *you*, so he could tell me when to go to the customs office.

"I can't answer that question," said Linda. "It depends on how Mr. Young reorganizes the office. He might find another office manager, and, if so, I hope he remembers to get approval from SunRise. My replacement might give you the information you need. If he can't find a replacement, or if SunRise doesn't agree with his choice, then shipments may stop coming and the entire scheme could collapse."

Frank kept folding and unfolding his napkin; he had taken only a few bites of his lunch. This was the moment he had feared the most—hearing

Linda tell him his job could end soon. *What am I going to do? I saved enough money that I can stay in Amsterdam for a while and try to find a job.* But what job? If it resembled his earlier data entry job, it wouldn't pay enough for him to stay. *I'll have to go back to Toronto. But as long as the authorities don't know I lost my job I can travel all over Europe.*

"I hope," he said, "I can stay in Amsterdam for a long time. For tonight, I have tickets to a classical music concert. I'm going with a friend."

"Wow, you've changed! I hope you enjoy your concert."

Linda wanted to probe what Frank knew about his role in the SunRise-YYZ scheme and asked, "Frank, tell me—what do you think your job *is* here in Amsterdam?"

Frank looked up from his meal, surprised. *She knows what I do. Why is she asking me this?* He didn't tell her the details of his job, but talked to her instead about his suspicions about the goods he cleared.

"For a while," he said, "I've suspected that there's something wrong with the Chinese goods YYZ ships. There's more to them than what you wrote in the paperwork. If these shipments were routine, we wouldn't have a dead agent. The reason I'm not *sure* we're doing something illegal is that you organized the trade, and you wouldn't make me part of an illegal activity. You told me YYZ was helping SunRise export their goods to Europe. I trusted you not to get me into trouble."

"I appreciate your trust in me, and I'm sorry Mr. Young and I involved you in an illegal trading scheme. This has bothered me for some time, and I am here to tell you what you agreed to do and to prevent you from getting into trouble."

Frank wanted to ask what trouble she was thinking of, but his mind had not yet absorbed Linda's message. Instead, he told the story of what had happened during his visit to Brussels: how a man called Z had roughed him up and how his partner carried a knife.

Linda interrupted. "Sorry to hear they mistreated you in Brussels, but the Transport Coordinator was right. For the European contacts and YYZ and SunRise, there was, and still is, a lot of money at stake."

"I figured that out. Any organization that employs a pair of enforcers like the men in Brussels must be into big money."

"The goods are fake brand-name labelled products—counterfeit electronics, jewellery, clothing, footwear, construction materials, and more —that SunRise sold to European customers for a while through the port of Antwerp. After they got caught, Mr. Young helped Mrs. Liu export SunRise goods under the YYZ name for a generous cut of the profits." She added after a brief pause, "And I agreed with this scheme, but no longer—no more illegal dealings for me. I want to live a normal life and share it with someone who doesn't obsess over making money."

Frank was quiet for a while. He felt a sense of betrayal, but then, as much as he grappled with the idea Linda had manipulated him, he realized, the SunRise-YYZ collaboration was less serious than it could have been. Linda's description of the goods matched the contents of the containers written on the paperwork, and they were all harmless. Frank didn't doubt selling fake brand-name goods was illegal, but because in his case there were no drugs, no weapons, or explosives, the trade wasn't too bad. If the containers kept coming, he would continue taking part in this illegal scheme. But what if the goods in the containers were of inferior quality and using them would harm people? He went over the clients he had recruited. Selling counterfeit adult briefs that weren't up to the usual standards wasn't serious, just inconvenient for the staff. But what about the construction materials and the car parts he had sold? If *they* were inferior, there may be serious consequences. Would he still take part in the trading scheme if that turned out to be the case? Where should he draw the line? This thought would keep him awake at night.

For now, he realized, he knew nothing about the quality of the goods he cleared through customs. The logical thing for him to do was to quit his job, to avoid the risk of participating in a harmful scheme. But Frank's thoughts weren't logical. His love for Amsterdam, his resistance to the idea of returning to a low-paid job, and his fear of Mrs. Liu influenced his thoughts. He wasn't willing to quit. If he had evidence there were harmful goods in the containers, he would consider leaving his job, but not now. This was what he told Linda.

"Good luck to you, Frank," she said. "I came here to inform you about your job, but the decision to leave or to continue is yours."

Frank watched Linda leave the restaurant. He lingered over a coffee, thinking about his life, which threatened to become complicated. *I must find out if her leaving YYZ spells the end of the shipments.* For him to continue to claim the containers, he needed reliable information about their arrival time. He realized because Linda no longer could give that information, he could do one of two things. The first was nothing. The old Frank, he realized, would have done that, nothing, and taken a wait-and-see approach, hoping Mr. Young would find a new office manager. But the new Frank, the one who enjoyed living the good life, emailed Mr. Young, informing him that he had met Linda and that she told him she didn't work for YYZ anymore. He asked Mr. Young to send him the information on the arrival times and the destinations of the containers. He would then inform the Transport Coordinator. *That will teach him a lesson. He'll realize he isn't as important as he thinks he is.* Frank felt good emailing Mr. Young. If the containers stopped coming, he was not to blame.

SEVENTEEN

FRANK's fear of the flow of merchandise being interrupted increased by the day. Mr. Young responded to his email thanking him for his commitment and agreeing to send him the information he had asked for. Since Frank's meeting with Linda, two containers had arrived, and more were on their way. The Transport Coordinator had balked at Frank emailing him about the arrival times and destinations but had no choice but to accept the information. But no more messages had come from Mr. Young since Frank had last cleared a container. He had emailed Mr. Young again, but was still waiting for an answer. Every day that passed, he became more convinced he was no longer part of the Sunrise-YYZ collaboration and that his good life in Amsterdam was ending. This became reality when his doorbell rang, and he found a well-dressed Chinese young man carrying a small suitcase standing in front of the door.

"Hello, are you Frank?"

"Yes, I am. Who are you?"

"My name is not important. May I come in?"

Frank hesitated a moment, but decided it must have something to do with the shipments. "Of course. Please follow me. Have a seat."

The young man placed the small suitcase on the coffee table. "Mrs. Liu sent me here to tell you that you are no longer working for SunRise Technologies or the YYZ Import/Export Company."

These words hit Frank as if the young man had swung a baseball bat at him. He developed an instantaneous headache, and his whole body hurt. *It just happened.* Mrs. Liu had ended his dream job. He thought she didn't have the right to fire him from YYZ, but she must have cleared this with Mr. Young.

The young man looked at Frank and waited until Frank had recovered enough to absorb more information.

"You are to vacate this apartment by noon tomorrow. You will take only your possessions with you. Leave the computer and any notes on the containers here in the apartment. Mrs. Liu thanks you for work well done and wants me to tell you this change has nothing to do with you. Your performance was satisfactory. She understands this sudden dismissal comes as a shock to you, and she realizes you might be angry with YYZ and SunRise Technologies. This might tempt you to talk about the containers with other parties. Of course, that is not advisable."

Frank heard only half of what the young man told him. He saw the man open the small suitcase and show him bundles of American hundred-dollar bills, but what so much money meant didn't sink in.

"Mrs. Liu wants me to offer you fifty thousand dollars to secure your complete discretion about what you might have seen and heard about the arrival and transport of the containers and their contents. By the way," he added, "Mrs. Liu also asked me to tell you that anytime you are in China, you are welcome to visit her. I don't know why, but she told me she will organize a guided tour of Shanghai for you. This is unusual. She never expresses sympathy for anyone. You must be somebody special."

Frank tried to say something, but he couldn't. He stood up and walked over to the sink for a drink of water. *My job is over, and I must leave and return to Toronto.* He stayed silent for a while to gather his thoughts. The young man waited for a response and after five minutes, to help Frank along, said, "Fifty thousand dollars should last you a long time."

Frank found his voice and protested. "I did my job well, made no mistakes and even brought in new clients."

"Why Mrs. Liu ended your job I don't know, but once more, I should stress that your termination is not because of anything you did or did not do. If you ask me, the decision came after Mr. Young phoned Mrs. Liu and told her there was a replacement for Mrs. Young. I am sure Mrs. Liu did not want the SunRise Technologies merchandise handled by someone she didn't know. At that point, Mrs. Liu took over the operations as much as possible. As a trusted employee, she asked me to replace you. A colleague of mine is replacing Mrs. Young to take care of the SunRise business. There will be a desk for him in the YYZ office, and he will oversee the shipments of our merchandise and tell me and the Transport Coordinator here in Amsterdam when the containers arrive and what their destinations are."

Frank heard the young man speak. He didn't catch the details. But the message that Mrs. Liu had reorganized the YYZ office, and he was no longer included came through loud and clear. *I am out. I must abandon this apartment and find another job in Amsterdam.*

"What about Mr. Young?"

"We cannot replace him for now, because we need YYZ to ship our merchandise to Europe. Mr. Young has agreed not to involve himself anymore in any business related to SunRise Technologies and only to offer the excellent reputation of YYZ and the services of his warehouse workers to us to enable the shipments to Amsterdam."

"I bet he doesn't enjoy being excluded."

"He has no choice, and we still pay him for using YYZ. He has no reason to complain."

"And me? Where do I go? I don't understand why I am being fired when things are getting busy. In the last month, I cleared four or five containers every week," Frank said, but he realized his claim of working hard would change nothing.

The young man, however, appeared to find Frank's numbers very interesting and repeated them. "Four or five containers a week? The lists of shipped goods show YYZ never sent more than three containers in any seven-day period. Are you certain there were times you had to clear four or five containers?"

"Yes, I am sure. It started a month ago."

The young man was quiet for a while. *Are my records incorrect?* he wondered. He didn't believe that. Mrs. Liu ran a tight ship. What could explain the discrepancy between what he knew and what Frank had told him? *This may be serious.*

"The times you cleared four or five containers," the young man said, "did you notice anything out of the ordinary? The size of the containers, the paperwork describing the contents, or their destinations, for instance?"

"Yes, in those weeks, containers were going to Belgrade and Warsaw. Two new destinations."

The young man looked pensive. There were no records of any SunRise goods being transported to Belgrade or Warsaw through YYZ. He had to investigate this—or better, tell Mrs. Liu about it and have *her* solve these discrepancies.

"Thank you for giving me this information," he said. "But now, to answer your question. Where you go and what you do is not my business. But when you take the payout in this suitcase, you agree to be one hundred per cent discreet about your dealings with SunRise Technologies. You will act as if this episode of your life never took place, and you will erase us and the containers from your memory. If I were you, I would be careful, because at the slightest mention of your activities here to anyone, we will know, and the consequences will be harsh. Do not think it is impossible for Mrs. Liu's enforcers to kill you. Do you accept the money?"

Frank shivered as if he felt the outdoor cold in his apartment. But, after a while, he pulled himself together. With the fifty thousand dollars and his savings from the two salaries he had received over the last seven months, he could stay in Amsterdam for a while and look for a new job.

"I accept the money," he said, "and I promise not to talk about my activities involving YYZ and SunRise."

"Good. Take it. Be careful with it. Don't attract attention by spending large sums of money and vacate the apartment. Lock the door on your way out and put the keys in the mail slot. I will enter the apartment with my spare set." The young man stood up and headed for the front door.

"Nice to have met you. I will let myself out. And remember: leave no later than noon tomorrow."

Frank moved into an affordable hotel near Dam Square. It took him a few days to come to grips with his new situation. He was out of work and his dream job was no more. He grappled with confusing feelings —regret about the loss of his job, the uncertainty that came with being jobless, relief it hadn't been him who had to decide to quit his job and that he had parted ways with Mrs. Liu without the threat of violence. After two days, he opened the small suitcase and started counting the money. Fifty thousand American dollars. *At least the severance pay is good.* The first thing to do, he decided, was to find work—here, in Amsterdam. He visited temporary employment agencies, but none offered him a job. "Sorry, we can't give you a job. Your current work visa allows you to work as a foreign worker for a specific company only." Frank realized his chance of getting a new work permit was small. *Whatever I can do, many Dutch people can do. Why should they give me a work permit?* Anyway, to apply for jobs, he would have to write a resume, and what was he going to write? His formal education comprised a high school diploma and a college degree in office management, which wasn't too shabby, but his work experience was spotty, with his employment at YYZ being the longest he had worked for any one company. Then there was the problem of listing his skills. Data entry was one, and he could call it "administrative skills" to make it look better, but lots of people entered data into computers, and it wouldn't help him much. Clearing containers through customs was not something he wanted to mention. And there was the problem of not speaking or writing Dutch. But he remembered how easy it had been for him to find new clients for YYZ in the Netherlands, so perhaps he should look for a sales job, or for a job promoting products at business meetings or events where many people came together, like international conferences where he was able to speak English.

Frank wrote his resume, but despite using a fourteen-point font and double spacing, he didn't fill more than three-quarters of a page. Besides, he couldn't give a permanent address. He would have to rent an apartment. His poor resume forced him to face reality. His chances of finding a job in Amsterdam or elsewhere in the Netherlands were small, and if he found one, it would be a low-paying job like what he would get in Toronto. So why not go back? With his fifty thousand American dollars and his savings, he might rent a decent place to live in downtown Toronto and start a job search. And he would, like he had here in Amsterdam, enjoy Toronto's rich cultural life—an enormous improvement over his earlier lifestyle.

Frank decided to talk with Herman about his chances of finding work in Amsterdam. They had tickets for an afternoon concert the next day, an excellent opportunity to discuss this subject with him. Frank was aware of the threat of violence from the young man who had given him a lot of money to be discreet. But if he didn't mention YYZ and SunRise or any specifics of the SunRise-YYZ trading scheme, he should be all right. Frank was ready to take the risk.

He had lunch with Herman before the concert. Although Frank wanted to ask Herman's opinion on finding a job, it took him until after they finished dessert to broach the subject.

"I want to tell you something, and perhaps you can give me advice."

"Sure. Speak, and I will see what I can do."

"Several days ago, I lost my job, and I need to find a new one. I tried temporary work agencies, but they need me to get a work visa first, and I'm sure I won't get one unless someone has promised me a job. But my resume is thin, and not likely to impress anyone."

Herman didn't respond. The fact Frank had lost his job disturbed him. Who had fired him? Mrs. Liu? But why? If Frank was out of favour in Shanghai, he could be a liability. Better to keep his distance until he had more information. But then, he didn't want to skip the concert.

"What I want to ask you," Frank continued, "is if you think I can get a job here, given my poor qualifications and lack of a permanent address."

"It depends on what job you want. Without a work visa, you won't find legal work, but the Netherlands has a vast underground economy that employs many illegal immigrants. I don't think you want to be part of that. There is no future in it, and immigration officials can arrest and deport you any time. Going back to Canada as a deportee would not help your future there."

Frank didn't answer. What Herman said was worse than he thought. No way was he going to be part of the underground economy and live in constant fear of being arrested! *I must go back to Toronto and make the best of it.*

Herman looked at his watch. "If we don't go now, we will be late for the concert. We can talk more later, but your chances of getting a decent job are small."

"Thanks for your opinion. It helped me reach my decision: I'll go back to Toronto. But let's go. No need to miss the concert."

It surprised Frank how calm he was. For seven months, he had not considered going back to Toronto. Living in Amsterdam was more attractive. But now, after he had lost his job and finding a new one appeared to be impossible, he was ready.

EIGHTEEN

AFTER she visited Amsterdam, Linda flew to Paris. She wanted to talk to Claudia. On the plane, she went over her discussions with Frank. He wasn't as naïve and innocent as she and Leonard had thought he was. He had caught on that there was something wrong with the SunRise-YYZ collaboration but had decided not to act. Linda suspected he had rejected the idea of leaving his job or contacting the authorities because of his loyalty to YYZ—to her—and because he liked his new lifestyle. Like her motivations. Loyalty to her husband and the promise of large payouts had made her go along with the illegal trading schemes. *Frank and I aren't that different.*

In the taxi to her hotel, Linda received a phone call from Mrs. Liu and learned of the changes at YYZ.

"I heard from Mr. Young you do not work at YYZ anymore," Mrs. Liu said. Her use of English surprised Linda. She had always communicated with Mrs. Liu in Mandarin. *She must have something important to say and wants to make sure I understand what she tells me.*

"Yes," Linda said. "I left both Mr. Young and YYZ."

"Mr. Young informed me he had a new office manager, but because I did not meet this person and Mr. Young does not know him well, I did not approve."

"What did he tell you about this new office manager? How did he find a replacement for me in such a short time?"

"Mr. Young met him in a bar a few days ago and liked him. So, the next day he hired him. Of course, I could not agree. What was he thinking?"

Mrs. Liu then told Linda that after she had left YYZ, SunRise Technologies took over some aspects of the trading scheme. "Because we trusted you, there was no reason to involve our people. But now that you are no longer there, we inserted our manager into the Toronto office and appointed our agent to replace Frank."

"Why Frank? He did well."

"Yes, he did, but I am in favour of putting as many SunRise employees in place as possible."

"And Mr. Young?"

"Because we continue to use YYZ, we are still paying him for his co-operation."

After a brief pause, Mrs. Liu continued. "Are you familiar with shipments to Belgrade and Warsaw?"

Without hesitation, Linda answered, "No."

"I don't believe you. Someone has been shipping merchandise, not allowed by SunRise, under the YYZ name. Because you were the principal organizer at YYZ, you should be familiar with these deliveries. You are a competent person. I cannot imagine you know nothing about these shipments. How many of these unauthorized shipments did Frank clear through customs in Amsterdam?"

"I am not aware of the shipments you mentioned. All I can say is, I noticed our warehouse workers were more active than normal, and when I asked Mr. Young about this, he told me it wasn't my business. Ask Mr. Young for more details."

"I did, and he didn't like it. He sounded panicked, scared. He was hesitant in his answers. I am sure he did not tell me everything he knows, which, most likely, means he shipped the extra containers. We will investigate further and find out if that is the case. Frank promised he will not talk to anyone about his work as our agent in Amsterdam, and for that, we paid him a lot of money. I hope you will give the same assurance of absolute discretion, and, of course, we will reward you too."

Linda took her time to plan her answer. The idea of accepting money from SunRise disgusted her, and after a while, she said, "I promise not to talk about the SunRise-YYZ collaboration. My interests are served by remaining discreet. I will take no money from you, as that would implicate me even more in this scheme to ship counterfeit goods."

Mrs. Liu was not happy with the answer. "I am not sure what you have told me. SunRise needs absolute discretion from you, and that is not what I heard you say."

"I said I will be discreet and do what is best for me. For now, those two statements overlap. Talking about the SunRise-YYZ business would only cause me problems. I hope we can leave it at that."

There was a brief silence, but when Mrs. Liu spoke again, her voice was threatening. "Be careful not to mention the trading scheme to *anyone*. There will be unpleasant consequences for indiscreet behaviour. We dealt before with talkative persons."

"I am aware of that, and you don't have to worry. By the way," Linda added, "if anything bad should happen to me, the police will investigate, so you better keep me safe."

Mrs. Liu hung up with no further comments, and Linda felt a sense of freedom.

She met Claudia in the lobby of the same hotel she had stayed in on her first visit.

"This is a surprise!" Claudia said. "I hope you're here for a good reason. Did you leave Leonard?"

"Yes, I did, and I don't work for YYZ anymore either. Let's find a comfortable place to discuss this. We can go to the restaurant we visited last time when I told you about me and Leonard."

"I'm curious about your departure from YYZ. You've put so much effort into running the office. Is YYZ going to survive without you?"

"I can't tell, and to be honest, I'm not concerned whether YYZ survives."

Linda took her time telling Claudia everything about her relationship with Leonard. The first part of her story was like the one she had told Claudia on her previous visit.

"Most of what I said, you already knew. When we separated, I was going to speak with Leonard. I did. Not the next day, as I'd planned. It took a week before I could engage him and raise the subject. He didn't want to hear about me leaving him—not because I'm his wife, but because without me, the YYZ office would not run well, and this would slow down the transport of the SunRise merchandise to Amsterdam. That was all he thought about, nothing about our marriage, not a single sign he valued our relationship."

Linda paused for a minute. Claudia kept silent. Although they had discussed leaving Leonard before, it still disturbed her to hear that her best friend's marriage had fallen apart.

"There is more," Linda said. "I told you YYZ did illegal business with a Chinese company."

"Yes, the last time we met you called them 'irregularities.'"

"I remember. I didn't want to use too strong a word. But whatever—our trading scheme with the Chinese company was illegal." Linda told Claudia everything about the SunRise-YYZ trading scheme. Not because Claudia didn't know already, but because Linda wanted to talk about her life over the last few years. Talking was a source of strength, and it led her to the same conclusion every time she talked about it: she had done well to separate from Leonard. She continued, telling Claudia about the parallel scheme and how she had gone along out of loyalty to Leonard and YYZ, and for the extra money.

Claudia said nothing. She had trouble accepting Linda as a criminal. It disappointed her that all those years they had been friends, her best friend had held out on her. After a while, Claudia asked, "How about Frank? I imagine he must enjoy living in Amsterdam. He always told me his biggest wish in life was to travel, but his income wouldn't allow him. Is he still working for YYZ?"

"I saw him in Amsterdam, not long before coming here, to tell him the true nature of what he did in Amsterdam. It turned out he already suspected we were involving him in the counterfeit goods trade. After I told him we *were* shipping counterfeit goods, I expected he would want to discuss how he could stop working as an agent, but he seemed not to find my information serious enough for him to quit his job or talk to the police. He likes his current life too much to stir the pot. He'll continue clearing containers. But this morning I got a call from Mrs. Liu and learned she fired Frank. It had to do with Leonard wanting to hire a new office manager and Mrs. Liu not agreeing with his candidate. She sent her office manager to the YYZ office and replaced Frank. She paid Frank for a promise to never talk about his stay in Amsterdam or mention SunRise. Indiscretion would come with severe consequences. I got the same message."

"Amazing. I wouldn't think Frank could do something as illegal as helping to trade counterfeit goods and *continue* doing his job after you confirmed his suspicions! I guess it shows the power of money and the good life."

"Frank has changed a lot since he worked for us in Toronto. He's more outgoing and more assertive. And he likes his life in Amsterdam too much to see it end. He has a friend he goes to classical concerts with, and he told me I *had* to visit the museums in Amsterdam."

"Are you telling me he has a girlfriend who teaches him about art and music, and he *likes* that? You must have misunderstood!"

Linda smiled. "I didn't say it's a girlfriend, but he was eager to meet his 'friend' to go to a concert."

"What's he going to do now? Is he out of work?"

"Frank told me before he lost his job he doesn't want to return to Toronto. He'll look for another job in Amsterdam. He didn't tell me what job."

There was a brief pause in the conversation, and Claudia gathered her thoughts. After a minute, she blurted out a question.

"Did you ever send construction materials to Paris?"

Linda saw that Claudia had a concerned look on her face. "Why do you ask?"

Claudia was eager to talk about the cheap, substandard fire-retardant insulation panels. Since she had received the test results a few months earlier, the pressure of knowing these panels were dangerous had weighed on her. To meet Linda was an opportunity to raise the subject.

"A while ago, a few weeks before your first visit to Paris, we found a supplier who could sell us cheap construction materials. The materials come from China, and the suppliers deliver them to us only a day or two after they arrive in Amsterdam. That sounded good, but the quality of the goods, in particular the fire-resistant insulation panels, concerned me. I had a sample of the panels tested. Guess what—they're of inferior quality and won't protect people from fires in the houses in which we've installed them."

Claudia fell silent, and Linda looked pensive.

"Have you mentioned this to anyone?" she asked.

"No, I haven't, but I've been worrying about it. I don't want to talk to my boss or the Toronto head office; I'm afraid the company will fire me. They might blame *me* for this disaster. As the project manager, I'm responsible for the quality of the materials we use, and I accept that. The problem is, the office manager didn't let me check the panels. 'We don't have to worry about testing,' he said."

"We shipped containers to Paris," said Linda, "but I don't remember how many, or what was in the containers. It's possible the fire-retardant panels were in those containers."

"Can we find out? Talk with the YYZ warehouse workers?"

"They only know what warehouse in Europe the goods are going to, not the final destinations. The warehouse workers in Paris have *that* information, given to them by SunRise, but I don't think they'll answer questions."

"You told me YYZ repacked the merchandise they received from SunRise, according to the destination. Are there no records of what those goods are?"

"Yes, we have records of what goods we imported from China and which warehouse we shipped them to, and the final destination, but I can't access the YYZ office computer anymore. I can ask Frank, but I don't think he knows either. He had no interest in the merchandise we moved. He only entered data. I can try to find the data entry clerk who replaced Frank to see if *he* remembers sending insulation panels to Paris. I have his private cellphone number—it was on his job application form and was an easy number to remember. But do you have to know the supplier of these panels? What will you do if YYZ distributed them?"

"I'll feel bad no matter where these panels come from. But if they came here through YYZ, I have an added reason not to talk about them —to protect you and Frank."

During her next get-together with Claudia, Linda told her she had contacted Frank's replacement in Toronto, but he remembered little of his work at YYZ. He told Linda there might have been *several* shipments of fire-retardant panels. "But," he added, "I'm not *sure*, and if we shipped them, I can't remember their destinations."

Claudia told Linda this didn't help at all. Linda answered that apart from breaking into the YYZ office and stealing the office computer, she couldn't think of any way to get the information Claudia wanted.

"Not a bad idea," Claudia said. "We can find someone to do that."

"I know. I was only joking."

"I want to disclose the test results," Claudia said, "but to whom? If I talk to my boss, he might ignore me and keep using the cheap panels. It wouldn't surprise me if he and the office manager pocket the money they save by using the subpar panels." Claudia paused for a few seconds. "I have no proof of this, but I noticed both men bought new cars and fashionable suits. The office manager told me he moved to a larger apartment in a better neighbourhood. My boss is also the company accountant, and if he were to show a big drop in expenses in the company books, it would attract attention from the Toronto head office."

"Are they aware these panels are defective?"

"I can't tell you. But if not, they don't have a strong wish to find out. They're hiding behind the stamp of approval of the French National Centre of Fire Safety."

"I see," said Linda. "If you can't talk to the Paris office, with whom can you talk? You can alert the police, but they will investigate where the panels come from and how they got to Paris. If YYZ shipped them —and we don't know that yet—there will be a police investigation of our actions, something we don't want, and several people, Frank and I among them, could go to prison."

Linda moved around in her chair, waved at the waiter, and ordered two coffees. Then she continued. "Assuming SunRise supplied these panels and imported them with the help of YYZ, many people will be, to various extents, familiar with their shipping and use. Everybody from Mrs. Liu down to the men in the YYZ warehouse, the Transport Coordinator, the European contacts, and the people in *your* office. But only Mrs. Liu and her co-workers at SunRise know that the counterfeit panels are subpar. YYZ, Frank, and all the other people do not, I am sure, although they may suspect as much. This means, if we can prove these panels were part of the SunRise-YYZ trade, the person to talk to is Mrs. Liu. What if we could convince her to stop shipping them? That would have minimal consequences for us, but still solve the problem."

"It would. That, and a promise to replace the defective panels that are already installed. But is it a realistic plan? Will SunRise agree to give up a profitable business?"

"Maybe not, but we should try. One approach is to offer them a profitable alternative."

"What do you have in mind?"

"I'm not sure yet. I'm only thinking out loud. The other thing I thought about is," Linda said, "should we bring Frank into these discussions? *He* might come up with a solid idea about what to do."

"Well, yes, he seems to be different now. He's going to classical music concerts, so he might have changed in other ways, too. The Frank I know never had good ideas. But let's try to get him here. Do you still have his phone number or email?"

NINETEEN

FRANK read Linda's email and decided on the spot. In his uncertain situation, he had missed Linda, and a trip to Paris to meet her was impossible to refuse. He checked out of the hotel and, pulling his suitcase containing all his possessions, including the money the young man had given him, walked to the central railway station. Before entering the station, he turned around, surveyed the cityscape, and felt a wave of sadness engulf him. *I am leaving Amsterdam. Will I ever come back? For sure, but as a tourist.* For a few minutes, he saw himself walking along the canals and standing in front of *The Night Watch*, then went inside and bought a ticket to Paris.

He arrived on an early January afternoon and met Linda in the lobby of her hotel. She told him they would see Claudia over dinner to discuss a delicate situation and what to do next. Frank's meeting with Claudia was cordial, including a perfunctory hug, and they exchanged the usual "How are you?" and "Thanks, I'm doing well."

They ordered dinner, told the server they weren't in a hurry, and settled in for an evening of discussions.

"Let me summarize," Linda started. "Frank and I no longer work for YYZ." She looked at Frank and continued. "I must admit, the chaos in the YYZ office after I left led to you being replaced by one of Mrs. Liu's employees. I am sorry for what Mrs. Liu did because I know your job meant a lot to you, but I had no choice but to leave Mr. Young and YYZ, and I hope you understand."

Frank looked at Linda and told her that he knew for a while what had happened, and it had not occurred to him for one second to blame her.

"You did what you had to do. Don't feel guilty."

"Thank you, Frank. I am glad you see it that way. Let's continue. Claudia still has a job as a project manager, but the office manager forces her to use cheap materials, which he orders from an unknown company at a steep discount. Claudia found out that some materials they use are subpar, and we suspect SunRise supplied these goods, with, of course, the help of YYZ."

Frank interrupted. "What are we talking about? Construction stuff? Electric supplies, windows, kitchen cabinets?"

"None of those. The specific items that are important to her, and us, are fire-retardant insulation panels for the building projects Claudia coordinates. The problem is, Claudia had them tested, and the results showed them to be defective. They afford no protection against the spread of fire and so put people in harm's way. The panels are counterfeit —cheap imitations of the real thing."

Frank asked Claudia, "Did you talk to your boss about this, or anyone else?"

"No, only to Linda. Talking to my boss would do us no good. I suspect using cheap panels is profitable for him."

Linda continued. "We aren't one hundred per cent certain these panels came from SunRise, or that YYZ shipped them to Amsterdam." She looked at Frank and said, "I phoned your replacement in Toronto, but he had nothing definitive to say. The problem is, he doesn't work for YYZ anymore, so he has no access to the office computer to check."

"When I was the data entry clerk," said Frank, "I wasn't interested in what was being shipped. I only entered the data. But if YYZ exported these panels on a regular schedule, I would have noticed. For instance, I know YYZ often shipped electronic toys, like Nintendo systems. Since I remember nothing about insulation panels, there might have been only a few shipments, if any, or the shipments might have started after I left Toronto, seven months ago. Why do we suspect YYZ supplied these panels? Other people import counterfeit goods."

"Well, the merchandise comes from China, and the manufacturer or the middleman imports the goods through the port of Amsterdam and sells them at a steep discount, like ours. I mean YYZ's."

Frank turned to Claudia. "Tell me how you found out your company is using cheap panels. What was your first suspicion? First suspicions can be revealing."

Frank was quoting a phrase from his Tuesday night crime series, and he was glad to try it out on Claudia.

"It started with a visit by two men, who, I noticed, spoke little French. They and our office manager holed up in my boss's office for a long time, and when they left, the office manager said we had received a twenty-five per cent discount on a lot of construction materials. I wondered who these men were. What firm could reduce prices by twenty-five per cent? Later, I found out the panels were among the items these men supplied, and that they came from China. Oh, and I didn't like the looks of these visitors. They were burly, and the one with the black-rimmed glasses looked like a criminal."

Frank was silent. He had put his head in his hands, and when he closed his eyes, he saw Z slamming him against the wall in the washroom of La Rose Blanche. After a while, Linda asked, "Are you okay, Frank? You don't look good."

"I recognize Claudia's description of these men. They're the same men I met in Brussels. I told you how one of them manhandled me. They're the ones who killed the Antwerp agent. Their visit to Claudia's firm is good proof the panels were part of the SunRise-YYZ scheme."

For a while, nobody talked but concentrated on their food. When Frank had finished his main course, he asked, "What's the purpose of our meeting? Are we looking for ways to dismantle all of YYZ or only its collaboration with SunRise? Or to stop the transport and use of the panels? Do we want the people who knew these panels were subpar to be punished by the law? And, if so, how are we going to avoid being implicated in this scheme?"

"Great questions," said Linda. "We have quite a range of actions we can take, but dismantling YYZ should not be our first choice, because it will involve the police, and they will scrutinize our role in the SunRise-YYZ scheme. And don't forget, Claudia might have a hard time convincing the authorities buying the panels didn't involve her."

"I'm not implicated in the SunRise collaboration with YYZ," Claudia said, "and I know nothing about where these panels come from other than what our office manager told me. I would have preferred not to know, but since I do, I accept I need to do something about the sale of these panels."

Again, for a while, nobody spoke. Frank restarted the discussion. "I feel somewhat the same as Claudia. I didn't know about these panels, so I didn't feel guilty about them. But now you've told me," he said, looking at Linda, "I agree—we need to stop their delivery, but without inviting the scrutiny that comes with going to the police. There's also the threat of violence from SunRise to consider. Mrs. Liu made it clear to me if I talk to anyone about the SunRise-YYZ collaboration, there will be dire consequences. Talking to the authorities is *not* a good idea. Mrs. Liu will find out who complained about her. Whatever we do, we must be discreet."

"I agree," said Linda.

"I don't like where this is going," said Claudia. "I don't want to get involved in anything that includes violence."

Linda said, "I guess we'll focus on the panels. We want to stop their use. We should also push for the defective panels Claudia's company already installed to be replaced with genuine ones."

Frank and Claudia agreed to this mission statement.

"Yes," said Frank. "Let's focus on the panels and see how we can get to our goal without harming ourselves."

"Okay," said Claudia. "We should do something about the panels but I don't want to lose my job."

"And I don't want to go to prison," said Frank. "I have no problem with YYZ. They've been good to me, and because of them," he looked at

Linda, "my life went from boring to interesting. Why would I want to dismantle them? SunRise is a different matter. I, and I'm sure you too," he made a sweeping gesture with his hand, "cannot support a company that kills people when they make a mistake. I have no reservations about destroying SunRise and seeing Mrs. Liu and the Transport Coordinator in prison."

A silence descended on the group. They realized how difficult a goal they had set for themselves: to rock the boat in a way that got the results they wanted, but with no collateral damage.

After a while, Frank spoke. "What we need is leverage to make SunRise stop shipping the panels. We can't visit them and ask without being able to exert pressure."

"Do you have something in mind?" asked Claudia.

"We need proof SunRise supplied the panels—not the proof we have now, which is good enough for *us*, but proof *nobody* can argue with, like computer files or emails. Without proof, we can't do anything."

"And if we get that proof, what do you want to do?" Linda asked.

"We could use the proof to force SunRise to stop selling the subpar panels. I'm sure SunRise doesn't want us to go public with data that shows they sell defective products. They can't afford the publicity—it may lead to investigations into other goods they sold and shipped."

Linda said, "You're right. SunRise makes most of its money from counterfeit goods. They don't want any scrutiny of their business. They might be sensitive to our blackmail, and from that point of view, your plan could work. But what bothers me is that Mrs. Liu's reaction might differ from what we expect. She might use her enforcers to *take* the data we want to blackmail her with or come after us out of spite. So overall I like the plan, but we need to do more thinking. Besides, we don't have any data yet to blackmail her. And we shouldn't forget that we don't know how many enforcers Mrs. Liu employs. The Man with the Black-Rimmed Glasses and his colleague who visited Claudia's office might not be the only ones."

Silence once again reigned around the table. Frank spoke first. He asked Linda, "Do you still have the keys to the YYZ office in Toronto?"

"Yes. When I left the office for the last time, I put them in my purse, and I don't remember removing them."

"Do you mind having a look?"

Linda rummaged around in her purse and, after a considerable time probing its depth, produced a set of keys.

"Here they are," she said, putting them on the table. "Please tell us what you're thinking."

"I remember from my time in the office, there was no alarm system—not in the building or the YYZ office suite. Did Mr. Young install one after I left?"

"Not unless he did it in the few days after *I* left, which I doubt. Leonard never enjoyed spending money on things he didn't think were necessary, and an alarm system would fall into that category."

As she spoke, she realized what Frank had in mind.

"You want to break into the YYZ office? What do you want to do?"

"Frank, you can't be serious," said Claudia. "Breaking in is a crime."

"Yes, I guess so, but not a difficult one when you have the keys to the front door and there's no alarm system."

Both women stared at him. They had difficulty taking in what they'd heard. Frank, a burglar!

"Have you done this before?" asked Claudia?

"No, of course not," answered Frank. "What do you think I am? A criminal? I'm only trying to work out a scheme to get to our goal of stopping these faulty panels."

"What do you have in mind, Frank?" said Linda. "Tell us, and between the three of us, we can come up with a working plan."

"The idea is to enter the office after work hours and steal the computer. At least in my time, it contained the details of all transactions involving YYZ and its suppliers, including SunRise. I bet my successor continued using the same computer. These records will back up our demands of

Mrs. Liu and give us enough leverage to stop SunRise from selling the defective panels."

Linda swirled her wine glass, and Claudia started picking the last crumbs of food from her plate. Both were aware of what Frank's plan was. A break-in, a criminal act, and they said nothing. They needed more time to decide.

Frank saw the indecision and said, "If we want leverage to convince Mrs. Liu to stop trading the panels, we need data. I propose I will go to Toronto and get data we can use. It shouldn't be difficult."

"I agree," said Linda. "That computer has everything we need. We can go ahead. But the plan isn't perfect—if SunRise doesn't give in, none of us will have the appetite to publish what's on that hard drive. And there's the possibility Mrs. Liu might guess as much and call our bluff."

They continued to discuss the idea and concluded the risks involved were small enough that they should go ahead with Frank's plan. They might find a better, safer way to use the data. Frank was to travel to Toronto the next day, enter the YYZ office with the keys provided by Linda, and copy the files onto a portable drive. Linda had insisted they leave the office computer and its hard drive in place so as not to alarm Mr. Young. "If all goes well, nobody, not Mr. Young, not the new data entry clerk, or the office manager will know we stole the data."

TWENTY

THE Transport Coordinator was unsteady on his feet as he walked home after a get-together with his buddies. He wondered why. *Am I getting fucking old and crappy and can't hold my liquor anymore?* He rejected the idea. *Getting old is no fun if it means I must limit my drinking to a few beers.* He pictured how his friends would react if he refused a drink. They would make fun of him, tease him by ordering drinks for themselves and a fucking soft drink for him. Self-pity enveloped the Transport Coordinator. He fumbled with the front door key and once inside the house, headed straight for the living room couch. He heard the object before it delivered a serious blow to the back of his head, but he had no time to get out of the way, and the world went black.

When the world returned, fuzzy at first, he saw Z and the Man with the Black-Rimmed Glasses sitting on the couch. He was sitting on a kitchen chair with his hands and feet tied.

"Welcome back," said Z. "Don't worry, soon you'll be okay, except for a splitting headache. Because of your size, we had to knock you out to make it easy for us to immobilize you."

The Transport Coordinator tried to move but couldn't. Z and the Man with the Black-Rimmed Glasses had done a good job immobilizing him, and his mind was racing. The two SunRise men's intentions were obvious. That's what Mrs. Liu paid them for, and in his tied-up state, he could do nothing to prevent being knifed. *How can I stall them? How can I convince them to untie me?* To his horror, he saw the Man with the Black-Rimmed Glasses take out his knife. *I hope it will be quick*, he thought. But he had heard that the enforcers liked to play with their victims for a while before killing them. *Disgusting people. Somebody should kill them as a punishment for the depraved things they do. Nobody in the SunRise organization is innocent, but the enforcers are at the bottom of the pile.*

The Transport Coordinator started talking about random subjects. "You remember the fun times we had in Paris, the drinking sessions with the French contacts? I have never been so drunk in my life. The current agent is okay, especially after you taught him a lesson. He's a fucking pussy, not meant for the work we do. I don't like Mrs. Liu. She's too bossy. You guys can do better if you leave SunRise. There's always a demand for skilled enforcers. Frank told me he disliked you and me. We are not sophisticated enough for him." The Transport Coordinator rattled on, but the enforcers paid no attention. "I made a lot of money, and I hid it for my retirement in Greece. I want to live on an island."

"How much?" asked Z.

"What do you mean, 'how much?'"

"We might have hit you too hard and damaged your brain. How much money did you stack away?"

"I haven't counted it for a while, but it must be over two hundred thousand euros. I worked with SunRise for a long time, and before the European Union started up and got rid of customs checks within Europe, I smuggled alcohol and tobacco. Very profitable. Much better than working with Mrs. Liu; I'm not my own boss now. I must follow her fucking instructions as if I am a school kid and she is the teacher."

"You can complain about Mrs. Liu as much as you want, but it won't help you. She's been good to you, but you didn't appreciate her generosity. Why did you compete with her? You have enough money already. She thinks you betrayed her, and you know what the sentence is for such terrible behaviour."

"You can never have enough money. I didn't compete with Mrs. Liu. My clients weren't SunRise's clients." The Transport Coordinator started again on random subjects. He talked about how great life was on the

Greek islands—the weather is sunny and warm, and the beaches are fantastic. He told the enforcers how he liked Amsterdam and how Frank was a tourist, not a full member of the SunRise network. "Herman wants to retire. To stop travelling all over Europe checking up on people. Herman doesn't like us. He goes to classical music concerts with Frank. I'm sure they are up to something."

"What are they planning?" asked Z. "Are they conspiring against SunRise?"

"I don't know, but going to classical concerts is not fucking normal. Listen, I have to pee. Cut me loose. I don't want to piss on myself."

"No way," said Z. "Hold it. You aren't going anywhere."

"How long are we going to listen to this nonsense?" asked the Man with the Black-Rimmed Glasses. "I want to go drinking, and the guy has only a few bottles of beer in his fridge. Let's get this over with as soon as possible."

The Transport Coordinator became desperate. *What else can I do to delay? Let's try the money again.*

"You aren't interested in the money? What if I tell you where the money is? Will you let me go to Greece and never meet Mrs. Liu again? She will never know I am still alive. Are you going to kill Mr. Young too? He was happy to work with me to export more merchandise. He has more money than I do. I'm sure you can convince him to give you most of it. Cut him a little with a knife, and he'll agree to anything."

"Where is your money?"

"I'm not telling. It is an exchange. You get the money and I walk. But first, you cut me loose. Why are you afraid? It's two to one. And I need to take a leak. I drank a lot of beer tonight."

Z told the Man with the Black-Rimmed Glasses to loosen the ropes and go with the Transport Coordinator to the restroom. "If we cut him, we don't want him to piss all over the place."

The Transport Coordinator moved slowly, and the Man with the Black-Rimmed Glasses pushed him ahead. "Hurry up. I want to finish our job." But the Transport Coordinator needed time; he needed a plan to get away. Maybe if he locked the door, he would have enough time to squeeze through the bathroom window. It would be tight, but worth trying.

"Don't come in," he said. "I can't fucking well piss if someone is watching," and the Transport Coordinator closed the door and locked it. His plan didn't work. The Man with the Black-Rimmed Glasses reacted right away by trying to bash in the door and calling Z, who came running. Under the weight of the two enforcers, the door lasted only five seconds before it flew open and hit the Transport Coordinator, who stumbled backward and fell into the bathtub.

"Enough games," said Z. "Tell us where the money is, and we'll kill you fast. Don't force us to kill you with a knife, one cut, one finger, one ear, or one eye at a time."

Nothing had scared the Transport Coordinator more in his life than the sight of the two enforcers. He felt defeated; he didn't have two hundred thousand euros stacked in a secret place. All he had to give them was thirty thousand euros he kept, together with his false passport, in his car for a quick getaway. He panicked when the Man with the Black-Rimmed Glasses pointed his knife at him. *No getaway today*, he thought. He realized he wouldn't get out of the house alive; he would die, right where he was, in the bathtub.

Z grabbed one of the Transport Coordinator's hands and laid it flat on the edge of the tub. "Cut off a finger," he said to the Man with the Black-Rimmed Glasses, who, in one fluent motion, severed the top of the smallest one. The Transport Coordinator let out a horrifying scream that echoed through the bathroom and disappeared out the window, where it scattered the birds sitting on a tree branch. He blacked out for a few minutes, but when he regained consciousness, he said, "Please, take all the money I have. It's in my fucking car. The keys are on the table in the hallway."

"Now we're getting somewhere," said Z. "Keep an eye on him while I look for the money. Where did you park?"

Despite the severe pain he was in, the Transport Coordinator responded in a weak voice, "In front of the house. The blue Nissan."

Z tossed two towels into the tub. "Stop the bleeding while I check your car. I hope for you, the money is there."

Z left and found the car. He unlocked the trunk and found nothing. He looked in the glove compartment and found nothing. *So, where is the money?*

"Can we help you?" someone asked. Z turned around and saw three men standing on the sidewalk looking at him.

"This is our friend's car," one said. "What are you doing rummaging around in it? Do you plan to steal it?" The three men took a few threatening steps toward Z. "Does he know you're searching his car?"

"Yes, of course. Your friend is inside the house. He gave me the key to find his first-aid kit. He fell and needs bandages."

"You better give us the key and come with us inside the house. We'll call Peter, one of our buddies. He is a paramedic. He knows how to deal with falls."

"Unnecessary—no need for a paramedic," Z said, but one man was already on the phone. *Three to two, and soon Peter coming over as well. The odds are not good. And when these men discover the injury of the Transport Coordinator, there will be hell to pay. Better try to get away. We can get to the Transport Coordinator later.*

The three men took a few more steps forwards and surrounded Z.

"Let's go—and hand over the car key."

Z had no choice. The three men crowded him and forced him into the house. Only one thing occupied Z's mind: how to get out of the house before the Transport Coordinator's buddies found out what the Man with the Black-Rimmed Glasses had done to him. As they moved through the corridor, Z, to his horror, heard a soft moan coming from the bathroom. He tried to cover up the sound by talking to the men. "It is not serious," he said. "You three don't need to be here. I can handle this."

"We'll see," said one man. "Where is our friend?"

"In the living room," answered Z, working off a plan that had popped into his mind.

The men entered the living room and noticed the Transport Coordinator wasn't there.

"Where is he?"

"I don't know!" said Z. "Maybe he left for the emergency room. If you want to know how he is doing, go there and support him. It must have been worse than I thought, for a powerful man like him to leave the house."

"Okay, what's happening?" Peter had come in, ready to administer first aid. "Where is the victim? Did he fall? Not surprising—he drank way too much. I noticed he had trouble walking straight."

"*This* gentleman claims to be a friend of Ed," said one of the Transport Coordinator's group, "and told us that Ed left the house and might have gone to Emergency."

"Oh, okay," Peter said. "Let's go there to see how he's doing."

Z felt better. *My plan might work.* Once the men had left, he and the Man with the Black-Rimmed Glasses would make quick work of the Transport Coordinator and leave in a hurry, well before the men found out they had gone to the hospital for nothing. But a loud whining sound reverberated through the house, quashing his hope for a good outcome.

"That's Ed, isn't it! Let's look for him."

The situation had turned critical again, and Z reacted by punching two of the four men in the face. One man fell backward and hit his head on the TV stand, leaving him lying on the floor, dazed. Peter kneeled beside him to see if he had sustained serious injuries. The second man had suffered a broken nose, and sat on the floor clutching his face, moaning softly. The third man was paralyzed by the sight of his friends suffering from the violent punch to the face. Z left him alone and ran out of the living room. He opened the bathroom door. "Let's go!" he yelled at the Man with the Black-Rimmed Glasses. "There are four of Ed's friends in the house."

"Who's Ed?"

"Doesn't matter. Move your ass, NOW." And he started for the front door. The Man with the Black-Rimmed Glasses followed closely behind. Once outside, they ran to their car, and by the time Ed's friends came out, Z and the Man with the Black-Rimmed Glasses had driven away. Peter, in the meantime, took care of the Transport Coordinator, who had succeeded, using the towels Z had given him and a lot of pressure, to stop the bleeding.

"I'll drive you to the hospital," Peter told the Transport Coordinator, who refused.

"Guys, thank you so much," he said. "You saved my life, and I'll be forever grateful to you, but I can't stay here. Those two idiots could come back tomorrow or next week or next month, so I'm leaving now, and don't ask me where I'm going. Once I settle in somewhere, I'll let you know. Please help me out of the bathtub."

Despite the many protests from his buddies, the Transport Coordinator insisted on leaving. Hiding in Italy or Greece, he thought, was the only way to survive. He knew that Z and the Man with the Black-Rimmed Glasses wouldn't give up trying to kill him; they couldn't afford to fail their mission. Mrs. Liu would not appreciate failure. Peter gave him a supply of Advil against his headache and bandages to wrap his wound. He said goodbye to his friends, and before he drove away, he explored, with his good hand, the underside of his seat, and found that the money and his fake passport were still there.

TWENTY-ONE

HERMAN sat in a cafe composing in his head an email to Mrs. Liu describing his plans to retire in a few months. He was aware this was a futile exercise—no one retired from the SunRise network unless Mrs. Liu told them to—but he enjoyed pretending. He would claim the stress of the constant travel around Europe became too much for him. *She might agree with me that old age is a good reason to retire.* He couldn't write about the *real* reason he wanted to retire. He could no longer stand his interactions with other members of the SunRise network and their focus on making money at any cost. Mrs. Liu would never accept *that* argument. And without her consent, she would see his retirement as a betrayal of his commitment to SunRise and come down hard on him. He would compose the email with care. But he might never send it.

Herman stared at a man and a woman a few tables over and wondered how people feel when they were middle-aged and married. Marriage wouldn't improve his life. He wasn't home a lot. He had a girlfriend in most of the places he visited, but he was tired of their constant demands for fancy clothing, handbags, makeup, and other gifts.

In the last few days, a feeling there was something wrong with the SunRise network crept up on him. Things were going on with his work —Frank was out of his job, and despite Herman's best efforts, he couldn't find the Transport Coordinator. It might mean nothing, he thought, but it reminded him of the situation the week before their operation in Antwerp was closed. Not knowing *why* Frank was no longer the agent or *why* the Transport Coordinator had disappeared made Herman wonder whether the time had come to leave SunRise, before the police came looking for him. But Mrs. Liu might have ordered Frank and the Transport Coordinator to leave. If so, abandoning SunRise would be a terrible choice. Mrs. Liu would not rest until she found him and punished him. *What to do?* The best thing was to do nothing, he thought. After all, he was only speculating something was wrong with the SunRise business. He didn't have enough information to make a rational decision.

Herman ordered a second coffee and decided, from now on, to check his surroundings and be careful with people he was not familiar with. As a precaution, he would carry his fake passport so he could, if needed, travel to Italy, where, as he envisioned, he would live out his life in comfort under an assumed identity with his favourite girlfriend. No one could say he was not prepared, but the fact Herman didn't know what was going on with Frank and the Transport Coordinator bothered him. He emailed them to find out more.

"Herman," Frank wrote back. "Nice to hear from you. I am in Paris, on personal business. I miss our outings and look forward to meeting up with you for a concert. Losing my job resulted from an upheaval in the YYZ office after Mrs. Young left. I learned about that when the new agent came to see me and told me he was taking over my job. He said I didn't lose my job because of anything I did. Mrs. Liu was happy with what I've done. She inserted her manager into the YYZ office and replaced me with a SunRise employee. That's why I am out of work. I also have an answer for you about the nature of the goods I have imported. Remember you asked me after our first concert, and I answered that it was possible the goods were counterfeit? Well, now I know for certain they are counterfeit, but I guess since I am no longer the agent, this shouldn't bother me."

The mention of Mrs. Liu stunned Herman. How could Frank tell him, in writing, about his link with her? Did he not realize writing such information in an email could be much more compromising than talking about it in person? *It's my fault. I should have known better than to ask him to email me. We should have set up a meeting somewhere.* He had sized Frank up correctly. Frank wasn't an asset to the SunRise network. He was too nice. *I guess that's why I like him; he's not cut out to be a criminal.* Herman had to admit he missed his outings with Frank. But Frank's loose lips, or fingers, might get them both into serious trouble. Was this the right moment to pack his suitcase? Herman took a deep breath. *Why is my life so complicated?*

Herman had come to Amsterdam to meet with the Transport Coordinator. On a recent trip to Berlin, during an evening of heavy drinking, friends of the Berlin contacts who had come over from Warsaw told them somebody who they didn't know had offered them cheap merchandise. Herman guessed it was the Transport Coordinator, who, against his advice, had gone ahead with his parallel trading scheme. He wanted to discuss this with him. He hoped he was wrong because if the Transport Coordinator sold merchandise in Poland, he was obliged to report this to Mrs. Liu.

Herman was waiting for the Transport Coordinator's email. When it came after an hour and another coffee, it read, "Dear friend. Many things have happened in the last few days, and my life sucks. I don't want to talk about it, but the important thing for you to know is that, with the help of my drinking buddies, I survived an attack from Mrs. Liu's fucking goons. I got away without one digit of my left little finger, but I'm still alive. Now I'm in hiding, far from the Netherlands. For now, we shouldn't communicate in person. We should wait till things settle."

Mrs. Liu is unhappy with the Transport Coordinator. He must have gone ahead with this parallel trading scheme. At least now I know what happened, and I shouldn't worry, because I am not part of that scheme.

The Transport Coordinator continued. "I found out that Mrs. Liu replaced Frank with a SunRise employee, but I didn't react right away to this change of agents, which was stupid. I told you about Frank, how he didn't commit to his work, but his replacement was the fucking opposite. Very professional. I should have noticed the new agent was more involved in the business than Frank and that it would be more difficult, if not impossible, to ship extra containers that weren't in the SunRise books. I should have talked with Mr. Young and stopped our scheme. But I didn't. I wanted more money to secure my future."

Herman thought about what he had read. He knew for a long time that the Transport Coordinator was looking for an increase in his payments and had talked to him about this several times, trying to change his mind. He was sure Mrs. Liu would not react well, and she might find someone else to organize the transport. If only the Transport Coordinator had listened to him! His earnings matched the work he had to do.

"Mr. Young," the Transport Coordinator wrote next, "had added an extra container to the regular SunRise-YYZ shipments, and Frank's replacement found out right away. The number of containers didn't match the information he received from the new office manager in Toronto. We never had a problem like that with Frank, who got his numbers from Mrs. Young. The extra container arrived a week after I looked for Frank and met his replacement. The same evening, I got a visit from Z and the Man with the Black-Rimmed Glasses, and I knew at once what that meant. But as I told you earlier, with the help of four of my drinking buddies, we scared them off. I was suffering from severe pain when I drove away but my wound has been healing well over the last two weeks. I am sure Mr. Young ratted me out. How else would Mrs. Liu know the extra containers belonged to him and me? I'm planning to visit him and cut off part of *his* finger. Why should I be the only one suffering? In the meantime, I will fucking well stay away from everything SunRise. It's too dangerous. You can say I'm retired."

Herman smiled. The Transport Coordinator, retired? No way. Herman was sure a new plot to make money was already brewing in his mind. *Good luck to you. Stay safe.*

He thought about what he had learned. The emails answered his question of whether he should quit. If YYZ was still operating, run by Mr. Young and the SunRise office manager, he was not in danger because he wasn't part of the changes at YYZ. If YYZ shut down, he also had nothing to worry about. Mrs. Liu would end his job, which was fine with him. For now, he would continue checking up on the distributors. Too bad he needed to travel again. But in his free time, he could work on his retirement email.

TWENTY-TWO

FRANK was nervous. The break-in would be straightforward, but still. He shouldn't worry. During the flight, he was wide awake and went over his plan multiple times. He would arrive midafternoon and stay at the airport until six o'clock. This minimized the chance of meeting someone he knew. Then, around six, he would take a taxi to the hotel where he was to stay that night. The hotel was downtown, close to the YYZ office. Only a pair of sturdy locks protected the outside entrance to the small, two-storey building and to the YYZ office suite. When Linda, Claudia and he were planning the break in, Linda had said that nobody was in the building after nine at night. He planned to enter the office around that time, copy the hard drive from the computer to a portable drive, return to the hotel, and fly back to Paris the next afternoon. *Simple*, he thought. *Nobody will know.*

Frank stuck to his plan. He stayed at the airport until six and then checked into his hotel. At ten minutes past nine, Frank walked by the office building for the first time and saw the ground floor and second floor windows were dark. Ten minutes later, he walked by again and saw the windows on the ground floor and the second floor were dark. When he walked by for the third time and saw the dark windows, he used his key and opened the front door. He closed it without unnecessary noise and walked up the steps. He opened the door of the YYZ suite, which comprised four separate offices, and waited a few seconds before entering to make sure no one was in the office. There was enough light in the offices from a large store across the road so that he didn't have to switch on the lights. He made his way to his old office, in which he had spent five years keeping the company records up to date, and switched on the computer, typed in the password, waited until the computer, an old model, settled, and hooked up his portable drive. He copied Excel files, starting with those from five years ago. Sitting in front of the computer, he thought about why he had never been interested in the data he entered. He realized he had trimmed his old lifestyle to the bare minimum and left no room for anything new. Sleep, eat, work, repeat . . . and dream of travelling. Amazing *that* life lasted so long! What did Linda tell him during that conversation after lunch? 'Your life seems boring,' or something to that effect. He didn't agree with her then, but now he couldn't imagine that his life before becoming an agent had satisfied him.

While the computer copied files, he allowed himself to relax. There was nothing to do but wait. It would take between fifteen and twenty minutes.

To kill time, he walked around to see the changes made since he had left. When he was still working for YYZ, they used the office next door to his as a storage room and a place for the coffee machine. Now it was a proper office, and wall decorations with Chinese characters suggested it belonged to the SunRise manager. The next office was Linda's old office, and her replacement occupied it now. Frank also peeked into Mr. Young's office; he didn't enter. Mr. Young had been his boss, and his office was still somewhat of a magical place he had only visited once. He returned to his old office and waited for the computer to finish copying the files. He thought back once more to the time he was the data entry clerk. According to Linda, he did useful work then. YYZ needed correct records of purchases and sales. *So, workwise, I was doing well. But why didn't I have more fun?* His low salary couldn't be an excuse for everything. There were plenty of free or low-priced concerts in town, noon organ recitals, jazz festivals, and lectures in the reference library or in community centres. Why did he attend none of these? Was he scared of events other than his work? When he mingled with people, he never talked about anything other than the weather or the local sports teams. Linda was right; he had been dying. Not anymore. Frank had never felt so alive as when he entered the YYZ office. He was taking action; he was contributing to the efforts to halt the trade in defective insulation panels.

Frank hooked his portable hard drive up to his laptop to search for the transactions involving fire-retardant insulation panels. He found none. He found no transactions with SunRise at all. This was a big setback, and puzzling. There must be files describing the extensive SunRise-YYZ business deals! He knew he had entered that data. But if the files weren't on the office computer, where were they? Had Mr. Young told the data entry clerk to delete them, so as not to leave a trail? *Unlikely, because for the correct accounting of the payments from SunRise to YYZ, a detailed list of transactions is necessary. Mr. Young will never rely on SunRise telling him how much merchandise they shipped.*

He was sitting with his head in his hands when he concluded that the SunRise office manager must have moved all SunRise-related files to a dedicated computer. A laptop, since Frank hadn't seen a second desktop computer anywhere in the offices. If the office next door belonged to the new office manager, the laptop might be there . . . unless the SunRise manager took the laptop home every night. Frank searched the SunRise manager's office. He opened the filing cabinets, searched a cupboard holding office supplies and the desk drawers, but found no laptop. He noticed, however, the SunRise manager had locked the bottom left drawer of his desk. Before he returned to Paris with nothing to show for, he should at least try to open that drawer. Frank inspected the lock. It didn't look solid; he should be able to open it with a sharp object, such as a knife. He looked in the desks of the office manager and the data entry clerk but found nothing suitable. Frank remembered Linda and Mr. Young sometimes ate their lunch in Mr. Young's office, so they might store plates, cups, and cutlery in one of Mr. Young's desk drawers. After hesitating for a second, he entered Mr. Young's office, searched his desk, and found a small knife. With this knife in hand, he returned to the SunRise office manager's office, inserted the tip of the knife in the lock, and, without much effort, turned the lock counter clockwise and opened the drawer. There was a laptop. He placed it on the desk and pushed the start button. That was as far as he got because the laptop asked for a password.

Frank thought about what to do next. To find the password at short notice would be impossible. He had heard of software that could discover passwords, but he didn't know how to go about that, and anyway, he didn't want to spend more time in the YYZ office. Frank took the laptop with him. This would cause a lot of commotion the next morning. But what else could he do? He put the YYZ laptop and his own together with his portable drive in a plastic bag so they would not be visible to anyone on the street or in the hotel. He switched the office computer off and, on his way out, locked the office suite door and the front door, then walked to the hotel, where he lingered at the bar. Frank was excited and tense after his first break-in, and he needed to calm down. He thought of something Herman had told him: "Classical music calms me down." But because there was no classical music, Frank decided he should follow the Transport Coordinator's recipe: one or two stiff drinks. He had to admit the Transport Coordinator was right; he slept well that night.

During breakfast, Frank went over his situation again. He thought it unlikely anybody would connect him to the break-in and the theft of the laptop. Because the weather was cold, he had kept his gloves on the entire time he was in the YYZ office. There would be no fingerprints. But he realized he had to scan his passport before being allowed to enter the country. This meant there was a record of his entry into Canada. If he was ever a suspect, it wouldn't be hard for the police to find out he had stayed one night in Toronto, the same night as the break-in. They might suspect him, but they wouldn't have a *direct* link to him. But who would suspect him, the quiet data entry clerk? That afternoon, Frank returned to Paris. Nobody at the Toronto airport asked questions or searched his luggage. Upon arrival the next morning, he emailed Linda and told her his mission had been successful. He was going to the hotel to sleep, and the three of them could meet in the evening for dinner.

TWENTY-THREE

Mr. Ho, the SunRise office manager, arrived at work around nine and within minutes, discovered someone had broken into his desk and had stolen his laptop. His reaction was instant and fierce. He stormed into Mr. Young's office, but Mr. Young wasn't there. He went to see the data entry clerk and Ethan, and gave them an earful about his missing computer in English and Mandarin, and shouted about how the theft of the laptop would jeopardize the SunRise-YYZ business and put everybody in danger. The data entry clerk and Ethan realized losing the laptop scared Mr. Ho, who, for the moment, was incapable of talking about what might have happened. "Who has taken the laptop?" was all he could say, but the two men shrugged and gave "I don't know" answers.

"Come with me to my office. I will show you the laptop is no longer there," Mr. Ho said, as if he wanted to convince his coworkers he hadn't made up the story. They made their way to Mr. Ho's office and examined the lock of the desk drawer.

"Someone broke the lock," said the data entry clerk, stating the obvious. "These locks are flimsy, so one can break them with little effort. All you need to do is insert a sharp object and turn it counter clockwise." He added, "This knife will do," pointing to the knife Frank had forgotten to put back in Mr. Young's desk. Mr. Ho grabbed the knife and started swinging it around as if the knife was a magic wand and the missing laptop would appear at any moment.

"What in the world is going on here? Why are you waving a knife around in the office?" Mr. Young had just arrived and saw Mr. Ho's panicked expression. "What did you two do that's so serious Mr. Ho needs to defend himself?"

"No, no. You got this wrong," said Ethan. "He's gone crazy because someone stole his laptop."

"Someone broke into his office last night," added the data entry clerk, "and disabled the lock of his desk drawer with the knife he's waving at us. Don't come too close. I don't know what he's thinking or what he's capable of doing."

Mr. Young panicked for a moment. Was this a targeted event? And if so, by whom? A SunRise competitor? Or a small-time burglar who, frustrated there was nothing valuable to steal, had noticed the locked desk drawer and, after opening it, had left with the laptop?

"Why are you two not at work?" asked Mr. Young. "I'll talk with Mr. Ho to find out why he's so panicked."

After the others had left, Mr. Ho started talking. "The stolen laptop has all the SunRise-YYZ transactions on it. Everything—the quantity of goods shipped, the nature of the goods, the suppliers, the warehouses the goods are going to, and the ultimate destinations. Our entire business is in danger of being exposed."

"Yes, I understand. Why don't you sit down in my office and try to calm yourself? I'll be with you in a minute."

Mr. Ho was moving towards the door when Ethan called from his office, "Did you make a backup?" Ethan was enjoying the situation. He had never liked Mr. Ho, and this could well be an opportunity to get rid of him.

Ethan's question set off another fierce reaction. Mr. Ho shouted. "No, I didn't, because Mrs. Liu asked me to keep as few records as possible." He fell silent and, as if ashamed by his outburst, started talking in such a low voice no one could understand what he said. Ethan, in the meantime, put more pressure on Mr. Ho. "It's not smart not to make a backup, because now you've lost all your data. I always make a backup. You're in trouble now."

Mr. Ho stormed into Ethan's office. "Shut up. This doesn't concern you."

"If losing your laptop leads to the demise of YYZ, it *does* concern me. I should never have agreed to turn over the SunRise data to a rookie manager. Look what happened! Who in his right mind leaves his laptop in an office without security? That's asking for trouble, and trouble is what you—we—got," answered Ethan.

Mr. Ho lunged at Ethan, but Mr. Young, who had followed Mr. Ho, restrained him and tried to defuse the tension. "Go to my office and relax. I'll be with you soon so we can talk about what happened. You two," he pointed at Ethan and the data entry clerk, "get on with your work unless you have insights beyond the obvious."

"I don't know who did this," said Ethan.

"Me neither," said the data entry clerk.

"Then get back to work. You've already wasted too much time."

Mr. Young and Mr. Ho settled into Mr. Young's office.

"What do you think is going on?" asked Mr. Young. "Do you have any idea who did this?"

"No, I don't, but it could be Ethan. He never liked my presence here."

"Don't accuse my people if you have no proof. Why would my office manager steal your computer? He has nothing to do with the SunRise merchandise."

"To make me look bad. You realize when Mrs. Liu hears of this, my stay in Toronto will end."

"I know, and maybe our business with SunRise will stop as well, but does that not suggest one of SunRise's competitors stole your laptop? Or was it a regular break-in? The laptop is password-protected, so it might be of no use to whoever ran off with it."

"There is plenty of password-breaking software on the web."

"If a small-time burglar stole the computer, and broke the password, that person would erase the SunRise-related files and keep the laptop or sell it to someone else."

Mr. Young's argument that losing the laptop would do no harm did not convince Mr. Ho. He kept fidgeting in his chair. Mr. Young continued to calm him.

"A lack of recorded transactions could have complicated our financial dealings with SunRise, but we settled our most recent bills. Buy another computer and start a fresh database."

"I have no choice but to tell Mrs. Liu."

"Why? This must stay between us. I'm sure if I ask my personnel not to mention the theft of the laptop, they'll keep it a secret. We're up to date in terms of payments, and you can visit the warehouse to find out which goods we need to ship. My only worry about the stolen laptop is if the break-in was the work of one of Mrs. Liu's competitors, the word might get out and she'll learn about the theft of the laptop. In that case, I guess Mrs. Liu will no longer trust you *or* me."

"I'm sure of that. If Mrs. Liu finds out, she'll cut her ties with YYZ and find another company to help her export goods to Europe."

"That's a possibility. We will see. I hope you think things over and decide not to call Mrs. Liu. That would be bad for you *and* me. In the meantime, I'll speak with my people and tell them they should keep this confidential."

Mr. Young made it clear the discussion had ended. But Mr. Ho lingered in his chair, reluctant to face the reality of what had just happened. Five minutes passed before Mr. Young asked him to leave. Mr. Ho stood up and headed for the door.

"Don't take it so hard," Mr. Young told him. Mr. Ho still looked agitated. "There's a real possibility nothing will happen, and if in the end Mrs. Liu finds out and she fires you, you'll find another job."

"You don't know Mrs. Liu. If someone uses this data against SunRise, they might kill me. SunRise does not tolerate failure."

Despite Mr. Young's calm appearance and soothing words, his mind was in turmoil. He couldn't afford more bad SunRise-related news to come out of YYZ. Not after the stern lecture he had received from Mrs. Liu about his initiative to sell more goods and split the profit with the

Transport Coordinator. He remembered her phone call. "I think you organized this parallel trading scheme with the help of the Transport Coordinator and Frank. I am sure the Transport Coordinator supplied you with clients and Frank cleared the containers, but I don't blame him. He must have thought they were regular shipments."

Mrs. Liu had issued a stern warning that competition with or disloyalty to SunRise would have serious consequences. She told him she had sent Z and the Man with the Black-Rimmed Glasses to find the Transport Coordinator and deal with him. A shiver had run down Mr. Young's spine when he heard those words. She said that for now, because he was difficult to replace, there would be no physical consequences, but she would reduce his compensation and warned him SunRise would tolerate no more missteps. Her steely voice had Mr. Young scared well after Mrs. Liu hung up the phone. *I cannot afford more bad news coming out of YYZ. Let's hope Mr. Ho doesn't fall apart.* Mr. Young wasn't worried about Ethan and the data entry clerk. They were solid and wouldn't talk about the computer theft. But Mr. Ho was different. He felt Mr. Ho could flee at any moment when his paranoia about Mrs. Liu got the better of him.

TWENTY-FOUR

"You did *what?*" asked Claudia after she heard Frank's story about his adventure in Toronto.

"You stole the laptop?" said Linda as if she had witnessed a miracle.

"Yes, I did. I had no choice. As I told you, the office computer had no transactions on it that involved SunRise. I'm sure after I left and SunRise installed their manager, they moved all SunRise-related files to a separate machine."

"That makes sense," Linda said, "and you did the right thing."

"I have to think about this," said Claudia. "Now we're fighting crime by becoming criminals ourselves. This isn't what I had in mind. You two are making me complicit in this illegal scheme of yours. Why don't we go to the police? We don't need to use the info we got by breaking into the YYZ office stealing laptops."

"I can't go to the police," said Frank. "They will realize soon that besides the faulty panels there was a lot of other counterfeit merchandise imported into Europe and find out I worked for YYZ and SunRise in Amsterdam, and Linda was one of the principal organizers of the operation. I'd lose the money we made and go to prison. Do you want that? *We* don't."

Claudia answered, "Now that you bring it up, what *about* all the other counterfeit goods? Do we know what they are and whether *they* pose a risk to people's lives? If you're going to choose to be a righteous criminal, shouldn't you dismantle YYZ and SunRise?"

Claudia's remarks upset Frank. He asked in an aggressive voice, "How can you call me a criminal? I could have ignored this entire business with the faulty panels. But I'm trying to correct *your boss's* actions. I knew nothing about the quality of the goods in the containers I cleared."

Claudia answered right away. "I don't believe you didn't know the goods were counterfeit. You told us you found new customers for Mrs. Liu, and the deep discounts didn't make you suspicious? The fact you found new customers shows you were more involved in this illegal scheme than just clearing containers. You worked to *expand* the trade in illegal goods. You're not as innocent as you believe you are, Frank."

"We have concentrated on the defective fire-retardant insulation panels," Frank answered, "and you agreed to that, so by *your* standards, you're a criminal too. You weren't interested in including other merchandise in this. And why should you be? The other stuff could be safe. If you buy kitchen cabinets from SunRise, the wood veneer may peel off in a year or two, which isn't good for the buyers, but in no way is it dangerous. You can't say all counterfeit goods are dangerous."

"I *didn't* say all goods are dangerous. 'Might' is the keyword. You can't tell whether the merchandise is safe. You prefer not to find out, because once you find out, you have a big problem, and you must decide whether you will ignore the facts or act on them and do whatever it takes to stop this trading scheme. It may land you in prison. Frank, you became a criminal—admit it. You helped import counterfeit goods, and you continued *after* Linda told you the goods were counterfeit. You don't have the *courage* to acknowledge what you did. Linda told me you got money from Mrs. Liu to keep quiet. If you had the least bit of moral rectitude, you would have refused to accept the money, but you didn't. I figure you want to hang on to it, even though Mrs. Liu got the money through criminal activities. You've changed, and I'm not sure I like the recent version of Frank better than the one I worked with in Toronto. You might feel good about helping us try to stop the distribution of the faulty panels, but it doesn't redeem you for what you did earlier."

Frank thought back to his conversation with Herman, with whom he had agreed not to do anything drastic since he wasn't *sure* the goods he cleared were counterfeit. But after Linda told him, he still hadn't wanted to quit. Did that make him an unscrupulous criminal? Did he have such low ethical standards that he saw nothing wrong with participating in the trade of fake brand-name goods? Or was it fear of what Mrs. Liu could do to him that made him continue? Frank wasn't sure now. After Mrs. Liu fired him, he'd been relieved the threat of violence had fallen away. So maybe it *had* been fear that had kept him going.

Frank looked at Claudia. "If I had a free choice, if Mrs. Liu hadn't threatened me with violence, I might have quit when Linda told me about the merchandise, but I didn't want to risk ending up like my colleague in Antwerp. Then Mrs. Liu fired me. At first, I must admit, losing my job disappointed me, but after a few days, I realized the fear of violence was gone and was no longer part of my thinking, not if I was discreet about my job and the SunRise-YYZ collaboration. I'm telling you this so you'll understand that the threat of violence was always with me and, I'm sure, determined a large part of my behaviour. Of course, violence wasn't the only thing that made me continue. Before Linda's visit, I used my ignorance of the goods in the containers as an excuse to continue my job, despite my strong suspicions. I decided I preferred being a well-off criminal over being an honest, but poor, data entry clerk. I stayed put and played along, and I must admit I *enjoyed* going out and finding new clients. As for the money, yes, I'll keep it, because it allows me to live my life more comfortably than a low-paying job would. And a low-paying job is my future. I have no second thoughts about keeping the money."

"But now it became clear to you that the trade in those counterfeit goods isn't finished. You have it in your power to stop that, to go the police and do the right thing."

"I agreed to stop the trade of the faulty panels," said Frank. "If that leads to stopping the rest of the business as well, so be it. But for now, going to the police is *not* something I want to do. We need to find another way, one that doesn't put Linda and me in danger."

Claudia wanted to say more, but Linda interrupted. "I'm sure Frank is wrestling with what you said, but he needs more time. Thank you for speaking up. Most of what you said applies to me too. There are personal choices to make, and when the right moment comes, Frank and I will decide what to do, but let's not stray now from our goal."

"Frank, you mentioned you can't access the data on the hard drive," said Linda. "How are we going to solve that problem? After all, we aren't sure the SunRise-YYZ transactions are on there."

"We need to find a hacker, someone who can run password-breaking software for us. It must be possible to find out what the password is on a laptop. People hack into mainframes from large banks and insurance companies, so it should be possible to get access to a simple laptop."

"Do you know such a person?"

"No," answered Frank.

"I can find someone," said Claudia. "My office is in a sketchy neighbourhood with computer stores that, I suspect, sell pirated software. Most likely I can find one that can help us copy the Excel files on the YYZ laptop to Frank's portable drive."

Frank and Linda looked at each other, smiled, turned to Claudia, and in unison thanked her for her offer.

Linda said, "Let's wait until someone has transferred the data and then get together again to decide on the next step."

Claudia was right. It took only two attempts to find a store owner who promised to copy the Excel files to Frank's drive. Claudia came back after work and paid the owner one hundred euros and insisted he not talk about the job with anyone. "Don't worry," the store owner said. "My business depends on discretion. By the way, I disabled the password on the laptop so you can access it anytime."

Frank had brought his laptop to the meeting and hooked up the drive. Claudia and Linda were sitting next to him and waited for the files to appear on the screen. When they did, both women sighed and Linda said, "Let's see what's going on with these panels." Frank scrolled through files, organized by shipment date, that described a wide variety of goods sent by SunRise to YYZ—plumbing and electrical supplies, electronics, chemicals, jewellery, medicine, handbags, clothing, shoes, and an assortment of construction materials. In the early files, they found no mention of fire-retardant isolation panels. Frank noticed recent files included shipments of adult briefs, and he felt proud. He hadn't *forced* Golden Pastures to buy these diapers. They had decided based on the savings he offered them, and he didn't doubt that if the quality wasn't satisfactory, Golden Pastures would go back to their earlier source. He was not responsible for what Golden Pastures decided. He stretched the truth when he told them a Chinese factory manufactured the briefs to exact specifications, like the ones Golden Pastures used, but that was not criminal behaviour.

Recent files also mentioned fire-retardant insulation panels. "Look," said Frank. "SunRise shipped those panels to YYZ. Now let's look at the files describing which goods YYZ shipped to Amsterdam." Frank opened files, starting with those dated a few days after the panels had first arrived in Toronto. After searching many files, he found what they were looking for: fire-retardant insulation panels destined for the Paris warehouse, with Claudia's company as the ultimate destination. All three were silent for a few seconds until Linda said, "Here we are—we did it, we have the proof we need."

"From the original source," said Claudia. "Now we can blackmail SunRise into abandoning the sale of these panels."

Frank kept silent. He kept opening files and going through their contents.

"So far," he said, looking at Claudia, "I found three shipments of those panels, transported to the Paris warehouse, with your company as the final destination."

"Now what?" asked Claudia. "How are we going to go ahead? Will we talk to Mrs. Liu in person, or stay anonymous and email her from an internet cafe? Are we sending her a copy of the data as proof that we have it?" Since neither Linda nor Frank responded, she continued. "I thought about this blackmail scheme. Blackmailing SunRise might be a dangerous thing to do. Mrs. Liu will suspect Linda because she had access to the office computer. She might also investigate her manager in Toronto, and she'll find out about the stolen laptop and know in her mind who's stolen it. You two are going to be her prime suspects."

"Yes, you're right," Frank said. "But we talked about that. Are you backing out of what we started? We have a lot of data on the counterfeit goods SunRise exported to Europe, so we'll try to agree with Mrs. Liu that in exchange for SunRise ceasing the shipments of the panels, we won't talk about any of their other illegal shipments. There's no reason she wouldn't agree to the deal."

"I'm not comfortable with that, for two reasons," said Claudia. "First, we'll be letting the trade in all the other counterfeit goods continue, and second, Mrs. Liu might *not* agree with us, and instead might punish us in a way that would make us glad to give her all the Excel files she wants. We're playing with fire."

"Frank is right," Linda said. "I worked with Mrs. Liu, and her interest is money, money, money. She doesn't care what products she sells. If we make a few copies of the data and make it clear *several* people know about these panels, we can tell Mrs. Liu if anything happens to one of us, the others will expose the whole illegal trade. I'm convinced she'll carry on with her business, but stop selling the defective panels. She can be vicious, but foremost she is a business woman, and violence may attract attention."

"What if she kidnaps one of us and demands the data for the life of whoever she holds prisoner? Her enforcers are more than capable of kidnapping one or two of us. That puts us in an impossible situation, one that would mark us for life."

Frank and Linda fell silent. Somehow, the scenario that Claudia had described was possible.

"There is a safer alternative," Claudia said. "Why don't we talk with my boss, or with the office manager? Now, we can prove *they* bought these defective panels. They'll have no choice but to stop using them.

We can agree neither they nor us will talk about the panels, and the whole affair will go away."

Both Linda and Frank were eager to respond. Frank said, "We *can* make a solid case now. We have actual proof, and they'll stop using the panels, but I wouldn't count on this going away. They can claim they didn't know the panels were subpar, and they'll blame you for the extra costs and time to replace them. After all, *you're* the project manager, and they'll argue it's *your* responsibility to make sure the projects finish on time and on budget. They'll tell the head office *you* ordered the cheap, faulty panels, and that's why you've sat on the test results for a few months. You might lose your job, and there may be legal consequences."

"I agree," said Linda. "Talking to your boss could be detrimental to you. You don't deserve that."

Claudia felt defeated. She couldn't wrap her mind around this problem. She hadn't come to Paris to get involved with illegal import schemes. But she could see how if she talked to her boss, he might make *her* the scapegoat and she could lose her job. She fell silent, and so did Linda.

Frank continued looking through the data on his drive. Linda ordered three coffees, and when the server left, Frank let out a triumphant, "Yes! I found six more files documenting YYZ-shipped panels—to *other* locations. There are at least two other construction companies in France that ordered them, and YYZ has shipped panels to Berlin and Barcelona to two different companies in each country. These shipments are recent, *after* the last shipment to Claudia's company. It looks like the trade in faulty panels is more widespread than we thought. Now it's clear: talking to Claudia's boss isn't enough. We need to talk to SunRise. We need to force them to stop selling the panels."

"I agree," said Linda.

"But going to China and talking to SunRise became more dangerous," said Claudia. "These panels are big business. What if Mrs. Liu isn't willing to stop selling them? There will be violence in the end, and I, for one, don't want to get involved."

Linda and Frank nodded. They agreed that there was much more money at stake than they had thought, and with that, the possibility of violence had increased. Mrs. Liu might send Z, the Man with the Black-Rimmed Glasses, and other enforcers for a visit to retrieve the Excel files. She might resort to kidnapping, as Claudia had said. It was no longer a matter of offering SunRise an alternative to the sale of faulty panels.

Claudia continued. "We need to work with the authorities—the police or customs—so that SunRise can't export the panels to Europe anymore. If YYZ becomes a victim in this approach, so be it. They were in on this criminal scheme; they were the conduit for these shipments. I realize you will get into trouble, and you might not want to contact the authorities, but it looks like that is the only way we can stop the panel sales. The alternative is to stop our efforts now and ignore the danger to the people who live in the houses in which my company has installed them. If your consciences allow you to do that, we don't have to meet anymore, and you will force me to go public. Not right away—you'll have time to travel to a place the police can't find you."

Frank and Linda wanted to respond, but at the last moment, they couldn't. They knew if YYZ was going to be implicated, they would be too.

"Do you realize what you're asking us to do?" asked Linda.

"Do you realize," asked Frank, "talking to the police or the customs office will get Linda and me in trouble?"

"Yes, I know that now, but I'm not here to protect you from your criminal past. I—and you, and Linda—are here to protect innocent people from the dangers of faulty insulation panels. I hope both of you will see it that way too and accept that you might have to pay for what you did."

Silence reigned around the table for a while, till Frank said, "Let me tell you *my* thoughts about this. There was a lot of time on the plane back from Toronto for me to think of different scenarios that could play out after I had the data, but I decided if we had to alert the police, we should. Maybe we could strike a deal with Mrs. Liu, but now it's clear that will be unlikely. This means if I want to return to normal life, I will have to face the justice system. I understand that now, and I'm at peace with it. But I want to prevent more violence from Mrs. Liu. She can't know *we* set in motion the process that will destroy SunRise and YYZ."

After a while, Linda said, "I agree. We might have to inform the authorities. We can't stop the trade in these panels by ourselves. If we don't come clean, YYZ, Leonard, and Mrs. Liu will be forever in my mind, preventing me from living a normal, happy, non-criminal life. I am, like Frank, ready to pay for what I've done."

Frank, Linda, and Claudia looked at each other, each realizing how important their discussion had been.

"I'm on board," said Frank.

Claudia and Linda only nodded.

Frank found several more files documenting shipments of faulty panels. He also found a file that listed all the companies that supplied SunRise with merchandise. Neither Frank nor Linda nor Claudia had any ideas on how to go ahead. They ate in silence until Frank said, "We need advice, and I know the person who can give it to us."

"Who do you have in mind?" asked Claudia.

"Yes, who do you know who can be helpful?" asked Linda.

"My friend in Amsterdam is an insightful person. I'm sure he can help."

"Is it a good idea to involve an outsider?".

"Talking to my friend involves risk, but we have a great relationship. We're good friends, so I'm confident I can talk to him. He gave me excellent advice earlier on getting a job in the Netherlands. I'll be discreet."

"If you think he's safe," said Linda, "I agree. We need help."

"Same with me," said Claudia. "I'll rely on your judgment."

"Okay. I'll leave tomorrow morning. I don't want to travel with Mr. Ho's laptop, Claudia, and I'll leave that with you."

TWENTY-FIVE

"FRANK! I was happy to see your email. I wondered where you had gone. You missed a marvellous concert the other day. Brahms's second symphony."

Frank had arrived in Amsterdam by train around noon and met Herman in a coffee shop close to the station. After they had talked for a while about the remaining concerts of the season, Frank said, "Listen, I emailed you not long ago about the circumstances of being fired. I told you I was working for YYZ and SunRise and was part of a scheme to import counterfeit goods. I want to talk more about that." He continued, telling Herman about his trip to Paris and how he had met Linda and how an old friend of his, Claudia, who was a project manager for a construction company, had found out that the fire-retardant insulation panels her company used were subpar and had wanted to discuss what to do.

"We found evidence that SunRise supplied these panels and YYZ imported them into Europe. The use of these panels is widespread, and we decided not doing anything about this would make us accomplices to whatever injury and death may result from these panels. Being involved in trading counterfeit goods is one thing, but selling materials that can put people's lives in danger is something else. It is a red line we don't want to cross. The three of us decided we need to stop the sale of the defective panels. After a lot of back and forth over different plans, we agreed to seek help, and I want to speak with *you* about this." Frank didn't mention the money he had accepted from SunRise, but he mentioned his promise to be discreet and how his successor had made it clear if he talked about the SunRise-YYZ scheme with anybody, there would be dire consequences for him. "Mrs. Young received the same message," he said. "That's why you can't talk about this with anyone."

Herman didn't respond, but nodded.

"We have solid proof," Frank continued. "YYZ received these panels from SunRise and transported them all over Europe. SunRise sold them in France, Germany, and Spain. Before we found out about the vast scope of the trade, we thought we could convince Mrs. Liu to stop selling the panels if, for instance, we offered her a lucrative alternative. But we identified a lot of other construction companies that use these panels, which makes it unlikely we can convince Mrs. Liu to drop that part of her business. But now we need advice on what to do. We're leaning towards involving the authorities, but we don't want Mrs. Liu to find out we talked to them."

Herman said, "I understand you cooperated for a long time with SunRise and YYZ, and I suppose that was because you didn't know what was in the containers. But now you do. You're no longer willing to stay silent because of the subpar fire panels? Right?"

"Right. We'll contact the authorities about them, but we *must* do it in such a way SunRise doesn't suspect the info came from us." He added, to make sure Herman saw the problem, "because of the violence that will follow."

"I'm sure you know," said Herman, "that if you mention these panels to the police or the customs office, the ensuing investigation will implicate you. You will face the justice system."

"Yes, Mrs. Young, and I can guess the consequences of going public. But we can't ignore the risks to innocent people that come with using the panels. Let's put it this way—we had a good run, but we don't want it to finish in violence and death. So, facing the justice system is a better choice than dealing with SunRise. We can negotiate with the prosecutors and maybe shave something off our prison times or fines by cooperating with them, but we can't talk with SunRise without inviting serious violence."

"I admire you and Mrs. Young. Both of you are taking a principled stance, and you're preparing yourselves for the consequences. What is your proof these panels came from SunRise through YYZ?"

"We got hold of computer files describing all transactions between SunRise and YYZ, including final destinations and shipment dates."

"How in the world did you do that? Did you steal the YYZ or SunRise office computer?" Herman's tone was light-hearted, but his thoughts were dark. *Is there no security guarding the data?*

"To tell you the truth," Frank said, "I did. I stole the YYZ computer and copied the transactions to a portable drive."

"Amazing. I cannot ignore what you told me, and I will try to help. It is serious, and if we go ahead, we need to divert any suspicion SunRise might harbour after hearing of the investigation away from you and Mrs. Young. Let me think this over for a while."

While Herman thought about what to do, Frank fidgeted with his empty coffee cup. "I'll get more coffee," he announced and left the table. When he came back, Herman said, "I have a plan, but before we go into that, I must tell you something important."

"Okay, what is the important news?"

"First off, I want to tell you something you already know. I am happy I met you. I can talk to you, and we attended great concerts together. Few people in my life appreciate the things I do, and if they do, they are people who see only my professional life. I have no friends who appreciate what I do in my personal life. Except . . ."

"Yes, we *are* friends," Frank interrupted. "My experiences are like yours. In my professional life, people appreciate what I do, but in my personal life, I have no meaningful connections with anybody except you."

"I appreciate our friendship," Herman continued, "and because we are friends, I must confess that I am not who you think I am. You have the right to know who I am. I work for Mrs. Liu."

Frank's vision blurred. Shivers ran up and down his spine, and he thought he was going to faint. Herman got him a glass of water, but

Frank's hands trembled too much. He couldn't talk. His mind had gone blank.

Herman waited. It hurt him to see Frank like this, but he had to make this confession sometime, and he didn't want to discuss Frank's plans without clearing the air first.

Several people came to the table to ask Herman if his friend was okay. Herman said, "Yes, nothing serious," but he had a hard time preventing them from calling an ambulance. After a good ten minutes had passed, Frank had recovered enough to ask Herman, "Why are you telling me this? I can't believe what you said is true!"

"I am afraid it is true. For many years, I have worked for Mrs. Liu, travelling around Europe to meet up with distributors. Sometimes I get special orders to check out specific people. That's how we met on the train to Berlin and then in front of *The Night Watch*."

"Do you still work for her?"

"Yes, but only in the sense that I haven't handed in my resignation yet. I want out. I want a regular life, not to spend my time with criminals anymore. The people who make up the SunRise network are interested only in money. They have no education, no culture. Their idea of a good time is drinking and going to strip clubs. The only person in the network I identify with is you. Please think this over before you decide you can no longer be friends with me. I couldn't tell you earlier I worked for Mrs. Liu. The risk of you telling someone else was too great."

Frank understood Herman was sincere. He believed Herman when he said he wanted to be friends. *But do I still want to be friends with Herman, someone who has lied to me for so long?* Frank stood up, steadying himself against his chair.

"I want to leave now," he said. "I want to go to my hotel." He named the hotel and added, "It's close."

"I'm familiar with the place. Allow me to bring you there. You are in no shape to walk there by yourself."

"I don't remember where to go," Frank whispered. "Everything is fuzzy right now."

Frank walked to the exit, leaning on tables and chairs. Herman was a short distance behind. Once outside, he turned Frank in the right direction. Frank felt weak, and all he wanted to do was stretch out on a bed and forget this entire episode.

The receptionist gave Herman the room key. "Your room is on the top floor. It is quiet there. The elevators are on your right."

The two men entered the room and Frank said, "I want to lie down on the bed. You don't have to stay." Without waiting for an answer, Frank stretched out on the bed and within seconds, fell asleep. Herman sat down in a comfortable chair and looked at him. He could see it wasn't a quiet sleep. *I'll stay with him to make sure he wakes up okay.* What was going to happen then, he didn't know. *I hope we can stay friends.*

* * *

Around midnight, Frank woke up. He was still tired but much better than in the cafe. At least he knew now who had been lying to him: Linda *and* Herman. He wasn't sure how he felt about that. *Should I stop seeing them? Should I ask for an apology? Would an apology change anything?* He had already accepted that Linda had acted as his boss and had told him only what she and Mr. Young had decided he needed to know. But what about Herman? He had been right not to tell me about his relationship with Mrs. Liu. He couldn't take the chance. *I would have talked about it. If I'd known earlier, I might have spoken with the Transport Coordinator, and Mrs. Liu would have fired or punished Herman for his indiscretion. But now he has told me. Because he trusts me.*

Frank looked around the room and saw Herman sleeping in a chair. That he had stayed with him meant a lot. It had taken courage for Herman to confess. *It means I'm important to him. Let him sleep. When he wakes up, I'll tell him we're still friends.*

TWENTY-SIX

"HERMAN, I have decided what we must do. We must send an anonymous note to the Amsterdam customs office telling them YYZ imported substandard, dangerous fire-retardant insulation panels from Canada through the Amsterdam container terminal."

Frank and Herman were in a good mood now that they had come clean about their involvement with the trading scheme. It had strengthened the bond between them and erased any doubts they were friends.

"Yes, I guess that would set an investigation in motion, but only if the note has enough detail. I'm sure customs receive a lot of anonymous notes from importers trying to make their competitors' lives difficult. Sending a note is not enough. You must make sure a customs officer *reads* the note and starts an investigation. Add as much detail as you can. You know almost everything about the SunRise-YYZ trade. It will be a powerful note and will be impossible to ignore."

"What if we make it look like someone *else* sent the note?" Frank said. "And we write the note in imperfect English—you know, insert a few grammatical mistakes—so if SunRise ever gets to see what we wrote, they won't suspect me or Mrs. Young. And if we want to make it look like either a SunRise employee or one of their competitors wrote the information, we mail the note from Shanghai, written on local letter paper. That would further diminish the risk of SunRise suspecting me or Mrs. Young."

Herman pondered Frank's proposal. "Listen, Frank, a note is a good idea. It could work," he said. "But the problem is, no matter what we write or where we mail the note from, you and Mrs. Young will always be the prime suspects. Mrs. Liu will suspect you, because she fired you, and in her world, that means you resent SunRise. And Mrs. Young will be an immediate suspect because she knows every detail of the SunRise-YYZ scheme, *and* she left YYZ. I have worked with Mrs. Liu for a long time, almost fifteen years, and she is the smartest person I have ever met. A fake note won't fool her. She'll come straight after you *and* after Mrs. Young."

"That makes things more difficult. We don't want to be in Mrs. Liu's crosshairs."

"You need to do something unexpected, something that has never happened in the SunRise universe, and stir up enough publicity for the police to take notice."

"What do you have in mind? Go to Shanghai and break into the SunRise office?"

"No, better to pull off something dramatic on familiar ground, right here in Amsterdam."

"Okay," said Frank. "We steal the agent's computer and deliver it to the customs office."

"No, that won't help. Not enough detail. You should know. What data are in the agent's computer? Only the arrival dates of the containers and general descriptions of the contents. You would have to add the data from the YYZ computer to make it interesting, which means there's no point in stealing the agent's computer."

Frank agreed his idea was not good. "Any other thoughts?" he asked.

"What if we get the French Institute for Fire Safety to start an investigation? They can't be too happy with these fake panels carrying their stamps of approval. Mrs. Liu would never suspect you or Mrs. Young of having given samples for testing."

"True, but she would find out that Claudia was involved, and Mrs. Liu might punish *her*," said Frank, "and that's not something we want to risk. Claudia has nothing to do with the use of the panels."

Herman closed his eyes to think better. After a few minutes, he said, "Yes! What if we hijack a truck transporting a YYZ container? That has never happened to SunRise. It will cause chaos when the goods don't arrive at the designated warehouse, and if we make sure the police recover the truck, they will open the container. That is what we want. They'll investigate where these goods come from and find out they are counterfeit, and a full-blown investigation into YYZ and SunRise will follow. And Mrs. Liu won't suspect you, or Mrs. Young, of stealing a container. She might suspect the Transport Coordinator, but she must find him before she can take revenge on him."

"How would the police find out the goods are counterfeit?"

"When they find the truck and open the container, they will think they found stolen or counterfeit goods, or both. The police will ask the companies whose names are on the packages to come and inspect the goods, and they will identify the merchandise as counterfeit. Once the police have established that, they will ask the Toronto police to investigate YYZ, which will lead them to SunRise."

"Okay, but we have a problem. The Toronto police won't find any SunRise data in Toronto because I took the laptop. During my time as a data entry clerk, we never backed up the data. Should I mail the portable drive with all the data to the Toronto police? We don't want them to miss the SunRise connection."

Herman thought about this for a while. "No, you should not. That would be the same as sending a note. Don't worry, they won't miss the SunRise connection. They will interrogate Mrs. Young, Mr. Young, the office manager, the data entry clerk, and the warehouse workers, and ask the Vancouver Port Authority for the import records of YYZ. They will piece together an accurate picture of the flow of goods. You don't have to put yourself in danger and give a detailed list of the SunRise-YYZ interactions."

"But how are we going to steal a truck? I do not know how! And I don't want you to get involved. It sounds dangerous."

"There's not much danger. I know two fellows from Spain—they sometimes work with me, and I am sure the police don't know them. They have never done anything serious, but they are part of the SunRise network. I think Mrs. Liu uses them to distribute samples to potential clients. They want to retire, like me. But they feel trapped. They are aware they need Mrs. Liu's consent, but they don't dare face her and ask. It would surprise me if they turned down a chance to dismantle SunRise. The operation is simple. Once my men have the truck, they can turn around at an exit and drive back to Amsterdam, where they can park the truck in a spot where it will attract the attention of the police. How about in Dam Square? Doesn't that sound good?"

"Wow! It sounds better than an anonymous note. And Mrs. Liu won't suspect that Mrs. Young and I are behind this?"

"No, she won't, but you can still expect a visit from her and her enforcers. She likes to deal with things in an organized way. She likes to make her way down a list. The advantage of this scheme compared to sending a note is you and Mrs. Young can tell her you had nothing to do with stealing the truck, and Mrs. Liu will believe you."

"It's an ingenious way to expose the counterfeit goods to the police. I agree with this plan. Do I have to do something?"

"No. Go back to Paris and explain the plan to Mrs. Young and Claudia. I will organize everything, and once my men have completed their task, I'll email you the word green."

"Why not Mozart? That is a special word for me."

Herman smiled, and said, "Okay—Mozart." He added, "Remember I told you I am planning to retire? I will write an email to Mrs. Liu *today* saying I want to retire next month, and I have thought a lot about what to say. I'll claim the travelling is getting too much for me. Old age will be the reason for my resignation, and I will add that I will retire only if she agrees. This should neutralize any thoughts of betrayal on Mrs. Liu's part. She might not even mind much, but you can never be sure. I hope she will see it as an opportunity to insert one more SunRise person into her network."

"I hope so. There could be nasty consequences for you. She might not like you retiring."

"Don't worry—I am sure she will understand."

"Why don't you wait until after the police complete the investigation? Then you won't have to ask Mrs. Liu for permission to retire."

"Yes, you are right, but I have worked with her for so long, I feel I need her blessing. But my time with SunRise will soon end."

"What are you going to do after you retire? Is there a chance this affair with the truck will impact you? We can't predict how thorough the investigation is going to be. The police might want to talk to you, and they might charge you because of your participation in the SunRise network."

"True, a risk like that exists. I will talk to the police and come clean and do my time. When you told me you were going to talk to the police, you inspired me to do the same. I prefer that over the alternative of living under a false identity and hoping nobody finds out."

"I'm glad to hear. In the long term, coming clean is better than trying to hide. When do you plan to pull off the robbery?"

"Sometime next week, after visiting the new Transport Coordinator to get the name of a driver and the day he will pick up a container. The best transport to target is one that drives to Barcelona, but a truck to Berlin will do as well."

"Won't the new Transport Coordinator be suspicious if you ask for those details?"

Herman looked at Frank, shook his head, and said, "You are right. There are risks associated with hijacking a truck, but I want to help you. I've adopted your goal as my own and I accept the risks. Helping you is like helping myself. Don't worry, I'll come up with a plausible excuse. I might tell him I want to check out the travel times of the transport trucks, so SunRise won't overpay."

"Still, after the news breaks that someone stole a truck, the new Transport Coordinator might remember your questions. It could implicate you."

"I don't think so. At the first hint that something is wrong, the new Transport Coordinator and your successor will run for the hills. They will recognize a police investigation is coming."

"I hope you're right. Mrs. Young and I want to go back to Canada before the Amsterdam customs office or the police begin their investigation. It's better to face justice in our own country. I'll ask our friend in Paris to discuss the panels with her boss in the coming week before we steal the truck, so she'll be on record as a whistleblower."

"Okay," said Herman. "I am glad you came to see me. We cleared the air between us and organized a scheme to stop the trade in counterfeit goods—*all* goods, not only the defective panels. And I have a chance to free myself from the SunRise network. Good luck to you, Frank. Take care of yourself. I will miss your company and our outings to concerts. We'll see how the justice systems in the Netherlands and Canada treat us. It could mean we won't meet each other for a long time."

"I hope once we've got through the police investigation, and whatever follows, we're free to move around again, and you'll come to visit me in Toronto."

After a long hug, the men went their separate ways. Frank returned to Paris, where he met up with Linda and Claudia and explained the plan. Both women had to adjust to the idea but agreed for them there were few risks associated with stealing a truck and Mrs. Liu wouldn't suspect their involvement.

"I'm okay with this plan," said Claudia, "but only if Herman's men don't hurt the driver. I—and I'm sure you two also—won't approve a plan that involves murder."

"The driver will be uncomfortable for a day or two," Frank said, "but he'll survive."

They agreed Claudia should talk with her boss and make sure at least one other person was present as a witness—if possible, not the office manager.

Their shared involvement in the plot to unmask YYZ and SunRise as suppliers of counterfeit goods had resulted in strong bonds between Frank, Linda, and Claudia, and their goodbyes were emotional and teary. Linda was going back to Toronto the next day. Claudia promised to talk to her boss soon, and Frank had realized he shouldn't travel with all the money he had in his suitcase and deposited the money in banks in Paris and Luxembourg. He also had to go back to Amsterdam to close his bank account there. Then he was free to return to Toronto.

* * *

Ten days after Frank and Herman had met and hatched their plot, Herman's men staked out the Amsterdam customs compound. They knew they would recognize the truck driver who was to take away the YYZ container.

"You'll have no problem finding him," Herman had told them. "His name is Piotr. He is an exception among truck drivers because he is the skinniest person I've ever met. You'll find him in the cafe next to the customs compound, where he waits for a phone call from the new Transport Coordinator to pick up the container."

Herman had been right. After a day of checking on the cafe patrons, they recognized the truck driver they were looking for and confirmed his name by talking to other truckers. The men waited outside the cafe, followed the driver towards his truck, and noted the number on the plate.

"The lead man said, "No problem following him."

After a while, the second man asked, "Where's he going?"

"East, towards the German border. Guess we're heading for Berlin. Why don't you check your phone for a suitable rest area to relieve the driver from his truck?"

After a few minutes, the second man pointed to a spot on his Google map. "Here is good, past the forested part of the highway, where most people will stop for a rest. But can't we do it at a gas station? At least we can stock up on coffee and sandwiches before starting our trip back home."

The lead man looked at his partner and rolled his eyes. "A service station is the *worst* place to hijack a truck. Too many people and security cameras. I imagine there may be truck drivers who recognize Piotr's truck and wonder why he isn't moving. They'll come over to check up on him. We do not want that. We want the police to check-up on him."

"Okay, so how do we lure the driver off the highway, and what are we going to do with him?"

"Here's the plan. We flag him down about a kilometre before the rest area, pointing at his rear wheels, so he thinks there's something wrong with his truck, like a flat tire. I bet you this has never happened to the driver, so he'll be curious and decide to pull into the rest area. If there are not too many other cars parked, we park our car right in front of the truck and point our guns at him in a way nobody else but the driver can see them, to prevent him from leaving the cab. We force him to sit in the back of the cab and strap his hands together, tape his mouth, and fasten him to a handrail or a bench. Herman wanted us to drive the truck back to Amsterdam and park it where the police will find it, but we should change that part of the plan. We should leave the truck in the rest area. It will be a day or two before the highway police get suspicious and investigate. This way, we will have more time to make our getaway than if we parked the truck in Amsterdam. If we did *that*, the police would start an investigation within hours."

"What will happen to the driver?"

"Nothing. The police will interrogate him, and he'll say nothing is missing. This will be a red flag. The police will understand whoever pulled this stunt left the truck for them to discover, and they'll open the container and start an investigation. From the paperwork, they'll know a company called YYZ exported the goods from Canada through Amsterdam. From there, the investigation will lead to SunRise and Mrs. Liu. Simple."

"What if the driver identifies us from pictures the police show him?"

"First, he'll be too scared to pay attention to our appearance, and second, the police won't have our pictures. We've never had a run-in with them."

"That's not true. I was with Herman in Antwerp when he got arrested. The police have my name and my fingerprints and my picture."

"No problem—Piotr doesn't have your name, and you'll wipe down the cab when we have restrained him. And believe me, he won't remember a thing. We never think about this, but being held up by guys with guns is traumatizing. You want to forget what happened, and you don't want to remember what the perpetrators looked like. Thus, if the police show the driver your picture—and there's no good reason for them to do that—we have nothing to worry about. We've done this once before, and the truck driver couldn't draw a picture that looked like us."

"Okay, this worked before, so why not this time? I'm not worried. But why do we abandon the truck? We can make a lot of money selling the merchandise. Shouldn't be too difficult to find a buyer."

"This isn't about making money. We want to attract the attention of the police so they start an investigation and SunRise and YYZ will be closed. We'll be free from Mrs. Liu and be able to pull a job whenever *we* want, not when *she* thinks we should."

Herman's men followed the truck and struck at the right moment. The plan unfolded without hiccups. They gagged Piotr and bound him to the seat in the back of the cab. Ten minutes after they had lured the driver into the rest area, Herman's men were driving away.

"That went well," said the lead man. "We were lucky there were only a few other cars parked at the other end of the rest stop, and I don't think they noticed what we did. Let's get out of here. We must drop the car off in Brussels, and tomorrow evening, we'll take the train, and by the time Dutch police open the container, we'll be home. We'll try to keep informed about SunRise. Oh, and I must email Herman. And did you wipe the cab?"

The second man didn't answer.

TWENTY-SEVEN

AFTER the theft of Mr. Ho's laptop, Leonard went back and forth on the danger Mr. Ho posed for YYZ. There were days when he paced his office thinking Mr. Ho might talk to Mrs. Liu, while on other days he took solace in the fact Mr. Ho showed no signs of distress and behaved as if nothing had happened. But the danger he would talk to Mrs. Liu about the stolen laptop was always in Leonard's mind.

The day the laptop had disappeared, Leonard had tried to calm Mr. Ho by talking to him in a comforting voice, but his thoughts remained far from reassuring. The most likely source from whom Mrs. Liu would learn about the laptop was Mr. Ho. What if he was one of these types who, when in danger, confessed, hoping for a less severe punishment to save himself, with no consideration for others? Mr. Young couldn't afford another misstep. If Mrs. Liu found out someone had stolen the laptop, she would blame *him* for not installing an alarm system and Mr. Ho for not taking the laptop home to keep it safe. The possibility all the trading data had fallen into the hands of a competitor would upset Mrs. Liu, and her punishment could be more than a further reduction in his payouts. Every time Leonard looked at the knife mark on his desk, it made him cringe and reminded him how scared he'd been when he'd met Mrs. Liu's enforcers. The question, "Do I have to leave YYZ?" kept him busy. He wasn't *certain* Mr. Ho would squeal, and after going over the facts and the risks and the possibilities, Leonard decided it wasn't time yet to close YYZ. But he should look for signs from SunRise whether he was falling out of favour.

The days after the break-in gave Leonard no reason to think something was wrong. Mr. Ho came in with his new laptop and worked in the warehouse making an accurate inventory of SunRise merchandise and supervising the shipments of four containers. Leonard relaxed. Everything appeared to be in order—shipment, clearance through customs, and transportation within Europe. He had underestimated Mr. Ho's resilience, and as days passed by, he felt better. *The shipments continue and more money arrives. Just as it should be.*

Leonard's confidence in the future of his collaboration with SunRise grew by the day. *Linda might have left, but I'm restoring YYZ. Because Mr. Ho is around, I don't have to spend any time on the SunRise business and I still get paid, and Ethan takes care of our legitimate clients. Soon, I'll be able to travel again, looking for new clients.*

Mrs. Liu, Z, and the Man with the Black-Rimmed Glasses found Leonard in his office in this great mood. Leonard's heart skipped a beat.

"Eh . . . Hello, Mrs. Liu . . . Nice to see you . . . What brings you here? Any problems I don't know?"

"No, nothing wrong," said Mrs. Liu. "I like to meet with my most important collaborators to make sure they are content and hear their suggestions on how to expand our mutual business. And I have something I want to discuss with you."

Leonard relaxed, but he remained worried. *No issues, good. No stolen laptop. But why is she here?*

"I'll be happy to discuss things with you," he said, "but do your enforcers have to be here? Can't they wait outside the office? To be honest, the sight of them makes me tense. That one," he pointed at the Man with the Black-Rimmed Glasses, "carries a knife."

"Mr. Young, don't be nervous. They won't do anything to you when I am here. They act only on my instructions. Just trust me."

"Okay, let them stay. Can I offer you a coffee or a glass of water?"

"No, let us get down to business. I am interested in the trading scheme you organized with the Transport Coordinator."

"We have discussed this already," Leonard interrupted. "I promised not to do it again, and you docked me twenty per cent of my fee. We settled that subject. I don't want to talk about it anymore."

"We won't. I trust you will not repeat your mistake. I'm here to get the details of this parallel scheme from you so we can organize something similar and expand our collaboration."

Mrs. Liu knows nothing about the stolen laptop. She wants to do more business with me. Great! "That sounds attractive," Leonard said. "What is it you want from me? My suppliers, the destinations? Anything you need!"

Mrs. Liu interrogated Leonard on the details of his parallel scheme and after thirty minutes, she said, "Mr. Young, I see opportunities here. You know we are a huge wholesaler, and we can find a manufacturer for whatever items our clients want. I'm sure we can do that better than you because we have access to the cheapest places to buy from. No need to involve other companies. You have shown you can handle the extra containers, so why don't we work on this together and broaden our client base in Europe? If you agree, you will find the new clients, and as a thank you, I will reduce your penalty to ten per cent. What do you think?"

"Of course," Leonard said. "I'll start with finding new clients in Poland, Hungary, Romania, and maybe later will look at opportunities in the Balkan countries. I'll tell you what they need. This could bring in a lot more money. I'll leave in a few days."

"Good. I am happy we agree. Please, send the first list in a week to ten days."

Leonard was in heaven. *This parallel trading scheme turns out to be good for me.*

"One more thing," Mrs. Liu said. "I want to speak with Mr. Ho. To remind him he works for me. Do you mind telling him to come to your office?"

"Sure, one moment."

Leonard felt unease creeping up on him. *Why Mr. Ho?* He was close to stepping out of his office when Mrs. Liu turned around and said. "Oh, and please tell him to bring his computer. I want to see how he organizes the data."

Leonard's legs trembled and his hands shook and with a weak voice, he said, "Will do."

He met Ethan in the corridor.

"Can you ask Mr. Ho to join us in my office and bring his computer?"

"That'll be difficult," said Ethan. "A few minutes after your guests arrived, Mr. Ho left with his laptop. He said he felt sick."

Leonard felt instant relief. *This could work out well for me. Now the disappearance of the laptop becomes an inside job, and I'm not responsible. It's my lucky day.*

"Your woman visitor had a brief talk with Mr. Ho before she entered your office," volunteered Ethan. "I don't know what they talked about, but the conversation disturbed Mr. Ho a lot. He left a few minutes later. I asked if he was going home, but he said it was better if he didn't tell me where he was going."

* * *

Mrs. Liu paced Mr. Young's office, her face distorted with anger after she'd heard Mr. Ho had left. "How can he do such a thing? We must find him and his computer. All our transactions are on there."

She turned to Z. "Find the laptop. Mr. Ho might have gone home if he is sick, but I don't believe he is. He would have let us know. One of you stakes out the train station, and the other the airport. Grab him and take the laptop. You can decide what you want to do with Mr. Ho, but don't go easy on him."

Z nodded and wanted to say something, but Mrs. Liu interrupted. "*Now.* Get going. *Now.*" Z and the Man with the Black-Rimmed Glasses jumped from their chairs and rushed out of the office.

"This is unfortunate," said Leonard, "but I guess we'll still go ahead with our new collaboration?"

"Of course. Get me that list as soon as you can."

"Can you send me a new office manager? Soon, please. We need to keep *our* transactions separate from my Canadian business. Do you have a candidate?"

"Not yet. I must search for a reliable person. Should we hire Frank as Mr. Ho's replacement? He did a good job for us as an agent. I'm sure he can do whatever needs to be done here. Or I can send you the current agent to replace Mr. Ho and ask Frank to resume his job. Do you still have his email address?"

Mrs. Liu looked at her watch. "It is time for me to go to the airport. Can you call me a cab?"

"My pleasure—anything to make you happy." A weight had fallen off his shoulders. Mrs. Liu wouldn't suspect him. The stolen laptop was all on Mr. Ho.

The next day, a phone call from Mr. Ho shattered his confidence in the future of the SunRise-YYZ scheme.

"Mr. Young, this is Mr. Ho."

"Good of you to call. You did the right thing yesterday. But why are you calling me?"

"Something happened you must know about," he answered in a panicky voice. "A truck with a container didn't arrive. The truck driver picked up the container from the Amsterdam customs compound, as usual, but he never made it to Berlin. He is more than a day overdue. Someone might have stolen the truck."

"How do you know this? Nobody told *me*."

"The Berlin contacts complained to the new Transport Coordinator, who is a friend of mine, and he emailed me with this news. I don't know who stole the truck or where the truck is. The situation might be as simple as the driver diverting to a different destination and selling the contents of the container. If that is the case, Mrs. Liu will find out, and she will send her enforcers to settle the score. Or one of our competitors stole the truck to disrupt our operation, or someone who is part of the SunRise network stole it to harm Mrs. Liu. The best way to do that, from their point of view, might be to make the police aware of the truck.

Everybody will be in danger if the police open the container. The paperwork in the truck leads straight to you and YYZ. That is the reason I am phoning. You treated me well when the laptop disappeared, and this is my payback."

"Thank you," said Leonard. "That *is* bad news. Thanks for calling. I hope you're in a safe place. I won't ask you where you are, but Z and the other man are trying to find you. Mrs. Liu was livid yesterday after she learned you had left and taken the computer with you."

"I'll be careful, and you should too. A police investigation could lead to criminal charges and prison time."

Leonard's mind was in turmoil. If stealing the truck was an attempt to attract the attention of the police to the counterfeit goods YYZ imported, he agreed with Mr. Ho—that would be the end of YYZ. The Toronto police would come and look at the relationship between YYZ and SunRise and arrest him for trading counterfeit goods. *I can't take that risk. I must leave. But what if it's a simple case of highway robbery? Then there's no reason to leave YYZ. What should I do? Is this the end of YYZ? Do I have to go to the Caribbean?*

Leonard phoned his contacts in Amsterdam. First, the new Transport Coordinator told him he was on the verge of leaving because the police had found the truck at a highway rest stop on the route to Berlin and had already talked to the agent, whose address they had gotten from the customs office. It was easy to predict what would happen next: a full-blown investigation of YYZ and SunRise. "Better disappear now, while you still can," said the new Transport Coordinator, "I'm on my way out." Leonard dialled the agent, but nobody answered. *He's thrown his phone away and disappeared. Time for me to do the same.*

TWENTY-EIGHT

THE first few weeks after his return from Paris were a time of reckoning for Frank. He had returned to Toronto without concrete plans, and the first thing he'd done was rent an apartment. Turned off by the high rents for downtown Toronto condos, he took a modest two-bedroom apartment in a North Toronto three-storey walk-up. Although he missed his downtown Amsterdam apartment, he was comfortable and mapped out a strategy to find a job. But at random times, he often thought about the decision he, Linda, and Claudia had taken, and how he and Herman had come up with a way to dismantle YYZ and SunRise. He was proud he had involved Herman, and he accepted that after the collapse of SunRise and YYZ, he would talk to the police and answer for his involvement in trading counterfeit goods. Frank tried not to speculate about what that would mean. Some days, however, he wondered whether he could have said no to Claudia and Linda. Couldn't he have told them those panels weren't his business? His job was to clear containers through customs. The responsibility for shipping counterfeit goods lay with Mr. Young and Linda, with Mrs. Liu for selling them, and with her clients for buying the cheap goods to save money. But he always came to the same conclusion. If he didn't talk to the police and set the record straight, the last seven months of his life would be with him for years, maybe for life. But despite his commitment, or possibly because of it, Frank often tried to minimize his contributions to the illegal trading network. He examined his role in selling counterfeit goods, and he realized that in the beginning, the argument that he occupied only a minor position in a complicated scheme was enough for him. But, as time passed, the argument that he only cleared the goods, a job anybody was capable of doing, was no longer compelling, and he'd admitted he was a criminal. But then, he argued with himself, he had agreed to stop the sale of the faulty panels. What criminal would do a thing like that? He doubted if Z, the Man with the Black-Rimmed Glasses, or the Transport Coordinator ever thought of doing anything about the counterfeit goods. Frank felt he was not like those men. Yes, he was a criminal, and for a long time, he hadn't wanted to give up his job, but he argued with himself being involved in the collapse of SunRise and YYZ was a partial redemption for what he'd done, no matter what Claudia had told him. *I'm a minor criminal—not one hundred per cent innocent, but, compared with other players in the scheme, not very guilty either.*

With these contradictory thoughts swirling around in his mind, Frank looked for distractions. He attended a Toronto Symphony Orchestra concert but couldn't concentrate on the music, and he missed Herman. He tried to find solace at the Art Gallery of Ontario but wandered around and didn't connect with any of the works on display. *When will this pass? When will life go back to normal? I hope the truck theft worked as planned.*

Frank's first sign something had happened in Amsterdam occurred when he walked by the YYZ office and saw no lights. At the end of the afternoon, this could mean the office was closed for the day, but another possibility was that YYZ was out of business. To find out, he returned the following day, midafternoon, entered the lobby, and pressed the buzzer next to the brass plaque with the YYZ name on it. No answer. He visited the print shop on the ground floor and asked the receptionist whether she was aware what had happened with YYZ.

"They might be closed—I have seen no one go upstairs for a week."

Fantastic, stealing the truck and making sure the Dutch police found the container worked. They had identified YYZ as the importer and had inspected the goods in the container on the truck and in the ones that remained, unclaimed, in the customs compound. They must have found out the contents were counterfeit and, through Mr. Tolman, identified me and his successor as agents for YYZ. No doubt the Amsterdam police were looking for him. It made sense to Frank the Toronto police would have gotten involved and talked with Mr. Young, which meant it wouldn't be long until they came to see *him*.

Frank learned more about what had happened at the YYZ office when he visited the Silver Beaver. He recognized Ethan. "Hey, did you find a new job?" he asked. "The last time we met, a long time ago, you weren't happy. I remember I told you I would try to find you a job at YYZ after I got back from Amsterdam, but I can't do that. YYZ will shut down soon if it hasn't already."

"I know," said Ethan. "Mr. Young made me his office manager, but he closed YYZ, and the data entry clerk and I lost our jobs. Let me tell you what happened."

They found a quiet corner and drank their beers.

"Listen," Ethan said. "Just over a week ago, the data entry clerk and I were having lunch when Mr. Young joined. He looked serious, and he told us, without introduction, 'YYZ is being dissolved. This is your last day at work.' We must have looked confused because he added, 'Don't come in tomorrow' and said he'd arranged for deposits of two months of wages to tide us over until we found new jobs. We protested. I told Mr. Young there were rules and legalities to follow when you dismantle a company. But he shrugged and said, 'I founded YYZ and now I am getting rid of it. Nobody's going to tell *me* what to do.'"

Frank was not able to hide his excitement. YYZ was no more, and he was sure that SunRise would follow. *I should find Herman and tell him his plan worked out as hoped.*

Ethan had more to say. "The data entry clerk and I were in a bad mood. We both felt shitty. I'd given up another job to join YYZ, and all of a sudden, I was out of work. The data entry clerk was close to tears. He took a few things from his desk and left without saying anything. I'm sure his agency will find him a new position. He was good at what he did."

"I can imagine being fired was hard on you two—so unexpected. What about Mr. Ho?"

Ethan told Frank about the visitors, a Chinese woman and two burly men, who could well be her bodyguards, and how Mr. Ho left with his laptop under his arm. "He looked terrified."

"I'll get more beer," said Frank. When he returned, Ethan continued.

"A few hours after Mr. Young fired us, I was busy cleaning up my office when two police detectives arrived, looking for Mr. Young. I told them he wasn't in, and I didn't know where he was. But I mentioned that, two hours earlier, Mr. Young had left the office carrying a small suitcase as if he was planning a trip. They asked me whether I was familiar with a Chinese company called SunRise Technologies and about shipments of counterfeit goods to Amsterdam. I told them I knew nothing about that, but we recorded all our transactions on the office computer *except* for the transactions involving SunRise. They were on a separate laptop, but somebody had stolen that laptop. The detectives asked if Mr. Young had reported the theft to the police and I said I didn't think so."

Frank's excitement grew. *Our plan worked!* Finding the truck with the container had sparked an active investigation.

"The detectives made a phone call," Ethan said, "and an hour later, they told me they got a warrant to search the office and take the computer. 'Sure,' I said, 'go ahead,' and I gave them the password. After a while, they thanked me for my cooperation and told me that for now, they didn't need me, but I shouldn't leave the city for the next two weeks. They got the data entry clerk's phone number from the personnel files and left with the computer."

"What happened to the guys in the warehouse?" asked Frank.

Ethan shrugged. "I phoned to tell them Mr. Young had shut YYZ down and they didn't have to show up for work anymore."

"The detectives will want to talk to me," Frank said, "but I know nothing about what merchandise YYZ shipped other than what Mrs. Young or Mr. Ho wrote on the bills of lading. Still, if they ask for me, you can give them my address. Here, I'll write it on this napkin. I hope you find a job soon because I feel responsible for your awful experience at YYZ. Believe me, when we talked that day before I left for Amsterdam, I didn't know YYZ was going to close."

"I'm sure you didn't. Don't be sorry. Buy me another beer and I'll forget about your promise to try to find me a job."

Frank and Ethan stayed for two more hours in the pub, drinking beer and having dinner.

"You know," said Ethan, "I've had enough of sending out my resume and not getting any response. People don't have the decency to acknowledge they received it or to send a simple email to let me know their decision. Don't they realize what it means to me to have a job?"

"I guess you have a lot of competition, so employers have no reason to be civil. They figure if you haven't heard from them for a couple of weeks, you'll understand they don't want you."

"You're right, but a sign they appreciate your interest in their company wouldn't kill them. I should start my own company, so I don't have to go around begging for a job anymore."

"Interesting idea," said Frank. "I've thought about that too."

Going home, Frank's excitement changed into relief. The truck theft had done its job. The SunRise-YYZ trading scheme was dead and the dismantling of the companies had begun. His fate would be determined by a prosecutor, and a judge, not by Mrs. Liu.

TWENTY-NINE

MRS. Liu received a phone call from the new Transport Coordinator, who, without wasting time on niceties, told her the truck and the container destined for Berlin were missing. The news silenced Mrs. Liu for a few seconds. This was something that had never occurred for as long as SunRise existed.

"How did that happen?" she asked.

"I do not know, but I thought I should inform you."

"Yes, you did well. Did you mention this to anyone else?"

"I told the agent."

"Isn't the truck equipped with a GPS?"

"Yes, and according to the company in Berlin that owns the truck, it stopped working almost two hours east of Amsterdam at a highway rest stop on the way to the German border."

"Why don't you go there? The truck might still be there. What if the driver suffered a medical emergency, a heart attack, or a stroke?"

"Could be, but that wouldn't explain why the GPS stopped working. Someone must have switched it off on purpose."

"We don't know that. Go anyway, and phone me the moment you find out more."

Mrs. Liu hung up and twirled her cellphone around. She needed more information. She phoned her agent, but despite several attempts, wasn't able to reach him. The new Transport Coordinator also didn't respond to multiple calls. This put Mrs. Liu in a foul mood. Her SunRise agent and the new Transport Coordinator in Amsterdam had disappeared. She realized that unless she could replace the two men, the containers that were on their way to Amsterdam would stay in the customs compound, unclaimed, which would lead to many unhappy customers. She would lose a lot of money. That was bad enough, but what got to her most was that two loyal SunRise employees had gone into hiding without telling her. She was still smarting from Mr. Ho's defection. What had made Mr. Ho decide to flee she could only guess, but it must be something serious. She wanted to find out, but she couldn't. Her useless enforcers were still looking for him.

Different ways a truck could disappear went through Mrs. Liu's mind. Hijacking and robbery were easy to deal with. She would find out who was responsible, and she would set things straight. Another possibility came to mind. Someone—a competitor or a member of the SunRise network—might have stolen the truck to attract the attention of law enforcement. Mrs. Liu realized her agent and the Transport Coordinator must have had similar thoughts, and that was why they'd gone into hiding. She wasn't angry at them for leaving their jobs. She understood they didn't want to be around when the police came calling. But they should have told her. Had she not always taken their interests to heart? Did she not overpay them for the simple jobs she had given them? Was there no more gratitude in this world?

Mrs. Liu stood at her thirty-second-floor office window and stared at the crowded street. Then her body stiffened, her eyes narrowed, and she breathed heavily. Mrs. Liu didn't register the comings and goings of the many pedestrians, cars, and buses. She thought of only one thing: police scrutiny must be the motive of whoever had made the truck and the container disappear. Someone wanted to break up YYZ and SunRise. Someone was challenging her, and she made a list of suspects. Frank was number one on the list; he might still stew over having lost his job. Mrs. Young was a suspect too. Mrs. Liu had not liked their last phone conversation. Too much independent thought. And then there were the Transport Coordinators, the new and the old one, her agent and Herman.

The first thing to do was to find Frank. He might be in Europe, but more likely he had returned to Toronto. She would send Z and the Man with the Black-Rimmed Glasses to Toronto. But this time, she would go with them. Mrs. Liu emailed Frank: "I want to meet with you to discuss an important subject. Are you in Toronto? If so, I will be there tomorrow evening, and we can talk."

If the police found the truck, their first focus would be on YYZ, giving her at least one or two days to deal with Frank. After that, she would have to be in Shanghai, answering questions from Chinese authorities. She knew the routine. The police would threaten arrest and prison time, but a few phone calls from her lawyer to the Chinese Ministry of the Interior would make them drop the case and apologize. Mrs. Liu saw no reason to worry.

* * *

Frank read the message with interest. Something important? *I should meet Mrs. Liu to find out.* He wrote back they should meet in the Silver Beaver.

The next evening, he sat in a booth in the Silver Beaver, but Mrs. Liu did not show. He waited until ten o'clock and was ready to go home when he received another email from Mrs. Liu, apologizing she hadn't made it in time. There had been a problem with the plane, and they'd made an unscheduled stop in Seoul. Was it possible to meet tomorrow evening, same place?

Frank wrote back, "No problem." He left the pub and got into the Uber he had ordered to go home. He didn't notice Z and the Man with the Black-Rimmed Glasses, who followed in a rental car.

Frank was expecting the Toronto police to track him down soon. So, the next morning, when there was knocking on his door, he expected to see police detectives. To his surprise, he faced Z and the Man with the Black-Rimmed Glasses.

"Hi, Frank, how are you?" said Z in the same friendly voice he had used during their lunch in Brussels. "Nice to see you again. Can we come in?"

"No," said Frank. "After what you did in Brussels, I want nothing to do with you two, so leave. I don't work for SunRise or YYZ anymore. I won't listen to what you have to say."

"Frank, is everything okay here?" A neighbour had appeared at the top of the staircase and looked at Frank and then at the two burly men, one of whom had a foot in the door.

"Shall I call the police. They can be here in a few minutes."

"No need," said Z and stepped back into the corridor. "We are here for a friendly visit, but Frank doesn't have time right now, so we are leaving."

After they had gone, Frank told the neighbour, "Thanks for helping me to get rid of those two. I've met them once before and didn't want them in my apartment."

"Well, that's why you have neighbours. Can't be too careful in these crazy times."

The visit from Mrs. Liu's enforcers had shaken Frank. What did Z and the Man with the Black-Rimmed Glasses want from him? Why were they here? Had Mrs. Liu's email been a way to find out where he lived? Should he go to the Silver Beaver this evening? Was she aware of his involvement in the plot to steal the truck? Had she sent her enforcers to punish him? He had to be careful. For all he knew, they were waiting for him outside the apartment building.

* * *

Z and the Man with the Black-Rimmed Glasses were plotting their next move. Mrs. Liu had ordered them to find Frank and to find out if he had contributed to the demise of YYZ.

"Ask Frank, and if he says no, and you think he tells the truth, *do* leave him alone, but if you doubt his answers, eliminate him." She had added, "Don't mess this up, like you did when you tried to silence the Transport

Coordinator. How the two of you weren't able to subdue a single man, I still can't understand. So what if his friends came to check on him? You got away, but you should have waited for the Transport Coordinator to leave the house, and have trailed and killed him. Do I need to hire more men to help you? And you didn't find Mr. Ho. I'll give you one more chance to prove yourselves. Find Frank, ask about YYZ, decide if you must kill him, and report back."

Mrs. Liu's enforcers understood they could not afford another mistake. They had to get to Frank. To minimize the risk of displeasing Mrs. Liu yet again, they would kill him, no matter what he said. They waited outside the apartment building, planning to intercept Frank in the driveway, hustle him into the car, and drive to a quiet spot. Much later, near the end of the afternoon, a car pulled up and someone stepped out of the building. "Hey," said Z, "it's Frank." But before Z was out of their car, Frank had entered the Uber he had ordered. "Clever guy," said Z, and the Man with the Black-Rimmed Glasses grunted his agreement. "Let's follow him and see where he's going."

They saw Frank enter the Silver Beaver and waited. Another car pulled up right in front of them, and to their surprise and discomfort, Mrs. Liu emerged. She looked around, recognized her enforcers, and made her way to their car. Z got out and opened the rear door for her.

"Mrs. Liu! Why are you here? We are following Frank, who is in the pub right now. We are waiting for a suitable moment to talk to him."

"Don't take too long. Are you going to speak with him inside the pub?"

"No, too many people. We need a quiet spot. Like the driveway in front of his apartment building."

Z's plan did not impress Mrs. Liu. He is *there.* Ask your question. At least you will find out whether you must kill him. What if he looks truthful to you? Then you have finished your job here and you can look for Mrs. Young. I have other things for you to do." And Mrs. Liu outlined her plans to find Mrs. Young, the old Transport Coordinator, and Herman.

* * *

Frank had settled into a booth. He was sure Mrs. Liu would not come. After a while, he spotted Ethan and waved at him.

"Hey, Ethan! Glad you're here. Can I buy you a beer?"

"Of course! You can do that anytime, but is something wrong? You look a bit . . . shifty."

"What does that mean, 'shifty?' How does that look like?"

"It means you're looking around the pub and over your shoulder more than at your beer. It means you have a problem."

"Yes," Frank confessed, "I have a problem. I'm being followed by two men. Earlier today, they tried to muscle their way into my apartment, but a neighbour came by, and they left. I took an Uber here, and I'm sure they trailed me."

"Very melodramatic. You read too many crime novels. Any idea what they want from you? Is this related to your job in Amsterdam or the shutdown of YYZ?"

"I can't be sure. All I know is these men work for SunRise. I met them before, and they're violent."

"What do you plan to do? Shall I call the police?"

"No. So far, they've done nothing wrong. The police won't arrest them."

"It might scare them."

"Believe me, scaring them isn't easy. Let me think. Let's order another beer. That might help us decide what we should do next."

Ethan noticed Frank had used the word *we*. "You mean what *you* should do next," he said. "I want nothing to do with this, other than discussing it—no action on my part."

Another beer later, Frank said, "Listen. Because they aren't going away without finishing their job, whatever that is, but involves me, confronting them might be a good idea—in a public space, to lower the risks. At least I'll have some control over what happens. Better than being jumped by them somewhere isolated."

"Sounds risky, but it's your choice. *I* would contact the police."

"I'd rather keep the police out of this. For my plan to work, though, I need your help. Nothing dangerous. Just go outside and tell them to meet me here."

"How do I recognize them?"

"Chances are they're sitting in a car parked not far away. You'll have no problem recognizing them. Two burly men, one of them wearing black-rimmed glasses. I think you've already met them. They're the ones who were with Mrs. Liu on her visit to Mr. Young. The visit when Mr. Ho left."

"Oh," said Ethan. "I *will* recognize those guys. After I tell them to come to the pub, what do I do?"

"Don't engage in conversation. Walk away. Go home. Or come back here and sit at the bar. I'll be in this booth."

Ethan decided he could do this. It didn't sound dangerous, and a little excitement would do him good. "Okay," he said. "When?"

"Right now."

Ethan stood up, wished Frank good luck, and left the pub. Frank waited, second-guessing his decision to confront Z and the Man with the Black-Rimmed Glasses. What if they carried weapons? The Man with the Black-Rimmed Glasses had a knife. Z might carry one too, or worse, he might have a gun. Frank needed something to defend himself. He ordered a coffee, "extra strong," asked for pepper, and stirred five small paper bags of it into his coffee. The server looked at Frank and declared, "Nobody ever puts pepper in his coffee."

"This is for special occasions. You should try it. It gives a kick to the coffee."

The booths in the Silver Beaver were perpendicular against one wall. Frank sat at the corner of one booth facing the entrance. *Easier to run away.*

Ten minutes later, Z and the Man with the Black-Rimmed Glasses entered. They looked around, recognized Frank, and headed his way.

"Move over," said Z. "I want to sit there. You can sit next to me, by the wall."

"I'm sitting here," Frank said. "You two can sit across from me, and then we can talk."

Z didn't appreciate Frank's commanding voice. *He's changed a lot since Brussels.* Not willing to attract attention the men complied. The Man with the Black-Rimmed Glasses took the seat against the wall, and Z sat across from Frank.

"Why are you bothering me?" Frank asked. "I stopped working as an agent in Amsterdam. I have no more business with you."

"We are not bothering you," said Z. "We want to ask you a question."

"Make it quick. The less I see you two, the better."

"We were told by Mrs. Liu what to ask, and she wants you to tell the truth."

"Why should I answer a question from Mrs. Liu? I don't work for her anymore. You two are barking up the wrong tree. You should know by now that the SunRise-YYZ trading scheme is dead. I found out because the YYZ office is closed. If you're interested in what happened, don't ask me. Ask Mrs. Liu . . . if the police haven't yet arrested her."

Frank's rant did not impress Z. "You are inventing this. Nobody told me YYZ closed, and even if it did, Mrs. Liu never gets arrested. She will deal with the Chinese authorities as usual. Nothing will happen to her. But she wants to know who made a truck which transported a YYZ container disappear. She suspects you. Was it you?"

Frank hesitated. He would, of course, deny he had anything to do with the truck incident, but what if Z doubted his answer? He picked up his cup of pepper-spiked coffee and said, "It wasn't me."

"I don't believe you. You have a motive. Being fired from your dream job still bugs you. You wanted to take revenge and make trouble for SunRise." Z looked at Frank and wanted to say more, but Frank, recognizing the threat, threw the peppered coffee into Z's face, and completing a sweeping motion, hit the Man with the Black-Rimmed Glasses hard on the side of his head with the cup. This disabled both men. Z groaned while struggling to rub the coffee and the pepper out of his eyes, and the Man with the Black-Rimmed Glasses fell sideways, banging the other side of his head against the wall. He groped around to find his glasses, but Frank had snatched them up and put them in his pocket.

Frank stood up and told Z, "You leave me alone. If I ever notice you lurking around again, I'll hire professional killers and we will chase you until you are both dead. Don't worry about your eyesight. In an hour or two, your vision will improve. I suggest you leave, go to wherever you are staying, take it easy for a few days, and then tell Mrs. Liu you couldn't find me."

The Man with the Black-Rimmed Glasses had recovered enough to take out his knife, and he squinted in Frank's direction. He wanted to follow Frank, but Z, with his head buried in his hands, blocked the way. Frank left the pub and was looking for a taxi when he heard a familiar voice call out to him. He looked around and saw Mrs. Liu standing on the sidewalk.

THIRTY

"FRANK, please come and join me in my car. I have little time. We need to talk."

Frank's first reaction was to ignore her, but he couldn't. He remembered the pleasant evening he had spent with her in Shanghai. He approached Mrs. Liu, who looked at him and smiled. "Please get in," she said again. "We can talk in the car."

"I'll drive," said Frank. "I disabled your enforcers. Z is out of business for a few hours, and I took his partner's glasses, but he might see well enough to come out and look for me. I don't want to meet him again."

"Good. Let's go." Mrs. Liu opened the rear door of the car.

"No, not there. I'm not your driver. Sit in the front. Easier to talk."

Frank drove away and after a few blocks, Mrs. Liu asked, "Can you drive me to the airport? I must catch a plane. I must be back in Shanghai as soon as possible."

Frank was reluctant. *Am I now her Uber driver?* But meeting Mrs. Liu had made him eager to find out what she wanted to discuss, so he agreed. "What is it you want to discuss?"

"I am disappointed in you, Frank. When we met in Shanghai, you were a nice, quiet, obedient young man who told me you don't dig into your boss's business. But now you have done something much worse. You worked *against* your boss and me. Thanks to you, YYZ has closed and I am losing money on the containers we shipped. We cannot clear them through customs. You caused a lot of trouble."

Frank stiffened. "Why are you saying this? What do you think I did? Even if I *wanted* to harm you, I wouldn't know how."

"I don't believe you. A few days ago, a truck transporting a YYZ container went missing. You knew about these containers and how we organized their transport, and I'm sure you played a part in the truck's hijacking, to attract the attention of the police."

"What a ridiculous idea. Do I look to you like someone who steals trucks? I have nothing to do with any truck disappearing." Frank relaxed. *She knows about the truck but is trying to find the people involved. She's fishing.*

"It's my turn," he said, "to tell you I am disappointed in you. Yes, we had a pleasant evening in Shanghai, and you pretended to be friendly and caring. You offered to organize a city tour for me if I ever came back. Then not much later, I learned you had the Antwerp agent killed, or, as the Transport Coordinator put it, you made her disappear. And your enforcers in Brussels were violent towards me. If that isn't disappointing, then what is?"

"What are you saying? Do you accuse me of ordering a murder?"

"Yes, I am, unless you don't control your enforcers. But I have no evidence that holds up in court, so you'll get away with it—for now, until Z and the Man with the Black-Rimmed Glasses talk to the police."

Frank continued. "The other reason I'm disappointed in you is that you lured me into an illegal trading scheme. You, Mr. Young, and Linda took advantage of me. I had organized a quiet life for myself, and Linda pulled me out of that with her invitation to come to Shanghai. I accept I had a choice whether to go or to stay in Toronto, but you told Mr. Young to offer me the position as the agent. Nobody mentioned that the job involved counterfeit goods. You made me a criminal."

"No, Frank, that is not true. It wasn't only me, and if you want to assign blame, consider Mrs. Young. She told me you were a quiet, hard-working person who never complained about his workload and that you were the perfect candidate for the job. She took you to Shanghai so I could check you out, and I agreed with her. But remember, there was only one person who turned you into a criminal, and that was you. The only person who said 'yes' to the job was you. You didn't think twice.

You agreed right away. Mrs. Young told me the only questions you asked were, 'What are my duties?' and 'When can I start?' Don't tell me that if I or Mr. Young or Mrs. Young would have told you the goods you were supposed to clear through customs were counterfeit, you would have refused the offer to become our agent."

Frank didn't answer. He had never asked himself that question.

Mrs. Liu noticed the hesitation and answered for him. "You would have accepted the job, Frank. Search inside you and see what kind of person you were. You were weak. You didn't want to take part in life. Frank, you were proud of having organized a life of routines, and if it were up to you, your dream of travelling the world would never have become a reality. So, we dangled a promotion in front of you, together with some European travel and a, for us, trivial amount of money, and you danced like a circus bear."

For the rest of the trip to the airport, Frank and Mrs. Liu were silent. Frank didn't know what to say.

At the airport, Mrs. Liu said, "You can keep the car for a few days before bringing it back to the rental agency. I prepaid."

This infuriated Frank. He wasn't her driver, and he wasn't taking care of her rental car. "I am leaving it right here, in front of the terminal. I am not your servant."

"Why do you dislike me so much, Frank? Compare your life in Amsterdam with what passed for one in Toronto before you got the job. From the Transport Coordinator, I learned you were interested in touristy things. I imagine you visited museums, walked through the city, and visited Berlin and Paris. And who knows what else you did? You were happy to be in Amsterdam. Frank, you might not like it, but I played an important part in your transition. What are you doing with the money I gave you?"

By now, Frank could not speak. The reference to the fifty thousand dollars was painful. He often wrestled with the question of what to do with it, but so far, he was not planning to give it away.

"You can leave the car right here," Mrs. Liu said. "The rental agency will find it and send the bill to an address in Beijing that does not exist. I am glad I came to supervise my enforcers. I learned two things. One, I must replace them with more competent men, and two, you changed a lot. The Frank I met in Shanghai could not disable two such men. You changed, Frank, and I am glad you did. As a data entry clerk, you had no life; you were dying. I was sad when Mrs. Young told me about you. Now you must work out how to undo your time as a criminal, without blaming others, and build a happy life—not a boring one, mind you. And by the way, I don't think you were involved in the collapse of YYZ. You don't have—how do you say it in English—the *balls* for hijacking a truck. I will call off my men."

Frank watched Mrs. Liu until she entered the Departures Hall. She had given him a lot to think about. *They played on my weakness, and I became a criminal.* The question that kept him busy was, why had he not quit? Was it the good life he enjoyed in Amsterdam? Did he possess a criminal streak? Was it because he didn't want to go back to his old life in Toronto? Or was he afraid of Mrs. Liu? How long would he have continued being the agent if Mrs. Liu hadn't fired him? Frank's mind went into overdrive. He left the car with the keys on the driver's seat and returned to the city by train.

Attacking Z and the Man with the Black-Rimmed Glasses had not been his intention. But now that he had, Frank was proud and confident. Payback, he thought, for what they did to him in Brussels. He felt a few inches taller. Mrs. Liu was right: he had changed. When he'd asked Ethan to let the men know he, Frank, could meet them in the pub, he wanted to convince them to quit working for Mrs. Liu because the Shanghai police were going to arrest her, and she was facing prison time. He'd wanted to tell the enforcers it would be no problem for them to find other jobs, and he'd hoped to finish their meeting with a mutual understanding. But Z didn't give him any choice. Frank smiled. To add pepper to the coffee was a brilliant idea. *It sure added a punch.* He found the black-rimmed glasses in his pocket and turned them over in his hands for a while, then threw them on the floor and cherished the cracking sound when he stomped on them and ground them into small pieces. Every time he put his foot down, he pronounced the name of someone—Z, the Man with the Black-Rimmed Glasses, the Transport Coordinator, and Mrs. Liu. *I'm done with you guys. I'm going to fix my life and do something useful.* Only a few minutes later, he realized he had not included Linda and Mr. Young in his exorcism. Why not? Linda had been the one who'd invited him to Shanghai and presented him as a perfect candidate to Mrs. Liu, and Mr. Young had handled the YYZ end of the collaboration with SunRise. Both knew they were offering him an illegal job. But they weren't like the SunRise people. Not violent like them. He couldn't include them in the group of despicable people from whom he had freed himself. *I still like Linda, and even Mr. Young, but they won't fit in my new life. Anything YYZ or SunRise is taboo.* With, of course, the exception of Herman. *I must find out what happened to him.*

THIRTY-ONE

THAT evening, there was a knock on Frank's door. "Police. We'd like you to come with us. We want to ask you a few questions." Frank opened the door.

"Are you Frank Cordelero?"

"Yes, I am."

"I am Detective DeWitt, and this is my colleague, Detective Peters. Please come with us to the station."

Frank wondered whether the questions would be about YYZ or the incident in the Silver Beaver. *It's going to be a long night.* The arrival of the police relieved him. All the tension about what would happen to him fell away. After Frank and the two detectives sat down in an interrogation room at the police station, Detective DeWitt asked, "Do you want your lawyer present? You can phone her now."

Frank decided he didn't need her. He was sure he could handle whatever questions the detectives had.

"Tell us what happened in the Silver Beaver this evening," said Detective DeWitt. "The barkeeper told us that you assaulted two men. With your coffee cup," he added, and couldn't suppress a smile. "Is that true?"

"Yes, that's true."

"Why did you assault them? Did they threaten you? Have you seen them before in the pub or elsewhere?"

"They threatened me, and yes, I have seen them before, and they were violent then, so this time I didn't take any risks. To hit them with a coffee cup was an excellent strategy to make them go away. It worked."

"Have you seen them before in Toronto?"

"No, in Brussels, when I worked in Amsterdam for the YYZ Import/Export Company. I was their European agent for close to seven months. I cleared containers with the merchandise they exported to Europe, through Amsterdam customs."

"Did you quit, or were you fired?"

"Someone else replaced me. I'm not sure why; I did a good job clearing containers."

"Where did YYZ buy its supplies?"

"Various Chinese companies, like SunRise Technologies, based in Shanghai."

Frank realized he had brought SunRise into the discussion. And why not? *They* were the actual source of the counterfeit goods, including the faulty insulation panels.

Frank continued telling the detectives about his involvement with SunRise and YYZ, starting with meeting Mrs. Liu in Shanghai right up to his dismissal as the agent. He told them how Mrs. Young had confirmed his suspicions about the merchandise in the containers. He mentioned his run-in with Z and the Man with the Black-Rimmed Glasses in Brussels and added that they might have killed a SunRise agent in Antwerp. The detectives asked him for more details of the murder, but the only thing Frank could offer was what the Transport Coordinator had told him. He also mentioned that Mrs. Liu, through the Transport Coordinator, had asked him to find new clients for SunRise. "I had no choice but to accept. If I had refused, I would have lost my job." He didn't mention the money he had received from Mrs. Liu. *I'm not giving the money back; I need it to organize my new life.*

The detectives listened, made notes, and asked occasional questions. When Frank fell silent, Detective DeWitt said, "To summarize, you say that Mr. Young, with Mrs. Young present, offered you an attractive job that included working for Mrs. Liu, and you were not aware the work was illegal? You stated that later you became suspicious, and that Mrs.

Young confirmed your suspicions. When did you get that confirmation? Was this before or after they fired you?"

"Before."

"Does that mean that what Mrs. Young told you didn't worry you enough to quit? You continued your job."

DeWitt was ready to get into the details of Frank's behaviour, but Detective Peters changed the subject. "Our colleagues in Amsterdam told us that one item YYZ traded was subpar fire-retardant insulation panels. Do you know anything about these panels?"

"I remember seeing merchandise described as insulation panels. I can't tell if they were fire-retardant. That doesn't mean YYZ didn't ship fire-retardant panels because I cleared many shipments. To remember all the different goods in the containers is impossible."

"You mentioned several people who had links to the SunRise-YYZ trading scheme and told us two of them assaulted you. We'd like you to look at a few photographs and tell us if you can identify these men."

Peters put two large photographs in front of Frank.

"Are these the men who attacked you in Brussels?"

Frank answered, without hesitation, "Yes. These men manhandled me in Brussels, and the same men threatened me in the Silver Beaver this evening."

The interview lasted another hour. The detectives asked no more questions about what had happened in the Silver Beaver, but they were interested in Frank's knowledge of who was part of the SunRise-YYZ scheme. Frank talked in more detail about his trips to Brussels, Berlin, Barcelona, and Paris, but couldn't answer questions about the names and contact numbers of the people he had met. "My contacts were secretive and never introduced themselves." He mentioned the Transport Coordinator and the young Chinese man who had brought him the message that Mrs. Liu had fired him. Frank didn't mention Linda, Claudia, or Herman. The detectives listened and thanked him for the information.

"How about this man?" asked Detective Peters after he put a picture of Herman in front of Frank.

"Yes, I know this man." He told them he had met Herman on the train to Berlin, and in the museum in front of *The Night Watch*, and mentioned the concerts they had attended together. He didn't speak about Herman's role in the SunRise network or his involvement with stealing the truck. "This man is my friend."

"We suspect that a while ago he was head of the network when they distributed the SunRise merchandise in Europe through Antwerp. What we don't know is whether he is still active. There is a possibility that after Belgian customs caught SunRise importing counterfeit goods, SunRise ended his job. Now, according to what you told us, the murder of the Antwerp agent might involve him." Frank squirmed in his chair. "No, that's not what I said. The two men who threatened me in the Silver Beaver, not Herman, might have murdered the SunRise agent in Antwerp. In fact, I'm not sure if there was a murder. The Transport Coordinator used the word 'disappeared.' I only guessed he meant 'murdered.'"

"We'll contact our colleagues in Antwerp and find out what they know about a potential murder around the time customs caught SunRise. Antwerp police can check their records for any incidents that took place then. For now, tell us if you know who might have replaced Herman, as you call him, as head of the distribution network."

"I have an idea. I dealt with the Transport Coordinator, and he could have been running the distribution network. Never heard him mention anybody *else* involved in transporting the containers, so he might be what you call 'the head.' But he received his orders from Shanghai, from Mrs. Liu."

Frank didn't feel bad about implicating the Transport Coordinator. He didn't owe him anything, and he was a more likely candidate to be the head of distribution than Herman.

"I don't know the Transport Coordinator's name," he added. "He told me I could call him Ed, but that is not his real name."

The detectives showed Frank another picture. "Is this the man you call the Transport Coordinator?"

"Yes, that's him."

"Thank you for your cooperation," DeWitt said. "For now, you're free to go, but don't leave Toronto until we give you permission. If the two men you assaulted don't file a complaint we'll forget what happened in the Silver Beaver."

Frank took a taxi home. He wondered, had he said too much? Or had he said too little? Should he have revealed his involvement in the truck hijacking? If he had to stand trial, the prosecutor might have counted that as a positive. Should he have mentioned Linda, Claudia, and Herman? He had decided against it. If the information got back to Mrs. Liu, she would react with a vengeance, something the truck theft was designed to avoid.

Frank asked the taxi driver to let him out as close to the front door of his building as possible. "Sure. We're having a chilly night," the driver said, and he mounted the curb and stopped a couple of feet from the front door. Frank looked around for any signs of Z and the Man with the Black-Rimmed Glasses but saw nothing out of the ordinary. He handed the driver a generous tip and entered the apartment building as fast as he could.

* * *

Z and the Man with the Black-Rimmed Glasses did not file a complaint against Frank. The effect of the pepper-spiked coffee wore off after an hour, and Z helped his partner find an optician who was open late to get a new pair of glasses.

"When will the lenses be ready?" asked Z. "My friend and I fly out in three days. We need the glasses to be ready in two days."

"Sir, I'm an optician. I can't prescribe lenses. But if you're here tomorrow morning at ten, I'll make sure someone is here to help you with the lenses, and I'll make sure they'll be ready in two days. Would your friend prefer a light-coloured frame?" the optician asked. "It would not hide his face as much as the black frame he is trying on now."

"He'll take the black one," answered Z. "We will be here at ten tomorrow morning."

Z guided his partner back to their hotel. He couldn't walk by himself; for sure he would misstep and land on the sidewalk, or worse, on the road.

In the evening, accompanied by a lot of beer, the men discussed what to do next. They realized that their tenure with SunRise depended on them being able to find Mrs. Young. Their failures were piling up. They couldn't find the Transport Coordinator or Mr. Ho, despite their many Chinese contacts, and now Frank had beaten them, in the worst way they could imagine—with a coffee cup. They needed to talk to Mrs. Young or they would have to search for another job.

"Plus," Z said, "we must seek revenge for what Frank did. We can't let this slide. If the incident with the coffee cup ever gets known, it will shred our reputation. Somehow, we must get to him."

The Man without the Black-Rimmed Glasses answered, "He better not relax, because I am going to cut him. To steal someone's glasses is a low thing to do."

"Okay. Tomorrow, after we order your lenses, we'll stop by the YYZ office. Frank said it's closed, but I want to see this with my own eyes. If the office *is* open, we will press Mr. Young for Mrs. Young's whereabouts. If it's closed, we can gain entry and search for documents with Mrs. Young's email address on it, and set up a meeting. Like Mrs. Liu did to find Frank. Then we can meet with her. We have Franks' address. We'll visit him later when he does not expect us."

Z had just finished his sentence when a ping on his phone told him he had received an email. The message was from Mrs. Liu and was short and blunt. "I don't need your services any longer. I have promoted two other men who have worked for me for a long time to represent my interests."

Z stared at his phone for a minute. "She fired us!" he told his partner. "Mrs. Liu doesn't need us anymore. She has two new people to do our job."

"Good. Then we don't have to look for Mrs. Young. We can concentrate on Frank."

THIRTY-TWO

INSPECTOR Mertens of the Antwerp homicide department looked over a message that had arrived that morning from Toronto.

In an interview yesterday, a suspect stated that two men with whom he is familiar might have murdered the agent of a company called SunRise Technologies in Antwerp. The agent is female, but we have no description of her. The murder might have taken place around the time Antwerp customs found out that SunRise sold counterfeit goods and barred the company from exporting goods to Europe. Please let us know if you have any knowledge of this potential murder. We are looking for the suspects. They were in Toronto at the time of our interview.

Mertens remembered the SunRise case. It had been less than a year ago, and it had made headlines. People had written to the newspaper and called radio talk shows complaining about the counterfeit goods, which they saw as inferior. When was the government going to stop the import of fakes? But a murder related to the SunRise affair? No, that he didn't remember. He headed for the archives and searched for unsolved murders reported within a month before and after customs had caught SunRise. No luck. His next stop was the office of the clerk who gathered the complaints, remarks, tips, and observations the police received from the public. Someone might have phoned in something relevant.

Mertens watched the clerk search the computer. Nothing special in the first twenty entries. Noise complaints, someone complaining the police had not done enough to find his missing dog, a car theft, and multiple mentions of vandalism. Then an entry caught Mertens's eye. The owner of a used-clothing store had reported that a homeless man had brought in a small pink suitcase he had found on the sidewalk. *A pink suitcase may be worth investigating. I should visit the store*, Mertens thought. He went through the rest of the entries but found nothing interesting.

"Yes," said the store owner in response to Inspector Mertens's inquiry. "I remember the pink suitcase. I bought it from Harry for fifteen euros, and I sold it and its contents over the last few months to three or four customers."

"Who is Harry? Is he the homeless man who brought in the suitcase?"

"Yes. Harry is a staple of our neighbourhood. Most nights he sleeps under a staircase on Harbour Street. That's where he found the suitcase. He also said, when he came into the store, that there had been two men, big men, pushing a young woman into a car that had been idling for a while, right across from his usual sleeping spot. I suspected he was making up a story to hide the fact that he had stolen the suitcase."

"In your report to the police, you mentioned only the suitcase. Nothing about Harry or about a woman being kidnapped. Why not?"

"I didn't want Harry to get into any trouble."

"Strange reasoning. You think Harry might have *stolen* the suitcase, but then you tell me he never causes trouble. Did *you*, by any chance, find the suitcase, not Harry?"

"No, Harry came into my store with the suitcase. I only wanted to tell you it's *possible* he stole it."

"Next time you deal with the police, try to be clearer. And more complete. If you had mentioned Harry or the kidnapping, we could have started an investigation right then, instead of now, months later. You better remember to whom you sold the suitcase and the clothing. *That* could be very helpful."

The store owner did not enjoy being bossed around by Mertens, but decided he better keep the inspector happy. "Sure, I will. I'll write a list."

"Good. Where can I find Harry?"

"Walk around the neighbourhood. You'll recognize him. For a homeless person, he dresses well, because I supply him with clothes. He's thin as a rail and never wears a hat. I guess that's why he lost all his hair. Believe me, you'll never mix Harry up with a regular citizen."

"Thanks. I'll take a stroll."

It didn't take Mertens more than fifteen minutes to spot Harry, who was busy rummaging through the garbage cans people had set out for pickup.

"Hello, Harry."

But before Mertens had a chance to introduce himself, Harry said, "No time, very busy. Garbage day. Looking for bottles and beer cans."

"Yes, I see. But I want to talk about something you might have seen almost a year ago. The pink suitcase you found."

Harry hesitated, but then said, "No time, have to fill up this bag." He held up a garbage bag half full with cans and bottles. "Worth a lot of money."

"How much do you get for a full bag?"

A sly smile spread over Harry's face. "Five euros."

Mertens knew that was too much, but he was willing to give Harry his five euros. He wanted him in a good mood.

"Listen. I'm from the police department, and I need to talk to you. You don't have to be afraid—you're not in trouble. I'll give you five euros if you agree to talk to me. What do you think?"

Harry considered the proposal. He didn't enjoy talking to policemen, but the five euros were attractive. Plus, he could still cash in his half bag of beer cans and bottles.

"Sure, we can talk. We can sit across the road in the park."

Mertens said, "Tell me everything about how you found the pink suitcase? How many people were present?"

"I didn't steal the suitcase. Two men left it on the sidewalk after they pushed a young woman into their car. I was sleeping in my usual spot, under a staircase on Harbour Street, and I woke up because a car was standing right across from me with the engine running. Then a young woman came along pulling the pink suitcase and two men jumped out of the car and pushed her into the back seat. After a while, one man cleaned his knife. The idea that they could discover me terrified me, but they didn't. They drove off, but they forgot the suitcase. I sold it for fifteen euros."

"Can you describe the two men?"

"It was dark. The street has little lighting. That's why I go there to sleep. The only thing I remember is both men were big and strong-looking, and the one who cleaned his knife wore dark glasses."

"You mean the lenses were dark, as in sunglasses?"

"No, not the lenses. The frame."

"How about the young woman?"

"I saw her for only a few seconds, so I can't tell you much. She looked pretty. A shame she got killed."

"Did you see the men kill the woman?"

"No, but what else would they be doing with a knife?"

"Can you show me the spot where this happened?"

"Sure, but I'm getting hungry. Difficult to walk."

"Okay. Let's have lunch. There is a diner at the end of the street. We'll go there."

Harry thought this was the best day since he had sold the suitcase. Mertens ordered a coffee for himself and a nondescript mix of potatoes, meat, and vegetables for Harry, who devoured his meal. When Harry finished, Mertens asked, "Tell me once more what happened that night in Harbour Street and how many people you saw."

Harry repeated what he said earlier. "Good, his story holds true, thought Mertens.

"Did you hear anybody talk?" he asked. "Do you remember what they said?"

"How about a coffee? Makes the meal much better."

Mertens ordered Harry a coffee. "Try to remember what the men and the woman said."

"I couldn't understand the woman. Her voice wasn't loud enough. But one man, not the one with the dark glasses, told her something like, 'We have our instructions. You worked for SunRise, but you couldn't handle the responsibilities.' I also remember he said, 'You mess with us, we mess with you.'"

Harry leaned back, enjoying his coffee and feeling good about himself. *I am doing something important. Why else would this police officer be paying me and buying me food?*

"Tell me again. The man used the word 'surprise?'"

Harry thought it over for a minute. *If that is what the police officer wants, I could say yes. But that's not what I heard.* "No," he said, "not 'surprise.'" He said, "'sunrise.'"

"Very good, Harry. Now show me where it happened." The men walked to Harbour Street, and Harry pointed out his usual sleeping spot.

"The car stood there, on this side of the road, and the young woman came from there. Then the two men jumped out of the car." Harry used his arms and body to re-enact what he had seen. "I was hiding here, under the staircase."

Mertens surveyed the scene. No street lighting and no apartment buildings, only warehouses and offices, deserted late in the evening. A perfect spot for a violent crime.

"No," said Harry, "I don't remember the time—late evening, but whether it was ten o'clock or midnight, I don't know. It was quiet, no cars, no people. That's all I know."

Harry wanted to go back to collecting beer cans and bottles.

"Thank you so much, Harry. You have been very helpful. And for now, we'll leave it at this, but I will call you to the police station. We'll record your story and make it official."

Harry winced at the idea of visiting the police station. "I'm busy. Can't go now."

"Not today—another time. Don't worry. You aren't in any trouble, and nothing will happen to you at the police station. We'll go for lunch again."

In his office, Mertens composed a message to his colleagues in Toronto. He described the two men, but the police hadn't found a body, so he had no proof the men had committed a murder. It could have been a case of sexual assault. "I have one witness, a homeless man who was present at the scene. He said one man, not the one with the dark glasses, mentioned 'SunRise.' Therefore, although evidence for murder is lacking, the proper police authority can arrest them for being part of a criminal organization."

* * *

Detectives DeWitt and Peters described Z and his partner to the car rental agencies at the airport, and one clerk confirmed that two burly men, one of whom wore black-rimmed glasses, had rented a car, and he gave the detectives the name of the hotel written on the rental form. When they asked at the hotel desk, they were told nobody who looked like the men the detectives described had rented a room with them. DeWitt and Peters were not happy. It meant a lot of legwork checking out other hotels. But one of the desk clerks told them that his friend, who worked in a hotel nearby, had told him that two burly men had checked in. He remembered because there had been a minor incident. One of the burly men had walked head-on into the glass doors, and this had attracted the attention of other guests. The other man had apologized and mentioned that he and his friend were planning to pick up a new pair of glasses.

DeWitt and Peters spotted Z and his partner in an optician's store near the hotel. They didn't arrest the men, but followed them to find out if they were planning more business in Toronto. They weren't. Z and the Man with the Black-Rimmed Glasses drove straight to the airport and bought tickets at the KLM Royal Dutch Airlines desk. "Destination Rome, with a transfer in Amsterdam," confirmed the ticket clerk. "The plane leaves in four hours."

The detectives made sure Z and the Man with the Black-Rimmed Glasses boarded the airplane, waited until the airplane was in the air, and then contacted Mertens. *He* could decide if he wanted the Dutch police to arrest the men at the Amsterdam airport.

THIRTY-THREE

FRANK didn't hear from detectives DeWitt and Peters for several months. He assumed the investigation was progressing at a slow pace, and he wondered often about how the collapse of YYZ had affected Herman, Linda, and Claudia. And how about SunRise and Mrs. Liu? He searched online for news of the truck hijacking and found a few small newspaper articles in Dutch, which he translated using a free web service. The police were looking for the perpetrators, but the driver could give few details of the men who had bound and gagged him. Some time later, Frank found an article that mentioned that the police had lifted fingerprints from the cab and were trying to find a match in international databases. *Herman's men should have worn gloves. What if the police find a match? That can lead to Herman.*

Other thoughts kept him busy. He couldn't help thinking about life in prison. Was it as rough as he had seen in crime movies? Or would he pass his time in a minimum-security facility? What would he do after he got out? His money wouldn't last forever; he had to get a job. But who would hire a convicted criminal? Frank struggled with these depressing thoughts. In addition, he didn't feel safe. He trusted Mrs. Liu to call off Z and the Man with the Black-Rimmed Glasses. But what if they ignored her? Frank understood how humiliated Z and his partner must have felt after being assaulted with a coffee cup. They would need revenge. Frank stayed in his apartment, and on the few occasions he went out, he ordered an Uber.

One of his outings was to the Silver Beaver to find Ethan. He had to talk to *someone* to quiet the thoughts swirling through his mind.

The bartender was not happy to see him. "If you're planning on assaulting more of my customers, you aren't welcome here. What in the world came over you to bring your problems to my pub? If you have a beef with other people, go somewhere else to settle it."

Frank apologized. He explained that he'd just wanted to talk to the two men, but they'd threatened him, so he'd had no choice but to defend himself. "These were dangerous individuals. They committed at least one murder. If they threaten you, you must strike right away and not give them time to hurt you. Don't worry—it won't happen again."

He spotted Ethan and joined him at his table.

"Hey, Ethan, how are you? How's your job search?"

"I sent out more applications but have heard nothing yet. What's up with you? You sure caused a commotion that day you asked me to tell those two guys to talk to you! Hit them with a coffee cup, didn't you?"

"Let's not talk about that. I'm trying to think what to do next. I need to find work. It's not urgent, but at some point, I'm going to run out of money. So, I came here to see if *you* had any ideas. I have no skills other than data entry, and I'd rather not take a simple job again."

Frank and Ethan drank their beers for a while in silence, until Ethan said, "You're coming off a great job, and I understand going back to what you did before you left for Amsterdam isn't attractive. So, don't. Let's try to figure out what else you could do. For example, could you be an office manager or a salesperson? Something more exciting than copying data into a computer."

Frank didn't answer. He had already thought of, and rejected, those ideas. "I want something different," he said, "more challenging. Before I became an agent for YYZ, I wasted my life on data entry."

Again, there was silence until Ethan said, "Here's an idea, and it needs much more thought and discussion, but are you ready to start your own business? Be the boss?"

"That's occurred to me, but I never explored the idea in depth. What business? Retail? Wholesale? A service company, like eavestrough cleaning or window washing?"

"Wholesale—that's it! Why don't you start up an import company to sell goods wholesale to Canadian customers? You're familiar with the wholesale business, aren't you? Imagine, you'll be the boss! And I can help you."

"The idea of starting a new company sounds good, but it needs a lot of planning. I need suppliers and customers." After a slight pause, Frank continued. "I could use the data from the YYZ computer to get started. But I can't start until I know the outcome of the police investigation. I might have to do prison time."

Ethan looked puzzled. "Prison time? Why? And how would you access the office computer? Remember, the detectives took it."

Frank realized Ethan was not aware of many of the events that happened while he was in Amsterdam. *I should tell him. As a potential business partner, he should be aware of what I've done.*

Frank explained the essence of the SunRise-YYZ collaboration, and what role he had played in this money-making scheme. He mentioned his visit to Mrs. Liu in Shanghai, his promotion to Amsterdam, his first discussion with the Transport Coordinator, who suggested that mistakes lead to serious consequences, 'like your colleague in Antwerp, who disappeared.' He talked about the rough treatment by Z and the Man with the Black-Rimmed Glasses in Brussels, and added, "Those were the men I assaulted with a coffee cup because they threatened me."

"Wow," said Ethan. "That's quite a story. When I arrived at YYZ, I knew not everything was straightforward. I dealt with only part of the business, and Mr. Ho had his things to do. He was secretive. I asked *several* times, but he wouldn't explain his work. He was very upset when someone stole the laptop he used to keep track of his part of the business. I guess Mr. Young told him to buy a new one. But one day, he disappeared with his new laptop, and I now realize he didn't want to risk a checkup from Mrs. Liu."

"You're right," Frank replied. "Mr. Ho handled the SunRise merchandise, which was counterfeit. You dealt with the part of YYZ's business that was legal."

"Good to hear. I don't want to be mixed up in counterfeit goods."

Frank didn't reply to that, but continued. "After I lost my job, I learned that fire-retardant insulation panels YYZ imported into Europe were defective and offered minimal protection to people if a fire broke out in their house or apartment. For me and my friends, that was the turning point. Trading counterfeit goods was one thing, but trading defective goods that put people's lives at risk was something else. We worked out a scheme to let the Dutch police know about the merchandise in the containers YYZ cleared. Our plan worked and resulted in Mr. Young leaving in a hurry, as you told me, and the shutdown of YYZ. SunRise will be next. My role in the illegal trading scheme is being investigated by the police in Toronto and Amsterdam."

"I understand," Ethan said. "You chose not to stay silent about those faulty panels, even though you must have known detectives were going to knock on your door someday. That was an honourable thing to do. You put other people's safety ahead of your interests. I'm not sure I could make the same choice."

Frank and Ethan didn't speak for a while, till Frank asked, on a whim, "Are you interested in starting an import company? We can work on this together and be co-CEOs."

A big grin spread over Ethan's face. "I thought you'd never ask. I'm tired of looking for jobs, and setting up a new company and making it grow sounds more interesting than sending out more job applications."

"Great! We should get together soon and talk about this more."

After a few minutes had passed, Ethan said, "You didn't tell me how you would have access to the YYZ office computer. Do you plan to ask the police to give it to you? That won't work. It's not yours."

"You mentioned the stolen laptop. I know who stole it, and I know the same evening, that person copied the Excel files describing the *legal* trades YYZ made in the last five years from the office computer. I can access that data."

Ethan stared at Frank, shaking his head in disbelief, and said, "That person was you, right? You copied the files from the office computer, and when you found out there wasn't any SunRise-related stuff there, you stole Mr. Ho's laptop." Ethan kept staring at Frank. "Are you aware of what you have done to Mr. Ho? Losing the laptop *terrified* him!"

"I'm sorry for Mr. Ho, but I've learned that your life is always in danger if you work with criminals. My friends and I wanted to use the data on the laptop as leverage to convince SunRise to stop supplying the faulty panels, but when we looked at it in more detail, the sale of those panels turned out to be too big for us to handle. So, we designed a plan to get the police to investigate YYZ and SunRise. And now I'm waiting to see what the consequences are for me. But whatever they are, having stopped the trade in defective fire-retardant insulation panels feels good."

Ethan got up. "I've got to get going. I need to digest the things you told me, and whether I want to drink beer—and work with—a criminal. Don't worry. I won't tell anyone what I learned here."

"Fair enough, Ethan. I told you all this because you needed to know. I came here to ask your opinion on what to do next, and you deserve to be aware of the person I am."

THIRTY-FOUR

AFTER the breakdown of the SunRise-YYZ trading scheme, Frank was obsessed with the question of what had happened to Herman. Where was he? Had police arrested him, or was he hiding somewhere? Frank resisted the urge to contact him, but he hired a lawyer, not only to defend him in court when the time came but also to find out whether Herman was in custody.

Frank found his lawyer on the internet after searching, "criminal lawyers counterfeit Toronto," and chose one whose name and address showed up on the third search page. *Can't afford a top lawyer.* He set up a meeting and hired her after making sure she had experience in handling cases involving counterfeit goods.

"I'm glad my credentials satisfy you," she said in her office, "so let's go over your case. Tell me why you are here."

Once again, Frank went over his story, starting with his trip to Shanghai and ending with the moment Mrs. Liu fired him. He talked about Herman and asked the lawyer if she could find out what had happened to him. "We're friends."

"Good," she said. "For now, I have enough to investigate your role in this case and start building a defence. I suspect there will be more to this story than you told me. Nobody ever tells me everything during the first appointment. I'll try to find out where Herman is. Let's meet again in a week or two and discuss what I've learned. Please, don't talk with anybody about what we've discussed here."

Ten days later, the lawyer phoned Frank. "Toronto police has arrested Mrs. Young and are investigating YYZ. The Greek police has arrested the Transport Coordinator, but Mr. Young and your friend Herman are still at large. Chinese police are investigating SunRise Technologies and Mrs. Liu. That's all they told me. I asked for details of the investigation but didn't get any."

The lack of news about Herman worried Frank. Herman had been clear: he preferred prison time over hiding for the rest of his life. So why had he not gone to the police? Was something wrong with him? Or had he changed his mind?

"I have a question for you," the lawyer asked. "Why are you so interested in Herman? Detective DeWitt said *you* suggested Herman was part of the SunRise network. How do you know?"

"Because he told me. We were and still are friends, and he wanted to tell me who he was. He travels around Europe to check up on the distributors of the SunRise merchandise, 'to make sure nobody skims off the top.'"

"DeWitt mentioned that the murder of the Antwerp agent might involve Herman."

"No, he misunderstood what I told him. He suspects Herman because he works for SunRise, but not everyone who's part of the network is a murderer. If you believe that, then you might as well believe *I* killed the Antwerp agent."

"Did you?"

"Of course not! The SunRise enforcers murdered the Antwerp agent. The Transport Coordinator told me. He wouldn't make that up unless he wanted to scare me."

"Okay, let's drop this for now. Nobody is going to prosecute you for murder. My guess is you will stand trial for being part of a criminal organization that imported counterfeit goods into Europe. The facts are obvious. You cleared the merchandise. In your defence, you claim that when you accepted the job, you weren't aware the goods were counterfeit. Correct?"

Frank nodded. The lawyer saying that Herman was a murderer had upset him so much, he wasn't able to concentrate, and he ignored his lawyer, who had to repeat herself: "I have a question and I need a straight answer. When did you become aware the merchandise in the containers you cleared was counterfeit?"

"Not long after I started my work as an agent," Frank answered. "I thought there was something wrong with these containers, and Mrs. Young confirmed my suspicions when she came to visit me in Amsterdam in December last year."

"And despite this confirmation, you continued your work?"

"Yes. I didn't want to give up my job. You must understand, there was no attractive alternative. I now see I should have quit as soon as Mrs. Young confirmed my suspicions. But it wouldn't have made much difference because a short time afterward, Mrs. Liu fired me."

"It would have made a *big* difference. If you had resigned from your job, it would count in your favour. It would have allowed me to argue that you are a man of integrity. But you continued clearing containers, so now the prosecutor and the judge might consider you a criminal, a person who knew he performed illegal acts."

Frank did not react. *This is the fourth time someone has called me a criminal.*

"One more question. Who is Claudia Anderson?"

The question surprised Frank. "Why are you asking about Claudia? I never mentioned her."

"I told you. My clients never tell me every detail in the first interview. That's why I do research. If you had searched the net for SunRise Technologies in the last few days, you would have found interesting facts about them. For instance, a Toronto construction company is planning to sue SunRise for supplying its French subsidiary with inferior counterfeit building materials: electrical components, kitchen cabinets, and fire-resistant insulation panels. It is asking SunRise for the cost of replacing the subpar materials and for large punitive damages. The articles I read named the project manager of the French branch as Claudia Anderson and said that she discovered the fraud and was aware these goods came from a Chinese firm called SunRise Technologies. I'm not sure how she knew the goods came from China, but her company hailed her as a hero for being a whistleblower and putting an internal investigation into motion. I wonder if you're familiar with her. You both connect with SunRise."

After a few seconds, she added, "From your facial expression, I suspect you know her."

Frank felt deflated. He realized Claudia must have used the laptop to show that SunRise was the supplier of the panels. How else could she have convinced her company she knew the panels came from SunRise? Had she added how she got hold of the laptop and mentioned him going to Toronto and taking it from the YYZ office? She might have. Her company would want to know how she got the laptop. He should have left it with Linda, or he should have destroyed it. He recalled how, during their discussions in Paris, Claudia had said more than once that she didn't wish to be part of a criminal scheme to stop the sale of the defective panels. She wanted to talk to the police or the company head office. "I don't want to fight crime with more crime." He and Linda hadn't realized what that meant for Claudia, or the potential difficulties her attitude could pose. Too bad. They should have known Claudia would cause problems.

The possibility of a lawsuit was terrible news. The last thing Frank wanted was publicity around the defective panels. It would expose the plan to dismantle YYZ and SunRise if Claudia had not already done so, and their efforts to make it look like they were not involved in shutting down the trade in defective panels would be useless. *Mrs. Liu will learn from the lawsuit that I stole the laptop and worked out the plan to hijack the truck with Herman. Herman and I, will be in deep trouble. Mrs. Liu will take revenge on us.* He thought about answering that he had never met Claudia, but concluded that was futile. The lawyer would find out.

"I am familiar with Claudia," he said. "More than ten years ago, we were students and worked together stocking shelves for a big Toronto supermarket."

"And you were aware she was working in Paris as a project manager?"

"Yes, after Mrs. Young told me during her Amsterdam visit. I was happy for Claudia. Being a project manager in Paris for a big construction company is a great job."

"Were you aware that Claudia used goods you cleared through customs?"

Frank became desperate. He was sweating, although he felt cold, and for a moment, he was sorry he had hired a lawyer. These questions were leading to exposure of everything he wanted to keep secret. Answering "yes" could force him to confess how he had stolen the laptop, how he had met with Claudia and Linda, and how he and Herman had hatched a plan to hijack the truck. But "no" would be a lie, and there was no guarantee the lawyer or the police might not discover their plot.

"I can see my questions upset you. Take your time. I'll get you a glass of water."

Frank recovered after a few minutes. "Yes," he said, "we talked about this."

"Good. Do you want to give me the entire story now, or would you prefer to come back tomorrow when you feel better?"

Frank took a deep breath. *I'm sure Linda, Claudia, and Herman will understand.* He took another sip of water and told his lawyer about the events that had happened after Mrs. Liu fired him. Frank described Linda's visit again, his trip to Paris, and how he learned about the defective fire-resistant insulation panels. He confessed he stole the laptop to find proof that SunRise supplied the defective insulation panels and YYZ imported them into Europe.

Frank's lawyer interrupted. "Don't worry about this lawsuit. It might never happen. The laptop is powerful evidence that SunRise was the supplier of the defective panels, but any lawyer can argue the laptop didn't come from the YYZ office and the data are fake. They need corroborating evidence. At least one person, other than Ms. Anderson, must come forward and testify that he or she took the laptop from the YYZ office." She looked at Frank. "Be prepared. The company's lawyer *will* phone you. Let me know if that happens before you answer. I don't think they can force you to testify if it involves you confessing to a crime. For now, please continue with your story. Tell me when you stopped the sale of the panels, and why you thought it necessary to destroy SunRise and YYZ to reach your goal."

Frank told his lawyer that finding out the fire-retardant panels were defective was a turning point for him and Mrs. Young. He described the decision they had made together with Claudia to stop the trade in defective panels. They had considered blackmailing Mrs. Liu with the data they had found on the stolen laptop, but had rejected that idea. Instead, they, with the help of Herman, had hijacked a truck loaded with SunRise goods to get the police involved. "This plan seemed more likely to be effective and to reduce the chance of violence. It worked," he added. "The police are investigating."

When Frank fell silent, he felt liberated, clean.

A week later, Frank got a phone call from his lawyer. "I have another question. We can discuss it over the phone, or you can come to my office."

"Let's do it now, over the phone."

"Detective DeWitt told me that not long ago there was a run-in between you and the SunRise enforcers, here in Toronto."

"Yes, there was." And Frank explained how he had disabled Z and the Man with the Black-Rimmed Glasses. He added, "these were the men I suspected of killing the Antwerp agent."

"I am not sure," said the lawyer, "but that might be why the Dutch police arrested them and extradited them to Belgium. They're in jail in Antwerp. I'll try to get more details."

"That is good news. I hope they stay there for a long time. At least for a while, I don't have to be afraid they'll take revenge for what I did to them. Despite Mrs. Liu telling me she would call off her enforcers, I didn't feel safe. I only got around by Uber and was always on the lookout to see if Z and the Man with the Black-Rimmed Glasses were hiding somewhere. I can relax now. Thank you for telling me."

"When did you talk with Mrs. Liu?"

"After I disabled her enforcers. We talked about private things, nothing that interests you. She told me then that she would call off her men and hire two new enforcers."

"For now, let's leave it at that. It may become important if this means you had a personal relationship with Mrs. Liu. Did you?"

"No. I have seen her only twice in my life. Do you know anything about the new enforcers Mrs. Liu has hired?"

"No, Chinese police are not forthcoming with details. If I hear something, I'll let you know."

The lawyer hung up, and for a moment, a warm feeling of safety enveloped Frank. *Safe.* No worries about Z and his friend. *Let them rot in prison forever.* But the good feeling didn't last long. He worried he hadn't met the *new* enforcers and wouldn't recognize them. How was he to know when he was in danger?

It did not take long before he realized Herman would not recognize the new enforcers either. Frank paced his apartment. He *must* break their no-contact agreement and warn Herman. He wrote an email. "Herman, Z and the Man with the Black-Rimmed Glasses don't work for Mrs. Liu anymore. The Belgian police have arrested them and they're in prison. Mrs. Liu has hired new enforcers, so be careful. You won't recognize them."

Frank waited for an answer, but after a week he knew that something had happened to Herman. He tried to imagine what Herman must have done after their last meeting in Amsterdam. Herman had work to do and had to travel around Europe and organize the hijacking. He must have taken his time before talking to the Dutch police, but Frank was sure Herman had returned to his house in Utrecht to deal with them. He asked his lawyer if she could contact the Dutch police and ask them to look for Herman in Utrecht.

"DeWitt showed me a picture of Herman," he said. "Ask DeWitt to give you a copy of that picture and send it to the Dutch police. It might help in finding him." But Frank felt he was too late. That Herman hadn't written back was an ominous sign.

Two days later, the lawyer phoned Frank. "You better take a seat; I have bad news for you."

After a long pause, she said, "Utrecht homicide recognized your friend Herman from the picture as a recent murder victim. The perpetrators shot him in the chest three times inside his house. Police analyzed the bullets and concluded there were two people involved, but for now, they have no suspects."

Frank felt faint and collapsed in his armchair. When he came to, his mind was empty, his mouth was dry, his vision was black, and his entire body appeared to be burning. Little by little, he recovered, and he could think. *This is the second time I have lost Herman, but this time it's final. He won't come back.* Why? The reason was obvious. Mrs. Liu had learned that Herman had organized the truck hijacking and had taken revenge.

Frank heard his lawyer speak through the phone, which lay next to him on the floor. He picked it up and tried to answer, but he could not express a single word, and he shattered his phone by hurling it against the wall as if he wanted to punish the bearer of terrible news. For a long time, Frank sat in his chair, not moving. He thought about Herman and the good times they had enjoyed in Amsterdam. Other random thoughts swirled around in his mind. Staring at the pieces of his broken phone, he thought he needed to buy another one and remembered having seen an advertisement for cheap cellphones in the morning paper. Thoughts of revenge popped up in his mind, and he started shaking with rage. He should go to Shanghai and kill Mrs. Liu. The Transport Coordinator came to mind; he should warn him. Together, they should finish the new enforcers. After a while, Frank stood up and walked through his apartment as if he had never been there. He inspected his bedroom, then the living room, and when he entered the kitchen, hungry, he ate half a tub of vanilla yogurt. Then he thought of Linda. Was she in danger too? Or was she safe in prison? He must see her.

His mind cleared, and his thoughts became more rational. Violent revenge was not a choice. Going to Shanghai and killing Mrs. Liu was not something he could do. He wasn't like the SunRise enforcers. He should say goodbye to Herman. His lawyer should ask for permission from Detective DeWitt for him to travel to the Netherlands. He ate the rest of the yogurt and, exhausted, he stretched out on the sofa and fell into a fitful sleep.

A loud and persistent knocking on his door woke up Frank. He looked through the spyhole and saw his lawyer. When he opened the door, she said, "I am worried about you. Your phone doesn't work. How are you?" Frank nodded and invited her into his apartment.

"Frank, is there anything I can do? Do you need help? I know a grief counsellor you can talk to."

Frank shook his head. "No, thank you. I'll work through this myself. But could you inquire with the Utrecht police when Herman's funeral is? And ask DeWitt for permission for me to attend? It would mean a lot to me to say goodbye to him. It would help me get over this horrific event."

"I will try. I don't think DeWitt will object if you promise to return to Toronto."

"Of course, I'll come back. I have nowhere else to go."

On the plane out of Toronto, Frank's thoughts were with Herman. Nothing else mattered. He went over all the wonderful concerts they had attended together, and how Herman had advised him to visit the many museums in Amsterdam. He remembered the music and the paintings, hummed his favourite compositions, and thought back to how he felt looking at *The Night Watch*.

Frank arrived too late to attend the funeral, and by the time he stood in front of Herman's grave on a cold, humid, windy day, no other mourners were there. There was a temporary tombstone with only Herman's name on it. Frank imagined what he would write: "He tried to improve his life, but dark forces stopped him." Standing in front of Herman's grave brought on a loneliness he had not experienced in his life. *Herman, my only friend, is gone, dead, murdered by Mrs. Liu's new enforcers.* Who could he still meet with, still talk to? Claudia, Linda, and Ethan. He would not talk to Claudia, and Linda was in prison. That left only Ethan, someone he had met only a few times.

Frank noticed a man walking in his direction, and his body tensed. Was this one of Mrs. Liu's new enforcers? He looked around to see if a second man was hiding close by, but saw nothing suspicious. The man approached, joined him in front of the grave, and said something in Dutch.

Frank relaxed. The man didn't look like an enforcer. "Sorry, I don't speak Dutch. I don't understand what you're saying."

"No problem, we can speak in English. I am Herman's brother. You weren't here when we buried him yesterday."

"No. I arrived early this morning from Toronto to say goodbye to him. He is—was—my best friend."

"Then you must be Frank. Herman talked about you every time we got together. I'm happy to meet you."

"Yes, that's me. I met your brother when I was working in Amsterdam. He was a wonderful man. He was in the wrong business."

"You are right. Herman always was a good person, but after he turned thirty, he fell in with bad people. He was making good money but greed killed him."

Frank didn't respond.

"Herman spoke often of you, but he never told me any details of what he did. He only hinted his work wasn't legal. Do you know? Did you work with him?"

"No, we didn't work on the same project. But he wanted to leave his job and lead a normal, quiet life. It's unfortunate his boss had other ideas."

Talking out loud with someone about Herman improved Frank's mood. He was ready to continue, but a glance at his watch showed him he had to get to the airport. DeWitt had allowed Frank to travel to the Netherlands, but only to stay for less than a day. He had to take the late-afternoon flight back to Toronto. As much as Frank wanted to go on talking to Herman's brother, he could not risk missing his plane.

"No problem. I can give you a ride. It allows us to talk more."

During the one-hour drive, the men continued their conversation.

"Tell me how you met my brother."

Frank talked about Herman and gave a detailed overview of how they met at the Rijksmuseum, the concerts they attended, and the many meals they enjoyed. "He was also the person I turned to for advice." Then he said, "Tell me about Herman."

"From his teenage years up to his mid-twenties, Herman was a cheerful guy. He had a few years of university under his belt and was looking for work. That's when the problems began. After several disappointing jobs, Herman became dissatisfied and angry. He complained he wasn't successful in his search to find any work with a decent salary. Then, as I told you, he fell in with the wrong people, and he got hooked on this high-paying illegal trade in counterfeit merchandise. As his older brother, I tried many times but failed to persuade him to stop with these shady activities. A year or so ago, Belgian customs noticed his organization and Belgian police arrested Herman, but there were no serious consequences. Again, I spoke to him, telling him that this was a good moment to change his life. For the first time, Herman responded. He wished to give up his job. That encouraged me, but he didn't leave the people he had worked with, and his next job disappointed me. Something to do with checking up on other people involved in this illegal scheme. Once again, he told me he wanted to retire but couldn't—he said he *couldn't* leave. When I said I didn't believe him, he invited me to come to a bar in Amsterdam the next evening and he would make sure I understood why he wasn't able to quit."

Frank interrupted. "I knew he wanted to leave his job. He wanted to turn himself in and do prison time."

Herman's brother nodded. "I met Herman in the bar, together with two other men. One of them introduced himself as Z. The other, a big man who wore a pair of black-rimmed glasses, said nothing. That Herman would meet with such men disappointed me. The two men drank Scotch straight. Herman and I drank beer. The conversation was general and not interesting, and, as expected, we ended up discussing women. The alcohol had made the Man with the Black-Rimmed Glasses talkative. He said that they'd had a good thing going in Antwerp, but it fell apart because their agent talked too much. Z tried to change the subject, but alcohol fuelled his partner, and, waving his arms around, he kept telling his story. 'We met this agent,' he said, 'a young woman. I wanted to have fun with her, but I couldn't because Mrs. Liu would not have agreed.'"

"That shocked me," Herman's brother said. "Then he said, 'Mrs. Liu told us to kill her but not to abuse her.' He slapped his hand hard on the table. 'I never liked Mrs. Liu; she thinks too much of herself. We should go to China and visit her.' Not long after, Z and the Man with the Black-Rimmed Glasses left. 'You see what I have to deal with?' Herman told me. 'One misstep and these two idiots will be after me.' Then I understood why Herman didn't quit his job. These were dangerous men. I tried to encourage him. Could he speak with this Mrs. Liu? Or make the entire operation public and get police protection? 'Herman,' I told him, 'you cannot continue this life. If you go on doing this, you will lose yourself. You will be a victim. The Herman I know will disappear.'"

Frank recognized that what Herman's brother had told him was important and wanted to comment, but Herman's brother continued.

"Whoever this Mrs. Liu was, the danger of her sending Z and his partner to kill Herman was real. I was sorry for Herman. I asked if I could help, but he didn't want to involve me. 'It is too dangerous,' he said. That was the last time we met."

"Did you report this conversation to the police?"

"No, I did not want to attract their attention to Herman."

"I understand. You were right. But things have changed. Are you now willing to tell what you heard to the Antwerp police, who have Z and his partner in custody on other charges? Your report could lead to a formal accusation of murder. I understand if you choose not to talk. There are risks. But you can, at least for now, stay anonymous. When the trial takes place, you might have to show your identity, but by then

SunRise will no longer exist and Mrs. Liu will be in prison. She won't care about her old enforcers anymore. She has already fired them."

The car stopped in front of the Departures Hall and the two men sat in silence, each with their thoughts.

"I will speak to the Antwerp police," said Herman's brother, "for Herman's sake. The men you are after did not kill my brother, but they are the same kind, despicable, rotten-to-the-core human beings. We should not allow them to walk free."

THIRTY-FIVE

"ETHAN, I'll keep the money. I'll use it in a way that I and others will profit from the money."

Frank and Ethan were having a beer in the Silver Beaver.

"Please backtrack," Ethan said. "What are you telling me? You make things so difficult for me! One day you tell me you must do prison time, then I hear you were in the Netherlands for a day, and now you say you want to keep the money. *What* money?"

"Sorry, sometimes I don't remember you weren't part of the SunRise-YYZ scheme, and I just start talking. I need that, and I'm lucky you want to listen. I was in the Netherlands to visit the grave of my friend Herman, to say goodbye. The new SunRise enforcers killed him. That's the penalty if you do something that threatens SunRise. As for the money, Mrs. Liu gave me fifty thousand dollars U.S. when she replaced me with a SunRise employee, and I accepted the money without thinking. But over the last few weeks, I've been wondering whether I should return the money. For sure, it's part of Mrs. Liu's proceeds from her criminal enterprise. And now that she's killed my friend, it's difficult to accept gifts from her. So, on the return flight from Amsterdam yesterday, I decided I *couldn't* keep the money. But then this morning, thoughts of Herman swirled through my mind, and I ended up convinced he would have wanted me to *keep* the money and put it to good use."

"How so? Why would Herman want you to keep money you got through crime? Did he tell you that?"

"No, not directly, but imagine this: if I give the money to charity and then do my prison time, I leave prison as a convicted criminal, with minimal savings. Who's going to give me a job? I'll be poor for the rest of my life. For sure, Herman didn't have *that* in mind when he told me, 'Take care of yourself.' That's why I decided we can use the money to start that import business we talked about and donate ten per cent of our profits to charity. Over time, that's more valuable for us *and* the charities."

"Your story is getting darker and darker, Frank. I had decided I could work with you because you're making a courageous effort to leave your criminal actions behind, and now you come up with this money gotten through crime. Why don't you give it away and make a clean break with your involvement in the SunRise-YYZ scheme?"

"I thought about what to do with the money, and I concluded that my break from the counterfeit goods business had started already and would be complete after I finish my sentence, whenever that may be. Giving back the money doesn't change that."

Ethan shook his head. "Completing your sentence is only one part of becoming a regular citizen again. Something your friend said inspired you to keep the money. I don't know him, but if he is, or was, part of SunRise, you're using the wrong marker. You can't set your moral compass by a SunRise employee. He was a criminal, and by following him, you will stay one."

This remark upset Frank. "You don't know Herman; he was a good man."

"In the same way, *you* are a good man, Frank. I'm sure you don't call an assassin or any other hardcore criminal your friend. You are, and your friend might have been as well, a criminal who doesn't want to be a criminal—a reluctant criminal. You want to leave the illegal activity behind, but you can't separate from its spoils. But you need to make a clear cut from the SunRise-YYZ scheme, *including* the money, or it will haunt you for the rest of your life."

Frank didn't respond. He recognized that Ethan's remarks were important, and he needed to think about what Ethan meant to tell him. *"A reluctant criminal." Is that a thing?*

"I'm going to chat with my friends at the bar," said Ethan, "and you can let me know what you decide. When I came into the pub today, I was eager to set up a business with you and do something other than a nine-to-five job, but I *will not* work with you if it involves Mrs. Liu's money. I have savings, and you might have too, from your *regular* job at YYZ. We can pool that and start small. Rent a small warehouse in the suburbs with space for an office and concentrate on importing and selling only a few products. I'll give it one hundred per cent and so will you, and we'll make it work. But we must start off on the right foot."

Frank nodded. "Let's meet tomorrow. You've given me a lot to think about."

Ten minutes later, Ethan came back with two beers, sat down again at Frank's table, and said with a big grin on his face, "Look. I'm not a saint —that's why Mr. Young hired me—and I'm okay if you want to bend the rules a bit and use the data you stole from the YYZ office. It's Mrs. Liu's money that sticks in my craw."

"Okay," said Frank. He raised his glass and said, "To reluctance." The two men laughed and touched their beer glasses. "To a new import empire."

THIRTY-SIX

THE next day, the police arrested Frank. Detective DeWitt came to Frank's apartment and said, "Frank Cordelero, I am arresting you for being part of a criminal organization. Please come with me to the station, where we will ask you questions, and you can state your case. Your lawyer is already there."

Frank was relieved. The arrest had been a constant presence in his mind, and he was at ease now that it was a reality. This was part of him paying for what he had done as a SunRise and YYZ employee, and once he finished his sentence, he could move on with his life and start, together with Ethan, their new import company. Frank had tried to imagine what a proper sentence would be for him. He accepted that his work with SunRise and YYZ had been serious, but he had come up with several attenuating circumstances. He never knew the nature of the merchandise he helped import into Europe. To him, this made his case less severe than if he had known that YYZ filled the containers with dangerous goods—weapons, or faulty medication, for instance. And once he was told by Claudia that he had helped to import faulty insulation panels, he had taken action to stop their sale. This should count in his favour. But then, the theft of Mr. Ho's computer and the hijacking of the truck negated these positive actions. He didn't envy the judge who had to come up with a sentence. He hoped his lawyer could sort that out. *If I were the judge, I wouldn't hand down anything less than one to two years in a minimum-security facility.*

The trial was a quiet, bureaucratic process. On the advice of his lawyer, Frank pleaded guilty to the charge of being a member of a criminal organization that imported counterfeit goods into Europe. He had accepted that he was a criminal, and he asked his lawyer if she could point out that he was only a minor player.

"How so? You might think of your role as minor, but if you had quit, the entire operation would have collapsed, or at least paused until SunRise could find a replacement."

"I know, but by 'minor' I mean I didn't make any of the decisions. I didn't control what was in the containers or the price or the destination. Not like the Transport Coordinator or Mr. and Mrs. Young or, of course, Mrs. Liu."

During the trial, Frank went over how he had become the agent, what had happened in the next seven months, and his efforts to stop the sale of the defective fire-resistant insulation panels. There were plenty of questions from the prosecutor, and Frank answered them all as well as he could. Yes, he had found new clients for SunRise, and he had stolen the YYZ laptop, intending to use the data as a tool to bring down YYZ and SunRise. He also answered questions about the hijacking of the truck.

"Why such a complicated scheme?" asked the prosecutor. "Wouldn't it have been simpler to talk to the customs office?"

Frank admitted that would have been better. At least Herman would still be alive. But he pointed out his fear of what Mrs. Liu would do to him. When, near the end of the trial, the judge asked if he wanted to make a statement, Frank addressed the prosecutor and the judge by saying he regretted that he was part of a criminal organization, but, he continued, "I have changed, and left this period in my life behind. I am planning to rebuild my life by starting a new import company, together with my friend Ethan Fisher."

"You were not the mastermind of the illegal trading scheme you were part of," said the judge, "and sending you to prison serves no purpose. We are here to support your reintegration into society, and no doubt you will be successful. I am convinced by your remarks in my court and by the arguments of your lawyer that you learned your lesson. You will not fall again into the trap of accepting a job or any other proposal with promising prospects before going over the details or going out again and stealing things. I am confident that you will become an honest citizen. Don't disappoint me. If you prove me wrong, I or one of my colleagues will give you a severe sentence next time."

The outcome of the trial surprised Frank: a six-month suspended sentence and a three thousand dollar fine.

Frank's lawyer argued that a three thousand dollar fine would wipe out his client's savings and make it more difficult for him to start a new life, but the judge refused to lower the fine. "When I said the defendant will integrate into society, I didn't mean he would live in affluence. Integrity is the goal to strive for, not money and luxury."

After the trial, Frank, his lawyer, and Ethan, who had attended all the court sessions, went for lunch.

"I can't tell you how I feel," Frank said. "All the dark history with YYZ and SunRise has ended. I feel light-headed and light-hearted and ready to start a new life. Thank you so much. I couldn't have done this by myself."

"That's why you hired a lawyer. The outcome was mild because you drew a judge with progressive ideas on the role of the criminal courts. He trusts rehabilitation more than punishment, but only for first-time criminals. Keep that in mind. You were lucky. You could have ended up with a two-year sentence if you had drawn a conservative judge."

"The judge won't regret his decision. I have no intention of committing criminal acts ever again. An honest life is what I strive for, and Ethan here is going to help me stay on track."

Ethan nodded. "I am looking forward to our joint venture, and yes, I'll keep you honest."

"What about Mr. and Mrs. Young and Mrs. Liu?" Frank asked.

"I got a message yesterday," his lawyer said, "that the police arrested Mr. Young in Mexico on drug charges. If proven, he is looking at ten to twenty years in a Mexican prison. If he behaves well, he can ask to be transferred to a Canadian prison after a few years, but then he must deal with his role in trading counterfeit goods. Mrs. Young is in prison for four years. Her judge found she was a principal player in the counterfeit goods trade, and she wasn't cooperative. She didn't want to disclose how much money they received from SunRise or where it was now. Out of misplaced loyalty to her husband, I guess. My colleague who defended her told me Mrs. Young put in a kind word for you in a character reference. She was sorry she lured you into this agent job without telling you about the merchandise you were dealing with. Her statement might have helped you."

"Four years is a long time," Frank said. "Can you make it shorter? Appeal the verdict?"

"No, not until she cooperates with the prosecutor."

Ethan said, "Frank, forget the YYZ and SunRise people. They did you enough harm. Purge them from your mind. Let's concentrate on the present and how we're going to start our new enterprise."

"I know. I exorcized the SunRise people, but—and I will say this only once and then forget it—I am grateful for what Mrs. Young did for me. She and Mrs. Liu told me that before I accepted the agent's job, I had no life. I was dying. I had mixed up contentment with happiness. And no matter what happened and how wrong it was, my stay in Amsterdam and my friendship with Herman changed my life. Without that experience, I wouldn't be sitting here planning to start a business. I wouldn't go listen to the Toronto Symphony or visit museums."

Ethan said, "Everyone has his journey in life, some more unusual than others, and I'm happy your journey landed you here, Frank. I look forward to working with you."

The lawyer said, "I'm always happy when cases I'm involved in end well. But one more thing, Frank. I received a phone call from a lawyer who works for the construction firm that wants to sue SunRise. They asked if I could talk to you about you testifying that the laptop Claudia Anderson has is the one you took from the YYZ office. Without that testimony, the construction company will have a hard time winning the lawsuit. Think about whether you want to testify."

"No thinking necessary. I will testify against SunRise."

"Frank," Ethan said, "you're not letting go. Please think about things before you answer. What does this lawsuit accomplish? If the construction company wins, they'll get reimbursed for their expenses. If they lose, they'll have to foot the bill. It's not an earth-shattering difference, and I'm sure the company has the money to replace the defective parts they used. And by the way, they are *not* innocent. Why *shouldn't* they pay for their bad corporate management? They should have had more stringent quality control procedures in place. You should also realize there are still SunRise enforcers. What if they decide to punish you for acting against SunRise? Why do you keep putting yourself in danger?"

Frank looked at his lawyer, who nodded. *Ethan is right. I shouldn't testify. I want to leave this period of my life. No big moral questions are at stake. Only money.*

"Okay, I won't do it," he said. "I won't risk being attacked by the SunRise enforcers. Tell their lawyer I won't do it."

"That's okay, Frank," the lawyer said. "Don't feel bad. One last thing. I received a phone call from Inspector Mertens, who is in the homicide department in Antwerp. He wanted me to thank you for the email address of Herman's brother who signed a statement identical to what you told me, and he will testify in the upcoming trial against the men accused of the Antwerp murder. Besides the testimony of Herman's brother, Mertens has a witness who was at the scene when the men hustled a young woman into their car, and someone referred to as the Transport Coordinator has agreed to testify too, but Mertens must find out if this man has direct knowledge of what happened with the agent or whether it's hearsay. Mertens got the name of the Antwerp agent from the customs office and tracked down her parents. He also tracked down the pink suitcase and most of its contents. The agent's parents will testify that the suitcase and the clothing belonged to their daughter. They will also testify they haven't been able to reach their daughter for more than a year. Their last communication was a day after the newspapers reported the SunRise affair and the agent told her parents she was coming home. But she never arrived. Too bad the police have not found her body, but the parents' testimony suggests the agent has disappeared and the prosecutor will ask the accused men to explain what they did to her. I'm sure that once the trials get underway, the court will convict them of murder, and they'll go to prison for many years."

"Do you know how Mrs. Liu is doing?"

"No, I don't. I contacted the Shanghai police department, but they told me that unless I have a direct interest in the case, they will not give me any details. Too bad. You can email her and see if she answers."

"I could, but I won't. I will not have any contact with Mrs. Liu. For me, she doesn't exist anymore."

"Perfect. That's the right thing to do. Forget about her," Ethan said.

The lawyer prepared to leave. "I must attend to another case. My secretary will send you my invoice. Please tell me if the money gets in the way of your plans to start a new business. We can work out a payment plan."

Ethan put up his hand and said, "I wanted to discuss with you something I saw during the trial. It won't take long."

"Please, go ahead."

"I attended all three days of the trial. There weren't many people present, so I noted that all three days there were two men sitting in the back row. Do you know them, and do you have any idea why they would spend their time listening to a court case?"

"I noticed them too. No, I didn't see them before, but many people attend court cases. Murder, rape, and kidnapping trials attract audiences. I guess for entertainment, or to find material for a crime novel, or to pass the time. But this wasn't a spectacular case. Although it's routine that a few people attend, most who show up won't be there all three days. I didn't like the looks of those two men in the back row. Too rough for my taste. But, sorry, I must leave. I am late. Good luck to you both."

After the lawyer had left, Frank and Ethan lingered over coffee.

"I didn't like the looks of these two men, either, said Ethan. They look rough. Like Z and the Man with the Black-Rimmed Glasses. Difficult to explain, but for sure you won't run into them at cultural events—concerts or book readings. More likely you'll see them in a bar, a strip bar. I can't put my finger on it, but they made me uncomfortable."

Frank thought this over for a while and then asked, "Are you saying they might be SunRise enforcers?"

"How can I know? But it's possible. You should be careful. Without them noticing, I took a picture. I'll forward it to you, so if you see them in the street, you'll recognize them and can hide or run."

Ethan took out his phone and sent Frank the picture. Frank studied it and said, "You're right, their appearance is off, rough. They don't look alive, more like robots. They may work for Mrs. Liu. I'll be extra cautious."

"Well," said Ethan, "let's hear your ideas about how to start our business."

"Before we get into that, I want to tell you I'm going to give Mrs. Liu's money all to charity. We won't need it. Together, we'll make things work. The only thing is, I don't want to do it right away, because neither the police nor my lawyer know about it, and I don't want to attract attention. I'll leave it in the banks for a year or two and then, at regular intervals, contribute to charities. Hope that's acceptable to you."

"Fine with me. I'll forget about the money as long as it stays in the banks."

"Good. Now let's talk business. We should first find out how much money we can invest. After paying my fine and the lawyer's invoice, I can contribute about ten thousand dollars. Those are from my savings as a YYZ employee."

"I can do the same, but what can we do with twenty thousand dollars? We need to buy supplies, and we need space to store them. And an office to keep track of our transactions."

Both men were silent, trying to come up with an idea of how to get started. Twenty thousand dollars was not enough to rent a warehouse and an office and buy supplies.

"We could start working from home," said Frank, "but I doubt the owner of my apartment will agree. My rental agreement doesn't permit commercial activity on the scale we want to do. I would have to move and find a suitable place to rent. Maybe we can sublet space from another import company. That would be cheaper than renting a whole warehouse."

"Unnecessary. I live alone in my house. I inherited it from my parents, who passed away a few years ago. If they knew I used their house to start a business, they would be thrilled. We can use the basement for storage, and I have a spare room for office space. We need a new computer, though. Mine is over five years old."

"Wow, starting in the basement! Romantic, but practical. We'll stretch our twenty thousand dollars further, buy more supplies. No need to get a new computer. I bought one last year."

"Good," said Ethan. "I can show you the space and we can think about how to get clients."

"Frank said," You don't mind if we use the data from the YYZ office computer, so why don't we look at that first? You must be familiar with it since it has only the legal transactions YYZ did with Canadian clients. I'll have to go home to fetch my laptop before coming over to your place. I propose we start tomorrow morning at nine. The trial is still occupying my mind, and I might not concentrate well on finding clients."

"Fair enough. Tomorrow morning, we will start our first regular nine-to-five workday. I'll give you the address." A few minutes later, he handed Frank a napkin. "Here is the address of our new business. You'll like it."

Frank took the napkin with both hands as if it was a valuable manuscript. He looked at the piece of paper and said, "I'm familiar with the street. It's easy to get to from where I live. Within walking distance. No more crowded subway rides." He folded the napkin and put it in the inner pocket of his jacket.

The men separated, each filled with positive thoughts about what was going to happen. They would start small but make the business grow and end up with a comfortable life. As a precaution, Frank took an Uber to go home. *I must be careful and be aware of my surroundings. We're launching our new business, and no SunRise enforcer is going to take that away from us.*

THIRTY-SEVEN

"HELLO, Frank. Good to see you. We want to talk to you, and what better place than here? Quiet, no witnesses."

Frank had walked into his apartment to find the two men he recognized from the picture Ethan had sent him. This stunned and scared him. He turned around and tried to flee, but one man had taken up position in front of the door. The other took him by the arm and walked him to the living room. With much effort, Frank asked, "How did you get into my apartment?"

"The owners equipped these old apartments with flimsy locks. No big challenge for my friend here. He picked your lock in ten seconds, leaving no signs of a break-in. So, here we are, and we have a lot of time to find out what we need to do."

This last remark confused Frank. "What do you mean? You're not here to punish me, to kill me?"

"We don't know yet. We reported the court proceedings to Mrs. Liu, and now we're waiting for further instructions. If she wants us to get rid of you, to punish you for your betrayal of SunRise and YYZ, we will kill you."

Frank labelled the men Assassin1 and Assassin2, since it was unlikely that they would give him their names.

Assassin1 continued. "That is the most likely outcome. I don't know why she couldn't let *us* decide. You must be special to her. This is like the day she had to punish a family member in Shanghai. She needed time to decide then too, but in the end, she told us what we expected. Dispose of, disappear, kill—whatever word you want to use."

Fear penetrated Frank's mind, his body, and his whole being. He shivered, as if the temperature in the room was below zero. He fell backward into his favourite armchair and tried to stand up, but couldn't.

For a while, the room was silent. Assassin2 had explored Frank's kitchen and prepared sandwiches and coffee. "Four o'clock is early, but let's eat a simple dinner. We need our strength. Hunger leads to wrong decisions. In this case, we might decide not to wait for Mrs. Liu to tell us what to do."

Frank was too scared to speak. His fate lay in the hands of Mrs. Liu, and now she knew he and Herman had plotted to hijack the truck and he had stolen Mr. Ho's laptop, she would take revenge. His thoughts drifted towards Herman. "Did you kill Herman?" he asked. "Did you wait for Mrs. Liu to decide then too?"

"No, she instructed us to find Herman and eliminate him. What he did was disgusting, one of the biggest cases of betrayal I have seen in my career as an enforcer. If he wanted out, he could have asked Mrs. Liu. She would have approved his request. Herman got too old for his job. Mrs. Liu would have given him a tidy sum of money as a farewell present, and that would have been the end. But the two of you dreamed up a scheme to attract the attention of the police and dismantle SunRise and YYZ. Did you expect to keep this a secret from Mrs. Liu? Of course, she would find out! The guys Herman asked to do the job were amateurs and made a crucial mistake. They left their fingerprints behind in the truck, and the police identified one of them. It took a week or two, but the police arrested him in Spain, and in exchange for a lighter sentence, he was eager to point out Herman as the organizer. Mrs. Liu had no choice but to kill Herman. The men Herman worked with were incompetent. I know them. They should have wiped the cab."

Frank tried to take in what the man had told him. *Herman died because he helped me and Linda and Claudia. And it's my fault. If I had refused to be involved with these defective panels, Herman would still be alive.* He put his head into his hands and tears welled up in his eyes. Desperate thoughts ran through his mind. *My fault. I should have dealt with this myself. Not ask Herman for help. Linda, Claudia, and I should have sent a note to the police. But we didn't. We were afraid of the violent consequences for us. Instead, we killed Herman. I hope they kill me soon; I deserve to die.*

But the moment these dark thoughts appeared, other, opposite thoughts took over. *I don't want to die. I want to work with Ethan to start a new company. I have a good life ahead of me. Why are these assassins after me?*

"Why do you want to kill me? I have nothing to do with the hijacked truck."

"That is not what you told the judge, and please behave like a man and take what is coming to you. Don't try to wiggle your way out of the punishment you deserve," Assassin1 said. "There's no reason to feel scared. You won't feel anything. We aren't like Z and the Man with the Black-Rimmed glasses, who use a knife and enjoy inflicting pain on their victims. We think death is enough punishment—no need to add torture. It will be over in a few seconds, so stop crying."

After a prolonged period of silence, Frank asked, "How about Mrs. Young? Are you going to kill her too?"

"Not now. She is in prison. We'll get to her when she's completed her term."

Frank had to express his disgust for the men who held him captive. "You guys are monsters, depraved to the core. How can you go around killing people just because Mrs. Liu commands you to?"

"That is *not* a nice thing to say," said Assassin2. "We work for Mrs. Liu, and we accept she tells us what to do. You may not like what we do, but that doesn't give you the right to insult us. Killing on command is common. Think of the military. Think of the man who works the electric chair. We're waiting for Mrs. Liu. It shouldn't be long now."

"I am sure," Frank said, "you know your examples are wrong. Killing your enemy in wartime or killing a depraved criminal convicted by a court of law—which we don't do in Canada—differs from killing Herman or Mrs. Young or me."

The men shrugged, and Assassin2 asked whether he should make more coffee. Frank realized these men were beyond reason. They lived in a different world with its own set of rules, its own standards of morality and duty. He lost the little hope he'd had that he could talk them out of their mission. After a long time, in which nobody said anything, Frank noticed both men were losing focus. *Let's take a chance*, he thought, and jumped up and ran to the door, but he had underestimated his captors. Both were at the door before him.

"Poor decision, Frank," said Assassin1. "I understand why you did it, but *we* are in charge here. Don't do that again. We may kill you and tell Mrs. Liu you tried to escape. Sit down and stay down."

Frank had never felt so lonely. Here he was, taken hostage by assassins waiting for their order to kill him or let him live, and there was nothing he could do. He had stopped thinking about Herman, Linda, and his time in Amsterdam. It was too draining. He had accepted that this was his last evening.

"How long are you going to wait for a response from Mrs. Liu?" he asked.

"A few hours. If by nine o'clock tonight we haven't heard from her, we'll make our own decision. I'm surprised she hasn't contacted me yet. She might be on a business trip and not have read our report yet. We'll wait."

Frank glanced at the big digital clock he had bought a few days earlier and hung above the television set: 7:05! Less than two hours left. Frank was alone in the world, alone except for two men who were waiting for his death sentence. 7:10! His body didn't function as it should. He was cold, he was hot, spasms made him shake, and he had a splitting headache. He tried to sleep, but of course, he could not. Unlike the men, who took turns napping. At 7:45, Frank considered forcing the men to act by attacking them, but rejected the idea. There was still a possibility, a small one, that Mrs. Liu would let him live. A glance at the clock told him another five minutes had passed. The blue numbers marched on their fixed path to the 9 p.m. mark. Frank clung to the idea that Mrs. Liu would pity him. Suddenly, he burst out in laughter. Assassin1 looked disturbed.

"Why the heck are you laughing? Shouldn't you think about your life, contemplate what you did, find out what you did right and what you did wrong, or whatever else people think about when their life is close to the end? I've never heard anyone in your position *laugh*."

"Sorry," Frank said. "You're right. I shouldn't laugh. But it struck me as funny that in the last hour of my life, all I'm doing is watching the clock. What if the power goes out, and the clock stops working? Does that mean I'm off the hook?"

Assassin1 shrugged. "I own a watch. It's 7:55. You didn't set the clock right—it runs two minutes fast. My watch is correct."

"Even though it's counterfeit? Is it a Rolex you picked up on the street for ten dollars?"

"For your information, I own a genuine Rolex. It's expensive. I don't deal with counterfeit goods. Most, if not all, are of poor quality."

Frank watched the clock on top of the television set. 7:57! He became convinced that he would die anyway, even if Mrs. Liu let him live. The assassins wouldn't leave him behind alive. They couldn't take the risk. Frank turned inwards, reliving his youth, thinking of his parents and the two trips they had taken together. He had visions of Death Valley and the Painted Desert. He remembered how that had stirred in him a wish to travel. A wish that had made him accept the agent's job without asking probing questions, leading to his impending death at the hands of two SunRise assassins.

At 8:45, Assassin1 became restless. He paced the living room mumbling to himself, "Why doesn't she answer? Something must have happened. I'd better inquire." He took out his phone, and Frank saw him tapping out a message.

"What are you doing?" asked Assassin2.

"I'm trying to find out if everything is okay with Mrs. Liu. Why doesn't she answer? The few times we did this before we waited only two hours. Maybe there is something wrong with her."

This conversation sparked a glimmer of hope in Frank. Something wrong with Mrs. Liu? *Maybe this time, the Shanghai police have arrested her? If so, I might negotiate a better outcome with the assassins.*

The negotiations started at 9:05. Assassin1 had received a message and, after reading it, sat on the couch and closed his eyes for a few seconds.

"What happened?" asked Assassin2.

"The Shanghai police arrested Mrs. Liu. They're accusing her of bribing Chinese officials and degrading the image of the Chinese state. Those are serious charges, and I doubt she'll wiggle her way out of them. Her friends abandoned her. We're on our own."

Frank gave the men time to adjust to their new reality. No more support from Mrs. Liu. He was sure they would soon realize they had to take care of themselves and do things that helped *them*. His mood improved. *This whole affair could finish well.*

Ten minutes went by. Assassin1 was staring at his phone, as if another message was soon to appear, one that said Mrs. Liu was okay. Assassin2 stood up and, in a low voice tinged with desperation, announced he was making more coffee. Frank's mood improved.

"Well, Frank," Assassin1 said, "the decision is ours. Let's go over our choices. We can kill you now. This time of the evening, there shouldn't be many people around, so we might leave the building unseen. Nobody will search for us, and we'll leave Canada as soon as possible. That is choice one, minimal risk for us."

Frank considered his answer. "You're wrong to think nobody will look for you. My business partner, who attended the trial, noticed you sitting in the back row for three days, and he took your picture. If you don't believe me, I can show it to you. He mentioned your presence to my lawyer, who had a good look at you too." *No reason not to embellish the situation somewhat.* "If you kill me, you will be instant suspects and the police will alert the border agents, making it difficult for you to leave Canada. My lawyer might identify you from the photographs taken when you entered the country. Then the police will know your names and where you came from and put out international arrest warrants for you."

"They won't know anything," Assassin1 said. "Our passports are fake. No criminal travels with his real passport."

"The police will have your pictures," said Frank.

A tense silence descended on the room. Then Assassin2 said, "What if we let you live? The situation would be worse for us. You'll alert the police, and the same scenario plays out."

"Except nobody charges you with murder. The charges would be much milder. You pay a fine, and that's the end of the story."

Again, there was silence, until Assassin2 said, "What if you talk about what we did to Herman?"

"I promise not to mention you told me you killed Herman."

"How can we trust you? Herman was your friend; you must want to take revenge."

"This talk about Herman isn't serious," said Assassin1. "It's Frank's word against ours. Two against one. Nobody will convict us for murder on that evidence alone." He addressed Frank. "But you must promise not to mention it to anyone, so as not to attract attention to us, and you also shouldn't mention we were here. That would allow us to leave Canada and put this entire mission behind us. I don't know what we're going to do without Mrs. Liu, but we don't want to stay here. The problem is, as my partner said, how can we trust you to keep your promises?"

The negotiations are shifting in my favour. Frank became more assertive. He saw an opening.

"Look at your situation. Not killing me lets you leave Canada without a problem and go wherever you want to go. Think about that. If you kill me, my friend will get suspicious, alert the police, and show them the picture he took of you, and leaving Canada will be much more difficult for you. Your two options are: one, kill me and bring a lot of problems upon yourself or, two, let me live and trust I'll keep my promise not to mention you were here. The second choice is the better one for all of us. The police won't be involved, and I promise I won't tell anybody you were here. If the police will ask me about you, I'll tell them you are old friends. We must get our story right to make it believable we have met before, but the second choice is the better solution of the two. For you, choice two is like choice one, but without the murder charges and police trouble. Reflect on that."

Frank stood up and went to the washroom. The men didn't stop him. They were discussing the scenarios Frank had laid out for them. When Frank rejoined them in the living room, Assassin1 said, "We decided based on what you said, and because we are no longer employed by Mrs. Liu and don't owe her anything. We will let you live because we don't kill for no reason. My partner and I trust you won't talk about us, and we will disappear from your life."

Frank's sense of relief was so strong, his legs turned weak, and he had to sit in his armchair. "I won't talk about you with anyone because I want to purge you—and everything that happened since I worked for SunRise —from my memory. I am going to build a new life."

The men stood up and Assassin1 looked at Frank. "I believe you," he said. "Good luck with your new life. I wish I could do the same."

Frank heard the front door of his apartment open and close, and it was as if those sounds switched on the lights and started his radio. He saw light and heard music. He saw his life ahead and was never so committed to his new life as at that moment.

* * *

The next morning, at nine, Frank showed up at Ethan's house.

"Wow," Ethan said. "You look like you didn't sleep the entire night!"

"I didn't, but don't worry. Everything is in order. Let's get to work."

ACKNOWLEDGMENTS

MANY thanks to my family, Marius, Jenny, Ilanit, and Ruben for their encouragements, suggestions, and the initial editing. Special thanks to Jenny and Ilanit for taking care of the digital aspects of turning the manuscript into a book. I am grateful to Catherine Marjoribanks from Wordplay Creative Services and Stephanie Fysh for their professional editing, without which the manuscript would not be publishable. Thanks to Steve Passiouras for the interior layout and special thanks to Ilanit Shohat for the cover design.

Manufactured by Amazon.ca
Bolton, ON

37473232R00155